TRACY

by

Mirabelle Maslin

AUGUR PRESS

TRACY

Author of
Beyond the Veil

British Library Cataloguing in Publication Data.
A catalogue record for this book is available from the British Library.

ISBN 0-9549551-0-2

First published 2005 by
Augur Press
Delf House,
52, Penicuik Road,
Roslin,
Midlothian EH25 9LH
United Kingdom

Printed by Lightning Source

TRACY

With thanks to
Vanessa, Norman, Bob, Imogen, Neil, Claire and Rebecca

Chapter One

Tracy lived on a housing estate just outside Bankbridge. Her parents had bought the house when they had got together. That had been before Tracy was born. As far as she remembered, people said that these houses had been built about twenty years ago. She didn't know how many houses there were on the estate, but there were several roads, and there were several styles of house. Of course, over the years some people had modified theirs by taking down an internal wall, or by adding a porch or a conservatory; and some with a garage had built an extra bedroom over it. She knew what each house design was like because she had friends all over the estate, and had been in and out of a number of their houses from as early as she could remember.

Tracy's home was semi-detached, with three bedrooms and a bathroom upstairs, and a kitchen and a living room downstairs. The living room went right through the house – from the front to the back. There was a small garden at the back, with a wooden fence round it. There wasn't much in it except grass. That was fine, because no one in her house was keen on gardening. They had sometimes talked of putting concrete slabs there instead, but they had never got round to it.

Tracy lived with her mum and dad and her sister, Paula. Paula had been born when Tracy was two, but you wouldn't think it to look at her now. She was almost the same height as Tracy, and looked almost the same age. But people who didn't know they were sisters had no idea that they were related. For one thing, they didn't go around much together when they were outside the house, and for another they didn't look like each other at all. As she passed the age of twelve years, Tracy had reached five feet. That was several months ago. She was of medium build, and had dark brown hair, which she liked to keep quite short: it was about two inches in length – all over. People didn't call her fat, but she felt lumpy. Yes, that was the word to describe it – lumpy.

Paula was only an inch shorter than Tracy, and was of a more slender build. Tracy could never quite work out what the difference

1

really was, because they could both buy the same size of clothes, and Paula was quite happy to help herself to the contents of Tracy's wardrobe. That was very easy for her to do, because she and Tracy still shared the room that they had slept in together, ever since Paula was big enough to move from her cot at the side of the double bed her mum and dad shared. Perhaps it was something to do with the shape of Paula's face. It was definitely fine-boned, and it was a kind of oval shape; and when framed by her auburn hair, which she kept quite long, she looked rather striking. By comparison, Tracy's face was round. This mostly seemed to Tracy to be a severe disadvantage; but if she was being honest with herself, she was glad that the dentist had admired her strong jawbones. He had pronounced that she would need no orthodontic treatment, whereas Paula was definitely heading for extractions and braces.

Tracy knew there was a certain amount of kudos attached to the wearing of braces; but since spending the summer holidays with her Auntie May and her cousin Flora, who was a couple of years older than herself, she had learned that braces could prove to be very painful. She was pretty sure too that she had overheard some adults saying that such treatment could even push the plates of the skull out of place. That sounded horrible. Tracy didn't want that to happen to Paula. She hoped she would learn something about all of this in her human biology classes at school, then she could be more sure of the facts.

The local primary school was adjacent to the estate, and it was situated between these newer houses, and the ones that had been a part of Bankbridge for a much longer time. It had been built at about the same time as Tracy's house, as the old one had not been big enough to accommodate the extra children the new estate would bring into the area. Tracy and Paula had attended this school from the age of five. Tracy had been away from it now for a whole year, and Paula had just one more year to go, before she joined her at Castlehill High.

Tracy had enjoyed the summer holidays this year, and she felt ready to go back to high school for her second year. Her time with Auntie May and cousin Flora had been just right for her in all kinds of ways. Paula had had two weeks by the sea with the family of one of her school friends, Jenny. Jenny's mum and dad had been keen to invite Paula along to keep her company. Jenny's older brother, Jack, went along too, but he just used the holiday house as a base from which to do his own exploring. After all, he was fifteen now. Jenny's family had been going to the same place for two weeks every summer for several years, and Jack had made friends with some of the local boys. He liked to meet up with them and go swimming and fishing; although sometimes his dad would take a group of them to try out something different, like archery.

The summer holiday had been quite different from the one that their mum and dad had originally planned. They had started talking about their ideas to Tracy and Paula a long time ago. It must have been before Christmas the year before. Their dad was in the police, and he had hoped to get his summer two weeks' holiday at a time when the girls were off, or just before the summer term ended. Mum and Dad didn't like the girls to miss any important lessons, and were always very careful about how they fixed their holidays. In the police, there were a lot of other people who had families, and who wanted their holidays to coincide with school holidays, so there was always a bit of anxiety about how it would all work out. But they did feel that the last week of the summer term was a time they could use, if necessary.

However, their plans for a holiday abroad hadn't worked out. Just after that Christmas, Dad had hurt his back, and he was off work for ages. No one could work out quite what had happened, but one day he slipped on some ice, and fell awkwardly. He seemed all right at first, apart from some nasty bruises; but a week or so later, his back had started to hurt badly, he began to limp, and he wasn't able to wear his police belt. He went to see the doctor, who gave him painkillers and signed him off work. Two weeks later he was no better, and he was referred to a physiotherapist. Week after week he had gone for sessions. Day after day he did the exercises the physiotherapist told him to do at home, but his back still caused him a lot of pain, and he had pains right down one leg too. After a while, he had tried to go back to work, as he had been offered light duties in the administration section. However, the pain he was suffering was too much for him. He had to be at home, so he could lie down whenever he needed.

Tracy knew that after some time had passed he did not get the same pay any more. She didn't like to ask about it, because her dad usually looked grey with pain, and her mum looked worried. All talk of holiday plans had long since stopped. Most of the talk was about

3

what might help Dad. She didn't mind this, except that she felt completely inadequate, as there was nothing she could suggest. Of course, she and Paula helped him all they could. They did any lifting or carrying that he needed, and he was always very grateful for their help.

Then one day, Mum had bumped into an old friend while she was doing some shopping on the way home from her work as a part-time receptionist at a hotel not far away. The friend had told her of someone she knew who had a good success rate when treating sports injuries. Mum had been surprised, and had said that Dad's injury had been from a fall. The friend had assured her that this didn't mean he couldn't see a sports injury therapist, and Mum had hurried home to tell Dad. The upshot of this had been that Dad had made an appointment, and had gone along the following week.

When he got back home, he looked quite a bit better. He had learned that something had got knocked out of place when he fell, and although the exercises he had been doing were good for strengthening all the right muscles, they couldn't put back what had been displaced. Tracy had been fascinated to hear about this. Not only did her dad look a lot better already, but also she was learning something she had known nothing about before. Perhaps she too could learn how to treat sports injuries when she grew older? The person Dad had been to was qualified in massage and in manipulation. He had certainly made a big difference to Dad's life, and because of that, to hers too. It had been so hard seeing him in so much pain for so long, and to see Mum looking so worried. If only they had known about this person at the beginning, he might have been able to help Dad right away.

He had gone back for one more appointment a few days later, just to get checked over, and then he had been able to go back to work soon after that. By that time it was half way through the summer term at school, and it was too late to book any holidays.

It was then that Jenny's mum had phoned to see if Paula could come away with them; and soon after that, Auntie May had invited Tracy to come for a fortnight. Tracy had jumped at the chance. But things worked out differently once she got there, and she had ended up staying nearly the whole summer.

She had always liked her Auntie May, although she hadn't felt completely sure about her cousin Flora. Auntie May was her mum's older sister. As far as Tracy could remember, Auntie May was about five years older than Mum. Apparently she and Mum hadn't done much together when they were children, but when they both left home, they travelled abroad together for a whole summer and had a wonderful time. Since then, they had been the best of friends, and they phoned each other at least twice a week.

Flora was an only child. Her dad had left when she was only a baby, and since then she had seen very little of him. Auntie May ran a bed and breakfast business from her big rambling house, and this meant that Flora had always had her mum at home, although she could be very busy at times. Easter to September was the time when things were most rushed, and Flora was by now used to helping over the summer holidays. At twelve, Tracy felt she could help out too, and she had looked forward with excitement to the day when Mum would put her on the train. Flora was to meet her at the station, and take her back home with her.

The way it worked out, that holiday was one of the best Tracy had ever had. The last time she had seen Flora was when she and Mum had gone for a weekend when Paula was staying overnight at Jenny's house, and she hadn't found Flora very easy to talk to. But this time had been different... entirely different. Tracy's mind went back to the moment when Mum had waved her goodbye on the train.

Chapter Two

'Bye, Tracy. Remember and phone when you get there,' her mum shouted.

'Okay. I promise I will,' Tracy called back.

Then it was ten o'clock, and the train pulled out of the station. Tracy leaned back in her seat. It had a 'reserved' ticket on it, and this made her feel more confident. Only four stops to go past, and then I get off at the fifth, she said to herself. She pulled a small writing pad out of her zipped shoulder bag, and checked the names of the stations. Yes, she was familiar with them all; but it was good to have them written down like this when she was travelling alone. She had promised Mum that she would send a text at each station, and then she would know she was fine. She was sure that was a good idea. She liked sending texts to Mum. She had her mobile in her bag, and she kept the long strap of the bag safely over her head. That way there would be no risk of accidentally leaving it behind on the train. She was rather proud of this bag. It was made of dark blue denim that was an exact match to her favourite jeans, and it was decorated with some strips of strong brightly multicoloured ribbons in a central panel on one side of it.

She was sitting in one of the seats a bit like those on planes. Not that she had been on planes very often, but enough to be familiar with them. She noticed that there was a reservation ticket on the seat next to her, but there was no one in sight so far. Mum had stowed her larger bag on the shelf above her head. That one had all her clothes in it. She and Mum had chosen it together at the sports shop. It was lightweight, and was made of a tough red nylon material. She was a bit worried about how to get it down again, but she had practised by standing on the seat while Mum was still with her, and seemed to manage all right.

She was just beginning to enjoy the feeling of being settled in her seat, watching through the window at the trees and houses flashing by, when she realised someone was in the aisle, next to the vacant seat. She turned and saw a large woman with a strangely shaped box, a

6

bulging leather handbag, and a suitcase on wheels. The woman dumped the box and the handbag on the seat next to Tracy, and proceeded to telescope the handle of the suitcase to its shortest length. There was a scuffle as a man insisted on helping her to stow it in a space between the backs of seats on the opposite side, and then the woman lifted the strange box up onto the luggage shelf next to Tracy's bag. After that, she wedged herself into the seat beside Tracy.

Tracy found this uncomfortable, and she felt hemmed in. The woman was the size of at least one and a half seats, and her warm flesh protruded under the armrest, and jammed itself against Tracy's thigh. She began to wish the journey would be over soon, when it had only just begun.

The woman sighed loudly, and then turned to Tracy and said, 'How far are you going, love?'

'Just a few stations,' Tracy replied, slightly evasively.

'Well, I'll be getting off at the one after next,' said the woman. 'Are you off on holiday somewhere?'

Tracy nodded her head, and the woman went on: 'I'm going to a wedding. You might have noticed the hatbox I put up on the shelf. It's my hat for the wedding.'

Tracy felt intrigued, and wished she felt free to ask to see the hat; but she had always been taught never to get into conversation with strangers, men or women, and she knew she should stick to that. It was all right to say a polite 'yes' or 'no', but it wasn't all right to encourage a conversation. That's what she had been taught, and from everything she knew, it was safer to stick to it.

The woman was speaking again. 'I can see the food trolley coming along. Do you want anything?'

'No, thanks very much,' said Tracy.

'Are you sure? I'm going to have a pack of sandwiches.'

Tracy shook her head in as polite a way as she could. The woman turned towards the aisle, and Tracy heard her ask for a pack of egg mayonnaise ones. Oh, no, my favourite! she thought, and her mouth started to water. She unzipped her shoulder bag again and pulled out some chewing gum, which she quickly fed into her mouth, and started to chew as unobtrusively as possible.

The woman was soon munching contentedly, and Tracy was able to return to her study of the passing scenery until the first station came into view, and she could send a text to her mum to let her know where she was. A text came back almost straight away. Tracy was glad she had put the settings to 'mute', as she didn't want the large woman to notice what she was doing.

'Tell you what, love,' said the woman between chews. 'I'll stand up before we get to the next station, and I'll let you have a look at my hat.'

'Oh,' said Tracy, unguardedly, 'I'd really like that.' She clapped her hand to her mouth, realising her mistake.

'Don't worry, love,' said the woman. 'I'm not about to do you any harm. There's some right rum people about these days, but I'm not one of them. I wouldn't harm a flea.'

Tracy thought for a moment how, if there was a flea on a seat where that woman was about to sit down, it wouldn't have a chance; but then, she realised, that would be true whoever was sitting on something so small, be it a large person or a small one. She waited, looking forward to seeing the hat.

The sandwiches finished, the woman stood up and put the wrapper in the bin. Then she put her handbag on the seat once more, and reached up to her hatbox.

'Here, love,' she said, placing it on Tracy's knee. 'Open it up and have a look inside.'

Tracy opened the fastenings, and lifted the lid. Inside the box was an amazing creation of feathers. In fact, it looked not unlike a bird, except that it had no head, beak or legs.

'Oh!' she gasped.

'Yes, it's beautiful, isn't it,' said the woman, proudly. 'Belonged to my aunt, it did.'

Tracy stared at the iridescent colours of the central feathers, surrounded by the many hues of brown in the surrounding feathers that framed them. She couldn't really work out which bit of it all would sit on the woman's head, but she decided that didn't actually matter. She would have liked to have asked which birds the feathers had come from, but not only was that outside minimal politeness, but also the train was slowing down as it approached the next station.

'I'd better shut it up,' said Tracy. 'Here's your station.'

Thankfully, she closed the lid and refastened it, while the woman collected her suitcase on wheels and extended the handle. She would feel relieved once the woman was off the train, not because she was in any way unpleasant, but it would remove the conflict Tracy felt about whether to speak to her or not, and if she spoke, what to say.

'Thanks for showing me,' said Tracy, as she handed the box across.

'Nice to meet you, love,' replied the woman. 'Bye.' And she pushed her way along the aisle to the automatic sliding door, which obligingly let her through to where the door out of the carriage onto the platform stood open.

Tracy took out her mobile once more, and sent a text to her mother including the name of the station. She added an abbreviated sentence about the woman and the hatbox, and her mother sent her a reply saying, 'Well done.' Tracy relaxed back into her seat and took a deep breath.

The rest of the journey was uneventful. The train was not busy, and no one else came to sit next to her. She sent texts to her mother at the next two stations, and then prepared to leave the train at the one after that. A young man in a railway uniform was making his way along the carriage, checking tickets, and as he saw her struggle slightly with her red bag, he reached up and lifted it down for her.

'Thanks,' she said, as she steadied herself, and prepared to make for the sliding door through which the large woman had left.

The train drew up at the platform, and she could see Flora waiting under a clock, exactly as had been arranged. She was taller than Tracy had remembered, but then, it was a year since she had seen her. Her hair was tied back in a ponytail, and seemed to be even fairer than it had been before. She was wearing a blue T-shirt, and denim jeans that looked not unlike the pair Tracy herself was wearing.

Tracy made her way out of the carriage onto the platform and greeted her.

'Hi!' she said, a little uncertainly.

'Oh, hi...' Flora replied. 'Sorry, I didn't see you getting off, although you were right in front of me.'

'Never mind,' said Tracy, as she put her red bag down for a moment to swing her shoulder bag round, so the back of her neck no longer took its weight.

'I could take one of the handles of this,' Flora offered.

'Thanks,' replied Tracy, relieved to be getting help with it. Although it wasn't too heavy, it was quite bulky and banged against her leg as she walked. Carrying it by taking a handle each would certainly improve things a lot.

'Mum's at the Cash and Carry, buying in all the breakfast cereals and cleaning things at the moment,' said Flora, as they made their way along the platform. She went on. 'This is a working holiday for you, you know. It's the busy season, and Mum's run off her feet she says. I've helped out before, of course. Last year and the year before it was just a few small jobs – carrying things around, and that kind of thing; but this year, Mum's paying me to work four hours a day. I usually do seven thirty to twelve, with a break of half an hour.'

She tossed her head confidently as she imparted this information.

'When Mum said Auntie May would be busy I had hoped I would be able to do something to help,' said Tracy. 'In fact, I've been looking forward a lot to coming; and it's because I'd like to learn as much as I can about the bed and breakfast business, as well as having some time with you. I expect you know that Dad was ill for quite a long time this year, and couldn't go to work. It's made me think a lot more about how I'll have to earn my own living when I'm grown up.'

Flora took in this information. 'That's fine, then,' she said. 'By the way, you'll be sharing a room with me. I'm up in the attic for the summer – that's so Mum can let out my room. We'll have plenty of space, because it's just one big room. I had to carry all my stuff up the stairs. It took me ages. But I've made it look quite nice,' she finished proudly.

By this time, they had passed through the station barrier and were walking along the road to a bus stop.

'It's only a few stops,' said Flora, 'but we may as well take the bus while we've got your bag.'

When they reached the stop, they both dumped the bag gratefully on the ground while they waited for the bus to come.

'What have you got in here, anyway?' asked Flora. 'A few bricks, perhaps?'

Tracy blushed. 'No...o,' she stammered. 'I've just got some changes of clothes, my nightclothes and...'

Flora butted in. 'I was just winding you up! You don't have to go through it all. Right? Look, here comes the number seven. We'll get on this one.'

They grabbed the handles of the red bag and climbed on the bus together; then Flora paid the driver, and they found a seat near the exit door.

A few minutes later, they alighted just outside a large church.

'This is St Peter's,' Flora remarked, despite the large board that stated this fact in bold lettering. She went on. 'I don't much like church, but I do like the Youth Club they have here. I usually go on a Friday evening. You can come along if you want. It's okay to bring a guest.'

'Thanks,' said Tracy. 'What sort of things do they do?'

'In the summer we usually go out. There's a putting green that some of us like. We can have a laugh there. One of the group leaders belongs to the golf club and sometimes takes us in to teach us a bit, and shows us how to practise shots. If it's wet, we stay in and have a discussion group. You know… talk about things like drugs, and how to help old people… that kind of thing. It's much better than soc. ed. at school.' She shuddered.

'What's that?' asked Tracy.

'Social education,' Flora explained. 'We get Mr Roberts. He's *so boring*! I think he must learn it all out of a book and then spout it at us.' She groaned loudly. 'It's *so* bad!'

Tracy giggled. The image of Mr Roberts spouting at a group of bored pupils who would be trying not to pull faces was too much for her. She noticed that this expression of her mirth led to quite a change in Flora. Although she had not been unfriendly before, Tracy had picked up a sense that Flora had not exactly been looking forward to her visit, and that she'd had reservations about having to spend much time with her. But after Tracy's unconcealed outburst of amusement, Flora relaxed, and turned towards her, smiling openly.

'Hey!' she said. 'We could have quite a good time together while you're here.'

In the knowledge of this, Tracy skipped a few steps.

'Hang on a minute,' said Flora, loudly. She had been taken by surprise, and the handle of the bag was nearly jerked out of her hand. 'It's the next road on the right.'

'Yes, I remember,' replied Tracy.

The two turned right and then almost immediately through a gate on the left hand side of the road into the short drive of a brick-built semi-detached house. It was the one on the left of the first pair. What had been the front garden had been turned into a patch of concrete for car parking. A signboard stood just to the side of the low wall that divided this area from the neighbouring house, and it bore the words Welcome Home – Bed and Breakfast. The house and its sign were well placed, because both were clearly visible from the main road the girls had just left, a situation that most certainly was of potential benefit to the business.

'There's no van, so that means Mum's still out,' Flora observed, as she took her key out of the pocket of her jeans. Tracy noticed that the key had a chain attached to it, the other end of which Flora had fastened to a metal loop on the waistband of her jeans. That's a really sensible idea, she thought to herself.

'I've got to remember to phone my mum,' she said. 'I promised her I would. If you hang on a minute I'll use my mobile.'

'No, don't do that, it can be so expensive,' replied Flora. 'Mum will be happy for you to use our phone.' She indicated a phone that was standing on a desk at the far end of the hall. 'On you go; I'll wait.'

Tracy soon heard her mother's voice.

'Tracy! You've arrived,' she said. 'Did you have a good journey?'

'Yes, thanks. I'll tell you more about it later. We're just going to take my bag up to the attic, because that's where we'll both be sleeping.'

'That's fine. Can I have a word with May?'

'She's out at the moment, but she'll be back soon. I'll tell her when she comes in.'

'No, don't bother. I'll give her a ring this evening. Bye for now, love. Have a good time.'

Tracy put the phone down. 'Right,' she said to Flora. 'Up we go. But will you show me all the rooms on the way up, so I get an idea of what's involved.'

Although Tracy had often been to this house before, she had only been in the rooms Auntie May herself occupied. She had a snug sitting room off the back of the house, with a view out into the garden, and her bedroom had its own bathroom and was located to the rear of the first floor. This bedroom was accessed by a small staircase leading up from the kitchen that was immediately to the front of her sitting room. The big dining room was of course the room with a bay window that was next to the front door. The room on the other side of the front door was used as the office. Flora's bedroom was usually the one next to her mother's, and was more or less over the kitchen; but, as she had already explained, this summer she had moved upstairs to the attic to allow her mother to let an extra room.

They put the red bag down on the landing of the first floor, and looked at the rooms. To their left was the door of a large room to the front of the house that contained a double and a single bed; and the walk-in cupboard had been converted to an *en suite* bathroom. The room was clean and airy, and was quite simply decorated with pale green wallpaper. The matching curtains and bed linen were patterned with pale green leaves on a white background. There was another room to the front of the house, the door of which came off the landing on the other side of the stairs. This room was relatively small, but contained a double bed. The walls were pale pink, and the linen was covered with a design of pink roses, and again there were matching curtains.

'I really like this one,' said Tracy admiringly.

'Come on, there's plenty more to see,' said Flora. 'You'll need to look round it all now, because the next guests will start to arrive soon I expect. All the rooms are empty at the moment. That's usually what it's like in the middle of the day on a Saturday. By the way, you might not like that room so much when you've helped me to clean it a few times!'

Immediately to the rear of the large green room was a narrow bathroom, which was covered in white tiles. To the rear of that was the room that was usually Flora's. It was another double room; and this one was painted in a delicate shade of pale yellow. The curtains were broad stripes of yellow and white, and the bed linen almost matched. The only difference was that the stripes were narrow.

'That's the first floor,' said Flora. 'Upstairs again, now.'

The second floor was smaller than the first. It had fewer rooms, and the ceilings were not so high. First, Flora showed Tracy into a very large cupboard, the door of which faced the top of the stairs. It was shelved nearly all the way round, and was full of things like cleaning materials, vacuum cleaners, toilet paper, ladders, and two dismantled cots. There was one large bedroom at the front, a bathroom which Tracy guessed was above the white one on the floor below, an extra toilet with a wash basin next to it, and a smaller bedroom to the rear. Both the bedrooms were double rooms. The one at the front had twin beds in it, and the one at the back had a double.

The décor of the room at the front startled Tracy. Its walls were a striking shade of bright blue, the duvet covers were covered in a bold modern design of blue, black and white, and the curtains were of the same design.

'I thought that would give you a bit of a surprise!' Flora said. 'Actually, we have quite a number of regulars who really like this room. I'll tell you about some of them later, if you want. One more room, and then we can go up to ours.'

She showed Tracy into a room that had pale blue walls; and she saw that the furnishings were patterned with small pale blue flowers.

'Now up to our eyrie,' said Flora, as she seized the red bag, and went up a steep narrow staircase to the attic space.

As Flora had already indicated, it was one room; and it covered the whole of the attic area. Because it was in the roof space, all the walls sloped down to the floor, and the area was lit by four Velux windows: two to the front, and two to the rear.

'I've put the beds at opposite ends,' said Flora, as she stated the obvious. 'But we could move them to be side by side if we wanted to,' she added generously. 'After all, we might want to chat after we come up to bed.'

'We can decide tonight,' Tracy replied. 'I suppose it'll depend on how tired we are.'

At this point, Tracy heard the loud jangling of a bell, and Flora started to race downstairs. 'It'll be some people arriving,' she called over her shoulder. 'I'd better let them in. Mum's not back yet.'

She jumped down the last six steps and ran to the front door, to open it as quickly as she could.

'Thanks, love.' Tracy could hear her aunt's voice.

'It's okay, Tracy. It's just Mum with the shopping. Let's help her to unload.'

Tracy joined her as she jumped out of the door onto the drive, and went round to the back of the van, which was full of large packs of all kinds of things. Tracy opted to lift an enormous pack of toilet rolls into the house, while Flora brought a large cardboard box containing what looked like a variety of packs of cereals.

'That's right, girls,' said May gratefully. 'You'll see there's one side of the van loaded with stuff for the kitchen, and the other's loaded with things to go upstairs to the store.'

Tracy and Flora worked energetically until the van was emptied; and a little while later the three were sitting round the kitchen table enjoying a lunch of toasted sandwiches.

'Well, Tracy,' said Auntie May, 'if you're wanting to help us out, there's plenty you can be doing.' She turned to her daughter and added, 'Isn't there, Flora?'

'Yes. Shall I get the diary from the office, and we can go through this week's guests with Tracy?'

'Good idea,' replied her mother.

She soon returned with the large black desk diary that her mother used for keeping all the details of bookings. She opened it.

'Right,' she said in a businesslike fashion. 'Today. Good job we got all the rooms ready, because we're completely booked up for the night. Oh, I'd better hang the "No Vacancies" on the bottom of our signboard. Hang on a minute, and I'll be back.' And she disappeared for a few minutes.

'I want to help, and I want to learn as much as I can while I'm here,' said Tracy to her aunt. 'Can I help with the cleaning and changing the sheets? I could help in the kitchen with the breakfasts too if you want.'

'Thanks very much, love. We've got a busy week ahead because all the rooms will be taken most of the time. Added to that, most of the people are only staying one or two nights, three at the most; and that means there are a lot of sheets to change and get washed.'

Flora returned and sat down again.

'Tracy's going to be quite a help to us, I think,' said her mother.

Just then, the doorbell went again, and May jumped to her feet and made her way hastily to the front door.

'Mr and Mrs Little? How nice to meet you. Do come in. My daughter will help with your bags. Can you just come over to this desk for a moment? I'll get you booked in, and give you your keys.'

By ten o'clock, everyone had booked in, and had been shown the dining room and their sleeping accommodation. The girls were yawning and could hardly keep their eyes open. They had helped a lot by taking luggage upstairs for guests. They carried the heavier pieces between them by taking one end each, receiving much praise from May, and appreciation from the guests.

'Better get up the stairs to bed now,' said May. 'I'll see you at seven thirty in the morning. There'll be the dining tables to set for breakfast, and I could do with a hand serving out.'

'Okay,' said the girls together, and made their way up the three flights of stairs.

Once in the attic, Tracy said, 'I hope you don't mind, but I'm too tired to chat tonight.'

'That's fine by me. We can move the beds some time tomorrow. I'll put my alarm on for seven.'

Chapter Three

Tracy woke to the unfamiliar sound of Flora's alarm clock. At home, she could hear her parents' clock through the thin wall, but it was muffled by the fact that it was in another room. This sound was harsh and loud. Flora moaned and put her head under her duvet for a moment before reaching out to switch off the noise. By this time, Tracy was already out of bed, and was putting on her zipped fleecy top.

'I'll just go down to the bathroom,' she said.

'Okay, I'll follow you down. Remember to use the small one that's next to the main one, and if that's locked, you can use Mum's.'

'Right. Yes, I remember,' replied Tracy, already part of the way down the steep stairs, carrying her spongebag.

She found the small bathroom was available and went in. She liked the subtle scent of the *pot pourri* in a small wickerwork basket on a shelf fitted into the corner of the small room; and she decided that when she got back home, she would persuade her mum to have something similar.

A few minutes later, she heard a tap on the door, and Flora's voice whispered, 'Will you be long?'

'I'm just coming out,' she replied as she grabbed her things and unlocked the door.

Not long afterwards, dressed in their jeans with clean T-shirts, the two girls appeared in the kitchen ready for work. They could see that May was looking a bit flustered.

'Good to see you,' she said, pulling things out of the large fridge that stood in a corner of the kitchen. 'Flora, can you show Tracy how to get the dining room ready, there's a dear. That would be a great help to me. The first ones will be down at eight because they're leaving early to catch a train. It's the two men from the dark blue room. Although it's Sunday, they've got work to go to somewhere north of here. I'll need to get a move on because they want a full breakfast.'

Flora led Tracy through to the dining room and showed her how

17

to put the cutlery out on the tables. Then she took the packets of cereal out of the dresser at the side of the room, and arranged them neatly on top. After that, she returned to the kitchen for piles of crockery and jugs of fruit juice.

By the time this was finished, the clock on the dresser showed it was nearly eight, and they could hear people coming downstairs.

The following two hours passed very quickly. The girls ferried food and empty plates efficiently back and to from the kitchen, holding polite conversation with the guests when appropriate, while Auntie May masterminded the cooking. By ten fifteen, the dishwasher was churning with a full load, and the girls were cleaning the last of the pans, while Auntie May was helping Mr and Mrs Little with directions for the outing they had planned.

'Whew!' she said, as she sat down heavily on a chair at the kitchen table. 'Now let's have our own breakfasts and plan the day.' She turned to Flora and said, 'Could you put some bread in the toaster for me, love?'

Flora got a pack of bread out of the freezer and fed slices through the slots of the toaster, and then went with Tracy to collect bowls of cereal.

When they were all seated round the table, May went on: 'It's always hard work when we're full,' she said. 'But we need to earn as much as we can in the summer months to help to tide us over the other times of year, when there aren't so many guests. That's why I asked Flora if she'd mind moving up to the attic for the summer holidays.'

Flora nodded, and said, 'I wasn't too keen, was I Mum? I like my own room a lot, and I don't like the idea of anyone messing it up, but I've discovered that now I'm in the attic, I like that too! To be honest, Tracy, I grumped a lot when Mum first suggested it to me, but it's worked out okay so far.'

'Actually, you were very angry with me,' May reminded her. 'And I could understand that. I would probably have felt exactly the same at your age. In fact, I wondered about moving to the attic myself, but my legs haven't been too good recently. I think it must be my age, and all the standing I have to do when I'm working.'

'But you aren't very old, Auntie May,' Tracy burst out. 'My mum's only forty, so that means you're only forty-five.' She blushed. 'Oh, do you mind me talking about ages?'

'No, not at all, love. I know some people still mind, but I think

18

that's a bit old-fashioned, and I'm certainly not bothered. What I should have said is that my periods are going a bit funny, and I think I'm heading for the menopause. Some people have all sorts of bother through that time, and it looks as if I might be one of them,' she said ruefully.

'I heard my mum talking to one of her friends about all that kind of thing,' Tracy said. 'I asked her about it afterwards, and she explained some more to me.'

Flora was looking a bit miserable.

'What's the matter, Flora?' Tracy asked her.

'Nothing much,' replied Flora, evasively.

'Come on, love,' said her mother encouragingly. 'There's something on your mind. Just say what it is. It's the only way.'

Flora's lip began to tremble a little, and she sunk her teeth into it and bent her head down.

May stood up and put her arm round her, but Flora jumped up and ran out of the room, and Tracy could hear her running up the stairs.

'Shall I go up and get her?' asked Tracy.

'Not just yet,' said her aunt wisely. 'I think she needs a few minutes first, but after that I think it would be a big help if you would go up. She certainly looks as if she needs to talk about something, but I'm not sure what it might be. I think I'll put my feet up for a bit before I do any more work. We'll have to do the cleaning later on, but we don't need to rush at it yet, because there are only two beds to change today. Everyone but those two men is staying on for another night. By the way, I won't be pushing Flora to tell me what's the matter. She'll come to it in her own time, especially if I don't rush her.'

Tracy thought through all that her aunt was saying, and it seemed sensible. Added to that, this bed and breakfast business was more complicated than she could have worked out for herself, and she knew she had a lot more to learn. After all, she had been here less than a day so far. She finished her piece of toast, and then went upstairs to see Flora.

She found her lying on her bed, staring at the ceiling with tearstains on her cheeks.

'Mind if I sit on the bed?' asked Tracy.

Flora shook her head.

'What's the matter?' asked Tracy. 'I'm sharing your room, and I

19

want you to tell me what's upset you.'

'I'm worried about Mum,' said Flora, miserably. 'She works so hard to get the money we need to live on, and she gets so tired sometimes. I just want to be ordinary going out with my friends, but she really needs my help, and now that I'm older I help quite a lot, but I could do more if I tried.'

'It's different for me at home,' said Tracy. 'But my dad was off work for ages recently, and my mum looked so worried, and I felt horrible. I was so relieved when he got better.'

'That's another thing,' said Flora.

'What?' Tracy asked.

'My dad.'

Tracy hesitated. She didn't know quite what to say. She knew that Flora saw her dad sometimes; but apart from that she knew nothing, and she was unsure about asking for more information. At this precise moment, she felt very lucky indeed that she had a home with a mum and dad in it.

Flora went on: 'I don't see him much. He always *claims* he keeps in touch with me, but he doesn't really. He's always too busy. I see him only when he happens to be passing through, and that's not very often. And he *never* sees Mum. Last time I saw him I asked him why, and he wouldn't answer!'

'That's not fair!' exclaimed Tracy.

'No, it's not. And actually... sometimes I hate him!' Flora burst out.

Tracy was a bit worried by the intensity of her cousin's outburst, but she thought it best not to say anything. I'll tell Mum and Dad about it when I get home, she thought to herself, they'll know what to do. For now, she thought it might be the best thing to change the subject.

'Can we do the cleaning together?' she asked. 'I'm looking forward to it.'

Flora started to giggle.

'What are you laughing for?' Tracy asked.

'Like I said before, you'll find it's quite fun the first time, but after that it can be a big pain. Anyway, let's go down and see Mum and get our orders. The sooner we get on with it the sooner it'll be finished, and then we might go out for a bit.'

Back at the kitchen table, they shared out the tasks.

'If you two will vacuum and dust round the rooms on the second floor, clean the bathrooms, and then change the beds in the dark blue room, I'll get on with the first floor,' said Aunt May. 'After that, you're free to go off out for a bit if you want. I've got to be on duty here. I might be able to fix for one of my friends to come and hold the fort for an afternoon later in the week, and we can do something nice together then. We'll plan it later.'

'Oh, good!' Tracy said enthusiastically.

'Right!' said Flora. 'Up we go. Where are the things for the beds, Mum?'

'They're in the usual place in that big cupboard in my bedroom, love. Just open the door, and you'll see them straight in front of you. There are plenty of clean towels there too – just take as many as you need.'

Flora led the way up the narrow stairway from the kitchen up to her mother's room and found the bedding.

'Here you are,' she said to Tracy. 'You carry the bedding, and I'll bring the towels. When we've finished, we'll go off out for a bit, and I expect we'll be able to find some of my friends. I'll introduce you.'

Having reached the dark blue room, Flora dumped the pile of towels on a chair by the door.

'Let's change the beds together,' she said. 'It's much easier that way.'

Deftly she whipped off the duvet covers, while Tracy struggled with the fitted sheets and pillowcases.

'Just dump them all in a heap on the landing,' Flora instructed, 'and then we'll take a side each.'

The beds finished, Flora dived into the large cupboard on the landing, and emerged with a black bin bag and another large bag that she identified as a laundry bag.

'Bedding and towels in here,' she said briskly, 'and empty the bins into the black bag.'

'Oh no!' she exclaimed as she went to get the bin from the dark blue room.

'What is it?' called Tracy.

'Mum told me to shut my eyes if I ever find one of these, so I don't think I'll show you,' said Flora firmly. 'I'll just tell you it's the sort of magazine that some men read, and we don't like them.' She dropped it into the bottom of the black bag, and sighed. 'Most of our guests are fine,' she pronounced, and then made her way to the bathroom, toilet and the other bedroom to collect the rest of the rubbish. She soon returned to the laundry bag on the landing, and dumped the black bag next to it. Then she said, 'Can you start the vacuuming in the pale blue room, and I'll clean the bathrooms because I've got rubber gloves.'

Tracy went to the cupboard and collected the upright vacuum cleaner she saw there.

'Hang on a minute, and I'll check the bag first,' said Flora. 'Ah, it's fine for today,' she pronounced, 'but we'll have to empty it tomorrow I think. When you've done that room, can you do the dark blue room, and then move onto the landing? And when you've finished that, we'll do the dusting together.'

The two girls worked determinedly. Having completed all the tasks, they returned the equipment and cleaning materials to the cupboard; and taking a sack each, made their way downstairs to where May was vacuuming the landing.

'Would you two do the dusting on this floor, and then that'll be us finished,' she said. 'Everything you need is in that box over there.' She motioned towards a large cardboard box that she had positioned to one side of the landing.

When everything was finished, they all met in the kitchen once more to make a drink and plan the rest of the day.

'So you're thinking of phoning Mary?' Aunt May said to Flora. 'That's a good idea. I expect she'd like a bit of company if she's in charge again today.'

'What might she be in charge of?' asked Tracy, puzzled.

'She's got a little brother, Tim. He's only one, and he's quite a handful,' Flora explained, grinning at her cousin. 'If I ever feel hard done by, I think of her when she's on duty. I really like Tim, but I'd hate to have to look after him on my own. It's good fun when we take him out in his buggy down to the special kiddies play park though. Do you fancy coming?'

Tracy nodded. It was a long time since Paula was small, and she remembered almost nothing of that time. There were people on the estate where she lived that had little children, and sometimes she would chat to them in their buggies at the shops, but she didn't have any opportunities to play with them.

'I'll ring her then,' said Flora, picking up the phone.

Chapter Four

By three o'clock, Tracy and Flora had met up with Mary, who had walked part of the way round to meet them with Tim in his buggy. He had dozed off on the way, and had flopped forward, but was held in his seat by his harness. Mary was a small dumpy person with curly brown hair and freckles, and she had a jolly manner. Tracy felt she liked her straight away.

'Hi,' said Flora to her friend. 'This is my cousin, Tracy. She's supposed to be staying for a couple of weeks, but actually I'm hoping she can stay longer. It's great having her.'

Tracy was much reassured by this show of enthusiasm, and the few remaining concerns she had about being a nuisance to Flora were finally dispelled.

Mary smiled engagingly at Tracy and said, 'I'm glad you could come.'

'Thanks,' said Tracy. 'Actually I'm quite lucky to have a holiday this year. My dad's not been well, so we couldn't fix anything. Then Auntie May invited me, and well... here I am!'

'Look,' said Mary, 'Tim's asleep at the moment. How about going for a walk first so we can chat? He'll probably stay asleep for about half an hour if I'm walking along with the buggy, but if I stop for long, he'll soon be wide awake. Once he's awake, we can take him down the toddler's park. He loves it there, but he'll be a handful, and we'll have to watch him really carefully. There won't be much chance for talking then.'

The others fell in with Mary's suggestion, and the three walked in the direction of the Memorial Gardens that were easily accessible by crossing a footbridge over the river.

'I've got to remember that Mum wants me to text her around four,' said Mary. 'She likes to know where I am, and I like keeping in touch. It means that I'm free to change my mind about what I've told her I've planned to do – especially when I'm out with Tim.'

Once over the footbridge, they lingered near the riverbank, watching the mallard ducks and drakes. There were families with bags of bread who were feeding the birds by throwing pieces into the water.

'I've noticed something about mallards,' Flora remarked.

'What's that?' asked Mary.

'You know how they usually go around in groups?'

Tracy and Mary nodded.

'Well, in some of the groups there can be many more females than males, and in others it can be the other way round. In fact, I have seen all kinds of combinations.'

'I feel a bit silly asking,' said Tracy, 'but I'm afraid I don't know which is which.'

'I expect you do really,' said Mary generously. 'Look at that one there with all the bright colours on it. What's that?'

'It must be a male,' replied Tracy.

'That's right. See, you *did* know,' said Mary.

'So the brown ones must be females,' mused Tracy. 'I must say I hadn't thought before how well they all get on in different kinds of groups. Thanks for pointing that out to me, Flora.'

'I wish it was like that in all our classes at school – everyone getting on well together in different groups,' Mary announced emphatically. 'Some of the boys can be a real pain.'

'What do they do?' asked Tracy.

'They get together in some of the classes, and start throwing bits of paper around, and giggling. It's *so* stupid.'

Tracy addressed Mary and Flora. 'Are you both at the same school?' she asked.

They nodded.

'Both in the same year?'

They nodded again. Then Flora added, 'But we aren't always in the same classes. Some of the subjects we do are different, and even when we do the same subject, we aren't always in the same class.'

Tracy absorbed this information, and then asked, 'How long have you known each other?'

Flora and Mary looked at each other, and giggled. 'Just about forever!' said Flora. 'Our mums say that we first met at playgroup when we were three, but neither of us remembers that. We remember playgroup a bit.' She looked at her friend. 'Don't we Mary?' Then she turned back to Tracy and said, 'But we don't remember each other being there.'

25

Mary took up the story. 'When we were about four, we started at the same nursery, and then when we were five, we went to primary school together. I remember that really well. My mum took us both on the first day, because your mum was expecting a lot of guests. You were howling because you only wanted *her*, and you didn't want my mum. I remember feeling really annoyed with you for making such a fuss, although I can sympathise now!'

Tim started to make snuffling noises in his buggy.

'Oh no,' whispered Mary, putting a finger to her lips. 'I was so busy talking, that I forgot to keep moving. Let's head towards the gardens and hope he settles down again.'

She swung the buggy round, and walked briskly up the path away from the river. The others followed behind her, hoping that Tim would fall asleep again.

As they reached the gardens, Mary said over her shoulder, 'It's okay, he's dozed off again. You can come alongside me.'

They wandered along slowly together in the warmth of the sun.

'This is quite a good place for us at the moment,' Mary remarked. 'The paths are quite wide, so we can all walk abreast, and the ground is firm, so it's easy to push the buggy along.'

'These plants are really nice,' said Tracy, indicating a formal layout in a bed to her left, which provided a blaze of red.

'Yes,' replied Flora. 'Mum says it's the Town Council that organises it, but she says there's a problem now about money, so they might have to cut back the number of beds they do.'

'Maybe they could turn some of them into grass, or plant some bushes,' said Mary thoughtfully.

'I wish I knew the names of some of these,' said Tracy in a wistful voice. 'I can see there are some deep red snapdragons, but after that I haven't a clue.'

'I'm not much help,' said Mary. 'I think Mum said some of them were Pelargoniums, but I couldn't be sure which, and she could be wrong.'

They walked along in silence for a while.

Then Tracy asked, 'Are you going to be away on holiday this summer, Mary?'

'I don't think so. Mum and Dad are so busy trying to build up their businesses. They said we might go away for a few days in the autumn, but to be honest, the age Tim is at, we're better at home. It's easier. Oh! I'm beginning to sound as if I might be his mum, and not his sister.'

'What do your mum and dad do?' asked Tracy.

'Dad used to be a nurse, but he decided to train to be a massage therapist and set up his own business. He's taken over the dining room in our house, and at the moment he sees most people during the evenings and at weekends.'

Tracy showed immediate interest. 'It was someone like that that helped my dad's bad back,' she said. 'It made a huge difference. Sorry, I butted in. What does your mum do?'

'Now Tim isn't a little baby any more, she's trying to set up a business selling herbal things to help people's health. To be honest I don't know much about it. I remember she was doing a course. It was mainly from home. Then she got pregnant with Tim, but she managed to finish it, and I know she's qualified to give advice to people about the things she sells.'

'Do you look after Tim quite a lot?' asked Tracy.

Mary looked at Flora, who nodded emphatically.

'Well... er... yes. I suppose I do,' said Mary.

Tracy digested this information as they sauntered past a fountain in the middle of an ornamental pool. Flora has to help out with the bed and breakfast business, and Mary has to look after Tim so her mum and dad can get on with their work, she thought to herself. That's quite a bit different from what it's like for me and Paula. Of course, Flora and Mary are older than I am. Then aloud she said, 'I wonder if I'll have some sort of job when I'm fourteen.'

But further conversation was cut short by a howl from the buggy.

'That's it,' said Mary. 'He's *definitely* awake now!' She stopped the buggy, and crouched down beside her brother. It's all right, Tim, I'm here,' she said, soothingly, as she stroked his head with one hand and held one of his hands in the other.

His howls soon reduced to sobs, and then to sniffs.

'Shall we go to the play park?' she asked him. 'Play park?' she repeated.

Tim started to bounce in his buggy.

'Come on, then,' said Mary energetically. 'Off we go. Wheeeeee!'

She swivelled the buggy round expertly, and set off, jogging with it back towards the footbridge. These actions resulted in Tim producing a series of crowing and chuckling noises, interspersed with shrieks of delight, while Mary made the trip sound exciting by making as many car and lorry noises as she could on her way to the bridge.

Tracy and Flora jogged along behind her, admiring the speed at which she propelled herself and the buggy. They all stopped at the riverside to look at the mallards; but Tim immediately started trying to get out of the buggy, so they continued across the bridge and headed for the play park.

'It's not far now,' Flora told Tracy, as they jogged along. 'It's just over there, beyond that fence.' And she pointed across the grassy area to a cluster of trees, where Tracy could see a low fence.

As they neared the fenced area, Tracy could see that there were a number of toddlers running about, being cared for by older children or by parents, who were helping them on and off the pieces of equipment. She could see that some of the little children could manage to climb up the steps of the small plastic slide, but that it was unwise to leave them unattended, because of the danger of them falling off when they got to the top. Although it wasn't far to fall, and she could see the ground was covered in a special kind of artificial matting, an awkward tumble could result in a nasty knock.

Mary stopped the buggy and said to Flora, 'Would you mind helping Tim out while I text Mum?' she asked. 'He hates waiting.'

Tim was already pressing against the straps that contained him, and was trying to stand up. Flora deftly unfastened him, helped him onto his feet and held his hand, while Mary sent the text. Tim made straight for a large plastic duck mounted on a big spring, and Mary lifted him up and sat him on its back, while he bounced happily for several minutes. It was difficult for Tracy to see how she could be of any use. Tim did not know her; and in any case, he already had two people to look after him, so she started to look round at the other people that were there. Everyone seemed happy, and the children were well cared for.

It was such a pleasant place, she thought to herself, and she sat down on the end of a short plastic bench at the entrance to the enclosure. It was then that she noticed that, although there were several litter bins, there was a considerable amount of litter around, most of which had ended up at the bottom of the fence. In fact, there were even some empty drinks cans; and she realised that if a small child got hold of one of them, a cut finger could result. She didn't fancy the idea of picking these things up with her bare hands, so after some thought, she approached a family who were eating a picnic on one of the other seats, to see if they had any spare bags she could use for gloves.

The mother was warm and friendly, just like her own mum and Auntie May; and she said, 'I have some spare bags I carry for emergencies, we could use those I suppose.' She thought for a moment, and then went on. 'I'm a bit worried about you doing it on your own, though.' She turned to the man who was sitting beside her, who Tracy supposed was her husband, and said, 'Jack, could you keep an eye on the kids, and I'll do some clearing up too.' She produced several supermarket plastic bags out of a small rucksack she had at her feet, and handed some to Tracy. 'Here you are,' she said. 'I'd put two on each hand if I were you.'

Together they made their way round the bottom of the fence. Tracy picked up several cans, innumerable crisp packets and many wrappers from chocolate bars. Then she came upon a broken bottle.

'Ugh!' she said.

The woman turned to look at what she had found and said, 'I'll do that one. It looks a bit tricky to me.' She scooped all the smaller pieces of glass into the one large piece, and deposited it in the nearest bin.

When they had finished, Tracy put her makeshift gloves into the bin, and went to where Flora and Mary were helping Tim to bounce on a miniature trampoline. She was amused by the expression on his face each time he went up in the air, aided by his helpers, and she wished her mum had been there to see. She was glad she would be phoning home tonight. It was good being here, but she realised she was missing her family a little.

Tim began to struggle and make signs that he had had enough of the trampoline. Flora and Mary lifted him off, and put him back on the ground to see what he would choose next. He began to run towards the fence, where a dog was pressing its muzzle into the wire inquisitively. Then he tripped, and Mary caught him just in time before he felt flat on his face.

'That was a close one,' she said. 'I don't want him banging his nose again. He's not very good at saving himself yet.'

'Hold on a minute!' said Tracy worriedly, 'I can see a sharp-looking piece of metal stuck into the matting here.'

29

She reached down to pick it up, but stopped when she heard Flora's voice.

'No, don't touch it!' Flora reached inside the pocket of her jeans and produced a piece of kitchen roll. She protected her fingers, and carefully pulled the piece of metal out of the grass. I'll tell Mum about this once we're back home,' she said. 'This is a hypodermic needle, *and* in the children's playground. Mum will know who to phone about it.' She dropped it in one of the bins, together with the piece of kitchen towel, while Mary swung Tim back into his buggy, and strapped him in. He did not protest, but reached one hand up in the air towards her saying, 'Uh, uh, uh.'

'I think he wants his drink,' Mary guessed. She pulled out a leak-proof beaker from the small bag that she had hooked onto the back of the buggy, handed it to him, and watched while he gulped the contents down.

Tracy and Flora said goodbye to Mary at the corner where they had met earlier that afternoon. Before they parted, Flora invited Mary to come round the following evening to watch a video, and to see the attic bedroom that she and Tracy were now sharing. She had tried to persuade her to come that evening, but Mary had been sure that her mum and dad needed her to feed Tim and put him to bed, so she couldn't be sure she would be free soon enough.

'It depends if he settles straight away or not,' she had explained. 'If he doesn't settle, I have to lie down beside his cot and sing to him. That works very well. He stops crying straight away, but sometimes I have to sing for quite a while. But it'll be great to come round tomorrow evening. I'll look forward to that.'

Back home, Flora told her mum about the needle she had found.

'It's a very good thing you've told me,' said May. 'I'll get on to the Council in the morning about that one. To be honest, I think they ought to send someone round to check the toddlers' park every week, and I'm willing to keep putting some pressure on them about that. But everywhere else…' she shrugged. 'I must say I worry about young people nowadays. It wasn't that there weren't drugs around when I was young. But now there seem to be a lot more people pushing them, and there are more different kinds, most of which are easily available.' She turned to Tracy. 'Do you talk about drugs at school?'

'Yes,' replied Tracy. 'Some of the teachers talk about them, and

30

we had someone round from the police at the end of last term as well, who gave us a long talk and showed some slides.' She shuddered. 'Some of it was really scary.'

'Well, I'll certainly put the needle on my list for tomorrow, so I don't forget. The last thing we want is for any little children to pick one up or get one stuck into them. Apart from getting stabbed you can pick up all sorts of things from them.'

She made a note on the long list of tasks she had already drawn up for the following day.

'Right, my loves,' she said briskly. 'What'll we have for tea? And after that Tracy can do her phoning. Oh... and remind me I'd like a word with your mum when you've finished.'

'Okay,' said Tracy. She was looking forward to speaking to her mum. Although she had been here only one day so far, a lot had happened that she wanted to tell her about. If Dad was at work, she knew Mum would tell him her news when he came home.

The girls opted to go to bed early that night. May had found their help at breakfast invaluable and had asked them if they would both be willing to help every morning that week, because of it being a 'full house'. They were quite tired, and they wanted to shift the beds round so they could chat. They didn't want to be too tired for that, as they had been the previous night.

Before they went to sleep, Tracy heard Flora say, 'It's great having you here. I wasn't looking forward to it much – with you being younger than me... but actually, it's fine.'

Chapter Five

Tracy and Flora woke once more to the sound of Flora's alarm. Tracy leapt out of bed straight away saying 'Race you'; and Flora, astonished, at first pulled a face and blew a raspberry, and then grabbed her wash bag and made for the stairs. Tracy got there a second before she did, and the two almost slid down the steep flight on their way to the bathroom. The door to the toilet was locked, so they made their way down to May's bathroom at the rear of the first floor.

'It's a bit of a trek, isn't it?' complained Flora. 'But it happens quite a lot when we're full up. Go on, you can go first.'

'Thanks,' replied Tracy, who then made sure she took as little time as possible.

Back in the attic they dressed as quickly as they could, and then vied with each other as to who would get to the kitchen first.

'Remember to watch out for guests on the main stairs,' Flora warned. 'It wouldn't look too good if we knocked one of them flying!'

May looked pleased to see them. 'It's good to see two pairs of nice pink cheeks!' she exclaimed.

'Oh Mum!' protested Flora in an angry voice. 'I *told* you not to say that. You know I hate it!'

'Sorry love,' her mother apologised. 'I'll try to remember. Now, we've got three tables coming down early this morning, so can you two do the same as yesterday?' Then to herself she muttered, 'Perhaps I should get them to put out the things each day so they're ready for the morning, but I don't like that. Sometimes a fly or two gets in, and might crawl on the cutlery.'

'What are you mumbling about, Mum?' called Flora from the dining room.

'Nothing love,' May said loudly. 'Well... I'll talk to you about it later.'

Tracy thought that Flora was being a bit rude to her mother this morning, but May didn't seem to notice, and if she did, she certainly didn't seem to mind.

The first guests arrived for breakfast. It was Mr and Mrs Little, who were hoping to set off early for their next destination.

'Good morning,' she said to them, and they smiled and returned her greeting. They were quite a bit older than Auntie May, thought Tracy, as she took a jug of milk to them. But she had no time to think any more about them. Others were coming into the dining room. She showed them to their tables, while Flora collected more things from the kitchen.

There were two men. They must have been in the dark blue room, she thought. She didn't remember them coming yesterday, and concluded that they must have arrived when she and Flora were out with Mary and Tim. Fleetingly she hoped that there wouldn't be another of those magazines to deal with; but if she was honest with herself, she felt curious about what yesterday's magazine had actually been. She was glad she had mentioned it to Mum yesterday, though. Mum had said something about 'Poor May, having to put up with it', but she had been interested in how Flora had dealt with it, and said to Tracy she had been glad she'd told her about it.

No more time to think just now, she said to herself, as a group of three people came into the room. There was a man and a woman about the same age as her mum and dad, and there was a boy. Well, she thought, not really a boy. He looked as if he was changing into a man, and was only half way there. She said a cheerful 'good morning' to them, and showed them to the same table they had occupied the previous morning. It was a larger table, and it stood in the bay window at the front of the house. It was the one that her aunt usually reserved for the green room guests. The man and woman thanked her, and the boy looked out of the window. He had ignored her the last time too, and she was glad. It was easier that way.

After that more people arrived, and she had no more time to think, as she was rushing to and from the kitchen, carrying plates and jugs, full and empty, and then making a start on the washing up. This morning all the breakfasts were finished by nine. Everyone was leaving today; and while she worked with Flora in the kitchen, she could hear Aunt May talking to some of them in the hall, as she helped them with directions and said goodbye.

Ten o'clock saw the three of them sitting round the kitchen table once more, eating their own breakfast.

'It's such a help having you both here,' said May gratefully. 'It isn't that I *can't* do the breakfasts without help, but I do feel quite stressed on the days when I'm on my own if I've got a full house, especially if it's day after day, like it can be in the summer holidays. And of course the guests don't get served quite so quickly.' She paused for a moment and then said, 'I've got to remember to give you a special "thank you" from Mr and Mrs Little, and to say they liked your cheerful service in the dining room so much that they've left you a tip!' She produced two five-pound notes from inside a stack of bills at one end of the table, and handed one each to Tracy and Flora.

'Oh wow!' said Flora and Tracy as they took the money.

May went on. 'I've been thinking. I pay Flora for four hours a day. If I didn't have her help in the summer, I'd definitely need to get someone in to help with the cleaning at least. But at the moment it's so good having an extra hand at breakfast that I want to give *you* some money for that, Tracy.'

Tracy looked startled. She had only thought of helping Aunt May because she was staying for a holiday, and it hadn't crossed her mind that she might get some money. Her mum had sent some money with her so she could pay her way on any outings, and she could put the five pounds with that. But Aunt May paying her for helping...? She felt uncomfortable, and she stuttered a little as she said, 'Um... perhaps you and Mum could have a chat about it... er...'

Her aunt looked at her, and realising how uncomfortable she was, said, 'All right, love, I'll have a chat with your mum about it next time we phone her.' She clapped her hands together and said briskly, 'And now, to work.' She looked at Flora. 'You know what we're heading for now, don't you love? All the rooms and bathrooms are to be cleaned, and all the beds are to be changed. The towels and clean bed linen are in the cupboard, of course. Can you start on the second floor, and when you've finished give me a hand on the first?'

Flora looked at Tracy. 'Race you!' she challenged, and ran out of the kitchen door.

The day was bright and sunny. Once in the dark blue room, Flora threw open the large windows as wide as she could, and then went into the pale blue room to do the same. 'Remind me to shut them up a bit when we've finished up here,' she said to Tracy as she grabbed a black plastic bag in one hand, and passed a laundry bag across to her.

'Can you start stripping the beds while I get the bins and the bathrooms over and done with? Then we can go and get the clean stuff and put it on together like we did yesterday, and finish up with the vacuuming before we go down to help Mum.'

The two girls worked quietly and determinedly. They both wanted to get finished so that they could help on the first floor. There had been seven people staying there, so it would be a lot more work than here, where there was only room for four. Tracy was pleased that she felt she was getting the hang of the work already.

An hour later they carried one of the vacuum cleaners down the stairs to the first floor.

'Ah, my trusty helpers have arrived,' May greeted them. 'I've done the pink room and nearly finished the green one. Can you start the dusting and vacuuming, please?'

It was after twelve thirty by the time everything was ready again for the next lot of guests; and they were just sitting down for a lunchtime sandwich when the phone rang. May lifted up the kitchen extension.

'Oh, Miss Maitland. How are you?' There was a long pause while she listened intently, and then she said, 'I *am* sorry to hear that. Yes, Flora's here, I'll hand you over to her.' She put her hand over the phone for a moment and said, 'Her home help is ill, and she needs a bit of shopping. She's hoping you might go round and see her.'

Flora took the phone. 'Hello, Miss Maitland. Mum says you need a hand.' She waited for a moment to let Miss Maitland explain, and then said, 'I've got my cousin, Tracy, staying at the moment. Would you mind if she comes too?'

After saying goodbye, she turned to Tracy and said, 'I hope you don't mind, I've said we'll go round at about two and pick up her shopping list. She isn't in a rush for the things. She says she'll be fine, just so long as she gets what she needs today. That means we can linger at the shops a bit. I'd been thinking of going round there this afternoon anyway – there's some makeup at the chemist's I wanted to look at. I thought you might be interested,' she added casually.

Tracy was impressed. She and Paula had some makeup they shared that Mum had bought them last year, but she hadn't really thought yet of looking for some herself. Most of her friends at school talked about it quite a bit, but she hadn't felt interested. Sometimes she wondered if it was because her mum hardly ever wore any. She just put it on sometimes when she went out somewhere special. But then, Paula seemed to experiment with what they had, so that couldn't be the whole explanation.

'Before you go, I wanted to suggest something,' said May. 'You told me that Mary's coming round this evening.'

'Yes, that's right,' said Flora.

'Well, I was wondering if you'd like to phone to see if she can come for tea. I could take a pizza out of the freezer for you all to share, and you can have the kitchen to yourselves for an hour or so if you want.'

Flora's eyes shone. 'That would be great Mum!' she exclaimed, and threw her arms round May impulsively. 'I'll phone and ask her now.'

'I think I'll put my feet up for a bit this afternoon,' said May. 'There'll be people booking in on and off from about four, but I'll get some time with my library book, and I'll be here to take enquiries. Although I'm booked up for the next two weeks, I've got some vacancies after that, and I don't want to miss a chance of filling them. I'll get on to the Council too about that needle you found!'

Flora and Tracy got up from the table.

'One more thing,' said May. 'Remember to bring your clothes down this evening. We can put a wash on in the morning, and peg it out after breakfast. We don't want you both running out of clean T-shirts!'

Flora phoned Mary from the hall, and fixed that she would come round at seven; and then she and Tracy set off down the road to see Miss Maitland.

'It's about twenty minutes' walk from here,' Flora explained as they strolled along in the sun, but you needn't worry because it's on the way to the shops we're going to.'

'That's fine, and I quite like walking anyway,' replied Tracy. 'Before Dad hurt his back we went on a lot of walks together. Sometimes it was all of us, and sometimes it was just me with him. For some reason we haven't done it again yet, and I've been missing it.' Here her voice cracked a little, but she gathered herself and said, 'So this is just great!' She thought for a minute about how her dad had been in pain for such a long time, and how worried her mum had been; then she pushed the images out of her mind and asked Flora about Miss Maitland.

'She's a friend of Mum's really,' Flora said. 'I can't remember how they got to know each other, but it must have been ages ago. She's quite old now, and she can't really get out. That's why she's got a home help. Mum goes round just about every week when it isn't the busy season, because they like chatting together, but at this time of year, Mum can't leave the business. It's too busy, and I'm not old enough yet to fill in for her with a lot of the things like booking in guests. I think I'll have to be about sixteen before I can do that.'

'What's she like?' asked Tracy.

'She's good fun,' Flora replied. 'She might be old, but she's really interesting to talk to. Her father was a farmer, and she and her sisters had to help with the work. They all lived there until their parents were both dead, and then they sold the business, and each of them bought a small house from the money they got. As far as I know, none of them got married. I like listening to some of her stories, and she always listens very carefully to anything I talk to her about. She comes out with quite useful things. Do you think you'll get married?'

Tracy was taken by surprise. She hadn't expected this question. 'I haven't thought about it,' she said. 'How about you?'

'Quite a few of the girls in my class have got boyfriends,' said Flora, 'but I'm not sure about it. After all, look what happened to Mum.'

Tracy didn't know what to say, so she kept quiet, and Flora went on: 'I sometimes think I'd like to try going out with a boy – just to see what it feels like,' mused Flora, half to herself. 'But there's nobody I fancy anyway. There's certainly no one in my class at school. They're either swots or stupid. There are some at the Youth Club, and one or two of the older ones seem quite good to speak to, but I don't really fancy them.'

Tracy was familiar with the word 'fancying', and it was used a lot between the girls at school; but she wasn't sure what it really meant when applied to boys, and she sometimes wondered if anyone else did either. It was a bit difficult to ask Flora, because although she seemed to know what she was talking about, maybe she didn't. This was another thing she must remember to talk to Mum about. She couldn't think why she hadn't thought to speak to her about it before. Yes, she said to herself, when I get home I'll ask her about it, and I'll ask her more about what happened to Flora's dad. After all, she realised suddenly, he is my uncle. It suddenly seemed strange that she had not met the man who was Flora's dad and her uncle. She had never questioned this before, but now it seemed so obvious that there was something odd. Auntie May never spoke about him, Flora was upset about him, and she herself had never met him. Had Mum and Dad ever met him? There were more questions in her mind, but no answers; and she didn't feel she ought to ask either Flora or Auntie May.

Flora was speaking again. 'We're nearly there. It's that little bungalow at the end of the road.' She pointed to a small rectangular building with a plain front door, and a window on either side of it. There was a very small garden to the front of it that had a few rose bushes, with a path up the middle to the door. Flora led the way up the path and knocked loudly on the door.

'She sits in a room at the back,' she explained, 'and you have to knock loudly so that she can hear. Then you have to wait quite a while to give her time to come to the door.'

After a few minutes the door opened, and Tracy could see a white-haired woman who was wearing a shapeless navy dress with a cardigan to match. She was not bent like some older people, but her skin was very wrinkled. She was about the same height as Flora.

'Come in, dears,' she said. 'How lovely to see you.' She led the way slowly to a room to the left at the end of the narrow hallway. 'Come in here and sit down for a while. Shall we have a cup of tea?'

'I'll put the kettle on,' said Flora, going into the other room at the back of the house, leaving Tracy with Miss Maitland.

'So you're May's niece,' she said. 'Yes, there's a bit of a likeness. I think I met your mother once, many years ago, but I hardly remember her. How are you liking it here?'

'I'm enjoying it,' Tracy replied. 'I arrived on Saturday, and I'm helping Auntie May and Flora with some of the work.'

'That's good. I'm sure May can do with a hand. And a bit of hard work never did a young thing any harm,' she reflected. 'I had to work hard when I was your age.'

Just then, Flora arrived with a tray bearing three cups of tea, which she handed round.

'Thanks, dear, that's a big help,' said Miss Maitland. 'I can be a bit shaky on my feet these days.' She turned to Tracy. 'How long are you staying?' she asked.

'Two weeks,' Tracy replied.

'But I'm hoping she can stay longer,' added Flora.

'I'm sure May would love to have you,' said Miss Maitland. 'Do you have to be back for anything in particular?'

'Not really,' said Tracy; and then she went on to explain how her family had planned to have a holiday abroad, until Dad's accident had intervened.

'I'm glad he found someone to help him in the end,' said Miss Maitland sincerely. 'Never mind about the holiday. It's good to have you here, and I hope you stay on for longer than two weeks. You're welcome here any time, if you want to come and have a chat with an old woman like me. When I was a girl I didn't know what holidays were. We just worked all the time!' She laughed. 'Mind you, there are people who pay now to go and live on a farm for a holiday. How things have changed!'

'Thank you,' said Tracy politely. Already she liked this person, and she hoped that Flora would want to come back again some time.

'Where's your shopping list?' Flora asked Miss Maitland. 'There are two of us to carry things, so just tell us exactly what you want.'

'Well, I need a new hot water bottle,' she began.

'But it's summer!' exclaimed Tracy without thinking.

'It might be summer, but an old lady like me can still get cold in bed,' Miss Maitland explained.

'But don't you need help to fill it?' asked Flora.

'Ah... I've got my ways and means,' said Miss Maitland. 'I prop it up in a bucket, I've got a plastic funnel that I put in the top, and I use both my hands to pour the kettle. Then, when I'm tightening up the stopper, I take my pair of pliers to make sure it's done up tightly enough.'

Tracy was impressed, and said so.

'We farm folk have to be resourceful you know,' said Miss Maitland with the equivalent of an impish grin on her face. 'The trouble is, I can't think of any way to get my old legs down to the shops, and so I have to rely on the likes of good people like you.'

'What else is on your list?' asked Flora.

Miss Maitland read it out. 'Porridge oats, carrots, cauliflower, and two rolls of toilet paper. That's it.'

'Are you sure there isn't anything else?' Flora pressed her.

'No, that's fine, unless...'

'Unless what?' questioned Tracy.

'Unless you wouldn't mind changing my library book for me.'

'Of *course* not!' Tracy reassured her.

'There is a housebound library comes round, but it's only once a month, so I try and get people to get books from the local library for me. The librarian knows some of the kinds of books I like, but here's a list you can show her in case they have any of them in.' She handed another list across.

Flora read from the clear round script. '*The House by the Dvina* by Eugenie Fraser. *A Childhood in Scotland* by Christian Miller. *Windows of the Mind* by G.M. Glaskin.'

'The book to take back is on the chest there.' Miss Maitland pointed across the room.

'Okay. We'd better be going now,' said Flora as she tidied away the cups and saucers. 'And if you aren't in a rush for these things, we'll take our time.'

'No, I'm not in a rush at all, and I'll look forward to you coming back later. Just let yourselves out and pull the door to behind you.'

Flora picked up the book, they said goodbye, and were soon walking down the street in the direction Flora assured Tracy led to the shops.

'It's about another ten minutes,' she said. 'We can go to the chemist's first, and get the hot water bottle and look at the makeup. They've got a really good range of testers.'

Once in the chemist's Tracy and Flora soon became absorbed in the enticing array of makeup and beauty products. At first Tracy was a bit worried about the fact that the woman in charge seemed to be watching them carefully; but after she had come across and said, 'Just take your time girls, it's nice to see you experimenting,' Tracy relaxed and followed Flora's example of putting streaks of lipstick on her hand, and blobs of nail varnish on the uncoloured artificial nails that had been put out.

'It's the only shop I know that does that,' whispered Flora. 'It's such a great idea. I come here quite often and try things out. I don't buy much because I'm trying to save up my money to put towards buying a computer. They are always friendly when I come, and they don't seem to mind me spending ages just looking.'

They became so engrossed in their experimentation that they almost forgot to buy Miss Maitland's hot water bottle. They were out in the street again before they remembered, and had to go back into the shop.

'She didn't say what colour she wanted,' said Tracy worriedly. 'Do you think it'll matter?'

'I don't expect so, or she would have said,' replied Flora. 'What do you think about getting one of these bright red ones for her? One of the sides is ribbed and one is plain.'

'I suppose if she really doesn't like it, we could come back and change it,' said Tracy. 'After all, it's not very far to come.'

'That's true,' said Flora. She looked at the pink digital watch that she had on her left wrist. 'We've still got loads of time.'

They paid for the hot water bottle and went out into the street again.

'I think we should go to the library next, then we aren't carrying the heavy stuff with us,' said Flora, as she led the way towards an older building that looked like an old-fashioned school.

Once inside, she handed the book and the list to the librarian who said, 'Oh, it's for Miss Maitland. Actually, I've got something here she's sure to like, but I'll check the list too for you.' She disappeared into a store cupboard set in the wall behind the desk, emerging a couple of minutes later with a hardback book. 'This is the one I put on one side for her. Excuse me a moment, and I'll see if I have any of these.'

The girls stood and watched while the woman checked her computer.

'Ah, yes,' she said. 'I have a copy of *A Childhood in Scotland* in at the moment. I'll just go and get it.' She picked a slim paperback off a nearby shelf, stamped the form inside each of the books and handed them to Flora.

'Supermarket next,' said Flora as they went out into the street once more; and it was not long before they were putting their groceries through the checkout.

Miss Maitland had been pleased to see them again, and had been delighted to have the books. The hardback had proved to be a selection of short stories of country life. When the girls had asked her about the other book, she had said, rather mysteriously, that she had read there was a bit about ghosts in it; and she had suggested she might read some of it out to them if they came round again some time.

She said she would mark the best bits just in case.

'Scary stuff,' said Flora as they walked back along the road towards her home. 'I wonder why it is that she's interested in things like that.'

'We should have asked her,' replied Tracy. Then she surprised herself by adding, 'I'd really like to go back soon and ask her to read some bits out and tell us why she's so interested.'

Flora stopped and looked at her. 'You're serious aren't you?' Then she laughed and said, 'Actually, that's exactly what *I* want to do too, but I wasn't going to admit it straight way. I feel silly now!'

Tracy started to giggle and couldn't stop; and Flora joined in almost straight away.

'What's so funny?' they asked each other between taking gasps for air. But neither of them could say.

Back at the house, they found May busy showing guests to their rooms, so they gave a hand with the luggage once more. Everybody seemed to be arriving at once, and May was glad of their help. This meant that she could stay downstairs doing the booking in, and handing out leaflets about local eating places for evening meals, while the girls took over the task of showing people to their rooms.

Once everyone was settled in, the three sat in the kitchen drinking tea, while May asked them how Miss Maitland had been.

'She was fine,' Flora reported. 'We got her shopping, and went to the library for her.'

'Oh yes,' said May, 'she never stops reading. She's always been like that. She never travelled much, but she's been everywhere in her reading.'

'How did you meet her, Mum?' asked Flora.

'That's an interesting story,' replied May. But she didn't say anything else, and Tracy noticed that she appeared reluctant to continue.

'Go on, Mum. Tell us,' Flora pressed her.

'Well…' said May, rather uncertainly.

'What's the big secret?' Flora persisted.

Tracy kicked her under the table, and said, 'I don't think your mum wants to tell us at the moment.'

'Hm!' said Flora, and got out of her chair, giving every indication that she was about to flounce out of the room. 'I *hate* Mum when she does this sort of thing,' she stormed.

'I'm sorry, love,' said her mother apologetically. 'Of course I'll tell you. Part of it is about your dad, so I need to ask you first if you would prefer to wait until we have time that can't be interrupted by guests.'

'Just tell me *now!*' snapped Flora irritably.

'Do you want me to go upstairs while your mum's telling you?' asked Tracy.

'No, it's all right Tracy. After all he's your uncle as well as my dad.'

Tracy was surprised that at this time, when Flora was so upset, she was able to think beyond her own relationship with her dad.

May began. 'It's quite simple really,' she said. 'As you know, your dad left us when you were about six months old. I was totally devastated, and didn't know which way to turn. You might think it odd, but one of the things I did was to go and see a medium that I'd heard about. She was having a group of people to her house one afternoon, and I wanted to talk to her about how she could see beyond what most people could normally see. I got in touch with her, and when she heard that I had a young baby, she said I could take you along with me. I was glad about that because I couldn't bear leaving you.' A tear slid down May's cheek as she recalled that time. She wiped it away determinedly and went on. 'So I went to that meeting, and it was there that I met Louise – Miss Maitland.'

'Oh *wow!*' said Flora, who was clearly impressed. 'Why on earth didn't you tell me about that before? That's really cool.'

'I don't know. Well, yes, I think it was because I didn't know what you would think about me being in such a state, and me trying to get that sort of help.'

'But Mum, I think it's absolutely great you did that. It helps me a lot to know you were so upset when Dad left. You've always been so matter-of-fact about it when you've mentioned it, and I thought you didn't care. And I'm so pleased you went to see that medium. What did she say?'

Her mother swallowed. 'Well, she didn't say anything about your dad,' she said cautiously. 'After the talk she gave, she had messages to give to quite a few of the people. Then she looked at me very intensely, and just said, very meaningfully, "You'll be all right", and that was that.' By this time tears were pouring down May's face.

'That meant a lot to me,' she said. 'And whenever I felt stressed after that, I thought of what she had said, and I felt a bit calmer.'

'Where did Miss Maitland come into all this?' Flora asked.

'She was sitting next to me during the meeting, and afterwards she asked me if I wanted to go back to her house with her for a cup of tea. She had seemed to sense that I was on my own, although I hadn't said anything about it to her. I went back with her, and found I was telling her everything about what had happened. She just sat and let me talk and talk. I knew she was really listening and trying to understand what I was going through, although she didn't say much. After that I got into the habit of going round for a chat. We talked about all sorts of things. We've always got on well together. You both know that your gran, my mum, died of cancer when she was quite young, a few years before you were born, Flora, so I hadn't got any family nearby that I could turn to. Miss Maitland is the youngest of three sisters, although neither of the others is alive now.'

Flora gave her mother a hug. 'Mum, you're just great,' she pronounced. 'The only thing that's wrong with you is that sometimes you don't tell me things you should. I can't wait to tell Mary when she comes round!' She consulted her pink watch. 'Hey, it's six thirty already. She'll be round soon. Where's that pizza? Oh, and can we watch a video in the sitting room later on? Mary says she's bringing one of a film she taped from the TV.'

'Of course you can. You won't mind if I come and sit in for a bit though, will you? I've got some mending to do, and it would be nice to do it in company.'

Chapter Six

Mary arrived at ten past seven.

'Sorry I'm a bit late,' she said, breathlessly. 'At the last minute an important phone call came in for Mum, and my dad was still out at some meeting. I had to stay with Tim until she was finished. It turned out that Mum's phone call was about quite a big order, but I must admit I felt really fed up. I know that it's important that Mum and Dad get their businesses off the ground, but all too often I have to change my own plans or they even get completely ruined.' She flushed as she said this, and looked distinctly angry and upset.

'Never mind,' said Flora. 'I waited till you came before putting the pizza in the oven, and you aren't all that late actually.'

Mary looked even more upset.

'What's the matter, Mary?' asked Tracy.

'In the rush, I've forgotten to bring the video. Shall I run back and get it?'

'No, don't do that,' said Flora and Tracy together. Flora giggled. 'You might find yourself having to do something else, and the pizza will get burned. We were looking forward to seeing you, and the video would have been good, but it's better to have you here without it than not at all! We can watch it another time I'm sure.'

Tracy nodded. 'Definitely,' she added.

'I'll heat up the oven,' said Flora in capable tones. 'Let's check what it says on the packet for the right temperature. They are usually all the same, but it's as well to check. Hey, it's one of those really nice ones with bits of artichoke in it. That's my favourite! If either of you two doesn't like artichoke, say so straight away, and I'll make sure you don't get any.'

'Um,' said Tracy. 'I'm not sure I know what it is actually. I might have had some. The name's familiar, but I can't think what it looks like.'

Flora pointed helpfully to the picture on the front of the packet to where half a baby artichoke heart was illustrated.

Tracy looked undecided, and then said, 'I just don't remember, but I'd like to give it a try, thanks.'

Flora pulled a face. 'Oh no! All the less for me,' she moaned in a fake voice; and Tracy, with her increased confidence about not only being included, but also accepted by Flora, gave her a playful push.

'Well you're in luck where I'm concerned,' said Mary. 'I've tried them, and I don't like them. So you can certainly pick *my* bits off.'

By now the oven was heated up, and Flora carefully slid the pizza out of its wrappings onto a flat baking tray, and put it on a rack in the middle of the oven, closed the door and set the timer. Then she went to the large fridge.

'I'm just looking to see if Mum's got any spare lettuce,' she said as she opened the door. 'I fancy a bit with my pizza.' She stopped. 'Hey, what's this!' she exclaimed.

'What is it?' asked Tracy, going over to join her.

'Look at this,' said Flora, pointing.

Mary joined them and peered into the fridge where they had discovered a large bowl with a plate on top of it, and a message on top of that, written in May's handwriting. It said, 'Help yourselves. Love, Mum x'.

Flora lifted it carefully out of the fridge and onto the table. Then she took the plate off the top and gasped. Inside was a large mixed salad, beautifully prepared.

'She must have made this while we were round at Miss Maitland's,' said Flora. 'And it means she must have been listening to me after all.'

'What do you mean?' asked Mary.

'Well, I've been trying to talk to her about how I'm worried about putting on weight, and how I'm worried about my diet. All she said was that I was a growing girl and that I was bound to be putting on weight. I felt angry with her because she just didn't seem to listen to what I was saying.'

'I've had that problem with *my* mum too,' said Mary. 'I'm growing out of all my clothes, and all she says is that I am still growing and that that's bound to happen. But it feels awful. I feel *so fat* and I want to go on a diet. I get really angry inside because there she is with her herbal treatments and all that, trying to get people well, and she isn't taking *any* notice of what's happening to *me*. And I can't say anything else to her because she's so busy and I've got to look after Tim.'

Tracy stayed quiet. She knew that there was something about her body that was bothering her, but she hadn't particularly related that to food. She had wanted to speak to her mum about it, but she didn't really know what it was, so she didn't know how to start or what to say.

'Do you know something?' said Mary.

'What?' asked Flora.

'Well, sometimes when Tim doesn't eat up all the food I've made for him, I just eat it up, even when I'm not hungry, and then I feel horrible!'

'Poor Mary!' exclaimed Flora and Tracy together, and they gave her a hug.

'Thanks,' said Mary. 'That really helps.'

Just then the timer on the cooker went off.

'Oh no!' said Flora. 'I meant to warm up the plates. Tell you what: I'll open the oven door and put them in for a few minutes with the door ajar.'

A few minutes later the three were sitting round the table, and Flora was dividing the pizza into equal portions, making sure she took the one that had two pieces of artichoke on it, and giving Mary the one that had none.

Tracy picked tentatively at the piece of artichoke in the middle of her slice.

'Don't waste it,' said Flora, a little irritably.

'I'm not going to,' replied Tracy. 'I was looking at it first,' she added defensively, before sticking her fork through the middle of it and putting it all in her mouth at once.

Flora watched her carefully with a mischievous expression on her face.

'Actually, it tastes really good,' Tracy pronounced.

'That means I've lost a chance of having a good laugh then,' said Flora with no real disappointment in her voice. 'Let's count all the things Mum's put in this salad. I'll start… cucumber.'

'Lettuce,' said Tracy.

Then Mary said, 'Tomato.'

'Those are all the easy ones,' mused Flora. She took the salad servers and lifted a generous portion onto her plate. 'Ah, there are some slices of avocado pear underneath,' she said.

'I think I can see bits of onion,' said Tracy triumphantly.

'And there's a lot of tiny bits of green leaves sprinkled all over it. I bet they're chopped herbs,' Mary added. 'I wish they taught us how to make things like this at school,' she complained. 'All that going on at us about five fruits and vegetables a day, and then they serve up chips at lunchtime, and give us no classes in food preparation! I saw a programme on the TV that said everyone at secondary school in Finland *had* to have classes in healthy cooking and eating, and it showed people of our age making berry soup. The soup sounded really weird, but if that's the sort of thing they're used to eating there, then that's fine for them.'

'Do either of you like French dressing?' asked Flora suddenly. 'I think Mum's got a bottle in the fridge that she likes.' She went back to the fridge and examined the bottles and jars in the shelves in the door. 'Yes, here we are. She's only used a bit, so I'm sure she won't mind us taking some.' She sprinkled a little on her salad and passed the bottle to Tracy.

'No, thanks,' said Tracy. 'I don't like that kind of stuff. Do you want some, Mary?'

'Not for me either. I'll put it back in the fridge for you, Flora.'

When they had finished, they sat on for a while, talking; then they cleared everything away, took an apple each, and went into the sitting room where May was busy mending some of the stitching that had come adrift on a number of pillow cases.

'Hello, girls,' she said. 'These pillowcases... this modern way of stitching isn't all that clever, you know. I often end up having to sew the ends by hand. But I suppose they are getting a lot of wear here.'

'Thank you very much for the lovely salad, Auntie May,' said Tracy. 'I really liked it.'

'Yes, we all did,' said Flora, while Mary nodded vigorously.

'Good,' May replied. 'Now, where's your video?'

'Well, actually, Mary forgot to bring it because she was in a rush, so we'll go straight upstairs.'

'Oh. All right. I'll put the radio on for myself instead. I see you've got apples. Just help yourself to as much fruit as you want, but do remember to bring any cores and left-overs back down to the bin in the kitchen, won't you.'

'Yes... definitely,' said Flora immediately. She turned to the others and explained, 'We've had mice in the attic in the past, and we don't want to encourage them by leaving anything around that they can eat. Ugh!' she shuddered, and then went on. 'Do you know, we had some candles up there once, and they ate *them*!'

'Oh no!' exclaimed Tracy. 'Well, I'll certainly be very careful. I don't want to think of them running over me when I'm asleep in bed at night.'

The three were soon settled in the attic, one at each end of Tracy's bed, and Flora sitting on hers, as they munched their apples.

'It's great being here,' Mary reflected. 'Being right away from the house in the evening makes me realise that when I'm there I'm always listening out for Tim in case he starts crying. Even when I'm watching TV or doing my homework, I'm listening out. Of course, I've got no homework at the moment because it's the holiday, but I wanted to work on a project I've been thinking about.'

'What's that?' asked Flora, sitting up eagerly.

'We...ll,' Mary said uncomfortably.

'You don't have to tell us if you don't want to,' Tracy reassured her.

'I want to experiment with drawing, using pencil or charcoal,' she said in a rush.

'I would never have guessed, Mary,' said Flora, who was clearly impressed. 'What have you done so far?'

Mary coloured a little. 'Well I found an art shop when I was in town with Dad in the Christmas holidays. He had parked the car with me in it, and had gone off on some secret mission. While I was waiting, I realised that he had parked just outside an art shop. Although I couldn't lock the car up, I went inside, trying to keep an eye on it at the same time. It was absolutely amazing! There was everything I had ever dreamed of, and more. I went back to the car quite quickly because I was worried about leaving it, but I promised myself I would go back as soon as I could, to have a proper look.'

'When did you go back?' asked Tracy, fascinated.

'It was about a week later. The holidays were nearly over by then. I'd done a lot of looking after Tim, even though he was only a baby then of course, and I managed to persuade Mum to let me go on the bus into town on my own. She agreed, so long as I took my mobile with me and promised to be back before dark. I took some of my pocket money, and went straight to the shop. I stayed looking at everything for as long as I could, then I bought a range of pencils, some charcoal, and two pads of special paper, and went home again.'

'What did your mum say?' asked Tracy.

'I didn't tell her. I managed to smuggle my things into the house, without her noticing,' Mary replied.

'Why did you do that?' asked Tracy, intrigued.

'I don't know why. I just knew I didn't want Mum or Dad to know anything about it,' said Mary emphatically.

'Wow! You're a dark horse,' exclaimed Flora. 'You didn't even tell *me* about it.'

'No, I didn't tell anyone,' said Mary.

'What have you tried so far?' asked Tracy.

'Oh… just little bits and pieces,' said Mary, her tone belying the importance to her of what she was saying.

'Tell us,' commanded Tracy. 'Go on. Please, please.'

'I did one of a rabbit,' Mary burst out. Her face reddened, and then she started laughing. 'I don't know why it's so difficult saying something to you two about it. I suppose I'm just not used to talking about it at all.'

'Tell us one more thing, and then we'll talk about something else,' said Flora. 'How was it that you were interested in drawing in the first place?'

'Yes…' said Mary. 'Actually, I'd really like to tell you about that. I've tried to remember how old I was, but I can't be exactly sure. I think I was about five. I think I must have been away on holiday with Mum and Dad somewhere. Anyway, I remember going into a huge museum or art gallery sort of place. It was absolutely massive. Whatever it was, and wherever it was, I remember it certainly had a lot of pictures on the walls and in glass cases. Dad had to lift me up to see some of the pictures, but mostly Mum and Dad were chatting to each other about them, while I walked along looking at the floorboards.'

'That doesn't sound very inspiring,' remarked Flora.

'Shut up,' said Mary, digging her in the ribs. 'I haven't got to the good bit yet.' She went on: 'I was following a dark-coloured floorboard that I had somehow noticed, when I found myself in a smaller place, a place where the lights were quite dim. It must have been a room off the main place, and my mum and dad were nowhere to be seen. The thing that really sticks in my mind about that was that I didn't feel scared. I didn't feel scared at all. There I was in this strange place, with my mum and dad nowhere in sight. I could see there were glass cases all around me, with lights in them, and the glass cases were full of drawings. I remember staring and staring at the drawings, and it seemed then as if the drawings were the only thing in the whole world that mattered to me. The drawings were amazing, and the feeling I had about them was amazing.'

'What happened then?' asked Tracy anxiously. She knew how worried her mum would have been if she had wandered off in a strange place when she was only five.

'I heard a voice shouting my name, but I didn't recognise it, and a man in a uniform came up to me and asked me if my name was Mary Field. I said it was, and he told me that my mum and dad were looking for me, and that he knew exactly where they were. He got a sort of radio thing out of his pocket and talked into it about me, then he took me back into the huge bit to where Mum and Dad were sitting, looking worried. The man in the uniform gave me to them, and they cuddled me a lot, then they decided we wouldn't stay there any longer.'

'Is that the end of the story?' asked Flora.

'No, there's one more bit,' replied Mary. 'When we were going out of the place, I saw there was a big rack of postcards, and I could see there were some of the drawings I had just seen. I asked Mum if I could have one, and she took no notice, so I asked Dad, and he just said "no". After that, I threw myself down on the floor and screamed, and kicked my legs up and down. I remember they were horrified and angry, but I didn't care. I knew I *had* to have a postcard.'

'Did they get you one in the end?' asked Tracy, fascinated by this account.

'Yes, they did. They *had* to,' Mary said with a set expression on her face, as she remembered back to what had taken place. 'I was determined not to leave without one, even if it meant being smacked.'

'*Did* they smack you?' Flora questioned her friend.

'No. They hardly ever smacked me. Only occasionally when they were very angry they might. What happened was that the man in the uniform came past, and he insisted on buying three postcards for me of the drawings, explaining to Mum and Dad that when he found me I had been looking at them.'

'Do you still have them?' asked Flora.

'Of course. I've kept them in my special box of treasures ever since.'

'If they're so special to you, you might not want to show them to us,' said Flora thoughtfully. 'But can you tell us who did the drawings?'

'Leonardo da Vinci.'

Tracy looked at Flora, and said, 'He's really famous, isn't he?'

'Yes, definitely.'

'Can we see some of what you've done so far sometime?' asked Tracy tentatively.

'Maybe,' replied Mary. 'I've never shown anyone else, but I might. Let me think about it. Can we talk about something else now?' she finished.

'Okay,' said Flora. 'How about we get out my collection of makeup, and try some things out on each other? It's all very well using a mirror to put it on with, but it's really good fun doing it for each other. We've done a bit before, haven't we, Mary?'

'Yes, and we had good fun with it,' Mary said as she remembered the evening they had spent in Flora's room downstairs. 'It's a pity I haven't got my own bag with me this time.'

'Never mind, we'll all share what I've got,' said Flora generously. 'I've got a few new things since we last did it, including some really fun colours. You'll see!' she finished, with a twinge of challenge in her voice.

Time rushed past, and when Flora glanced at her pink watch, she saw it was ten o'clock. 'Oh, help!' she exclaimed. 'What time do you have to be back, Mary?'

'Oh no! I'm late. Mum told me to be back by ten at the latest. I'd completely forgotten about the time. You usually have a clock somewhere in your room, and there doesn't seem to be one around today.'

'I think my alarm clock must have got knocked under the bed,' said Flora, fishing around for it. 'Yes. Here it is. Tell you what, I'll run downstairs for a damp cloth. It'll help to get that purple lipstick off you,' she said, jumping into action. She knew of old that Mary's parents could be quite restrictive if she didn't stick to the rules they laid down for her.

She was back quickly, and helped Mary to clean her face. 'We can phone your Mum and say we're just on our way,' she suggested. 'Tracy and I can walk you back I think, but I'll check with Mum first.'

She disappeared again, and Tracy picked up the dish of apple cores and followed her more slowly, with Mary close behind.

Flora found her mum asleep in the sitting room, and not wanting to wake her, she tiptoed out again. Mary phoned her mum, who fortunately had not realised how late it was. She was in a good mood because of the big order she had taken just before Mary left, and she said she would come round for her in the car. The girls waited at the front door until the car drew up, then Flora and Tracy waved goodbye to Mary as the car disappeared down the road.

'We'd better get to bed quickly,' said Flora to Tracy. 'We've got an early start again in the morning. And next time we see Mary, remind me to tell her what Mum said about Miss Maitland. We had so much to talk about this evening, I forgot!'

Chapter Seven

Although she was tired, Tracy didn't sleep well that night. She kept waking up to the sound of rain hammering on the velux windows, and there was a strong wind whipping round the house. It was never like this at home, she thought; but after all she was sleeping two floors higher up than the bedroom she shared with Paula at home. Flora seemed undisturbed by it all. Perhaps she was used to it, so it didn't affect her.

When the alarm clock went off in the morning, she felt tired and dopey, whereas by contrast Flora seemed to be full of energy.

'Come on, sleepyhead,' she teased.

Tracy groaned. 'Oh, leave me for a minute. I was awake a lot in the night.'

'That's no excuse,' teased Flora. 'If you aren't up in five minutes, I'll go and get some cold water to help you.' And she ran towards the top of the stairs.

When she had gone, Tracy got out of bed very slowly. Her body felt sore in places, and she wondered if there was something wrong. As she made her way down the stairs, she met Flora on her way back up.

'Ah, avoiding the wet flannel treatment,' she said, as she squeezed past Tracy.

On her way back up the stairs, Tracy felt that all the muscles in her thighs were sore, and it was then that she realised that she must be stiff from all that cleaning she did the day before. Although she often helped Mum with the cleaning at home, their house was tiny compared with this one; and she had done work on both the second and first floors yesterday. Feeling reassured that she wasn't about to be ill, she was able to speed up a little, and she joined Flora and her mum in the kitchen only a few minutes after Flora herself had arrived.

The breakfasts and cleaning tasks were much the same, but were less fraught today, because not so many guests came down first thing, and only two couples were moving on. In the bin in the dark blue room, Flora found two newspapers – the Guardian and the Times.

As they sat round the kitchen table finishing their own breakfast, May told them that she had fixed that a friend, Pat, was going to come in for a few hours the following afternoon to cover for her, and she planned to take Flora and Tracy out somewhere.

'So where we will go?' she asked.

'I'd like to go up to the town to look at the shops,' said Flora, without hesitating. 'How about you, Tracy?'

'I would too,' she replied. 'I can look for a present to take home for Mum and Dad and Paula, and I'd like to see that art shop that Mary told us about.' She clapped her hand to her mouth.

'Don't worry, I'm sure she didn't mean that we had to pretend the shop didn't exist!' Flora reassured her.

'What's all the mystery?' asked May.

'Oh… it's just something Mary was telling us yesterday,' said Flora with an air of studied casualness.

Her mother took the hint and didn't ask anything else. 'I'd hoped that you'd both want to go to town,' she said, 'but I didn't want to push you into it. I've got things to see to there, but I could have taken you somewhere else if you'd wanted.'

'No, the town will be great!' said Flora enthusiastically.

'Well that's it agreed, then,' May concluded. 'Now, as you know, there's not as much cleaning this morning, so it won't take so long.'

The cleaning was certainly less of a task this morning. But the rain continued unabated, so being outside was not a good idea. May had produced some old pots of paint from the garage, together with some of her old clothes as overalls, and had suggested that the girls might like to paint a mural on the far wall of their attic room. Tracy and Flora had been surprised and excited by this proposition and had moved all the furniture well away from the wall. In the end they had produced a bright scene depicting a field of large yellow sunflowers, with some buildings in the far distance.

They were well satisfied with their work, and invited May up to see it. She was suitably impressed, and sent Flora downstairs to fetch her camera so she could photograph what they had done, intending to let Tracy have a print to take home with her so that she could show everyone.

After that, Tracy and Flora had spent the rest of the day arranging and rearranging the room so that it was laid out more to their satisfaction; and the evening had been spent curled up in front of the TV together.

The following morning, the girls both leapt out of bed energetically, keen to get on with the work so they could then enjoy the afternoon out with May. The morning was slightly overcast, but Tracy noticed that it was clearing by the time she was throwing open the windows of the yellow room before vacuuming the carpet.

Downstairs in the kitchen, May was gathering up a few things she needed.

'We don't need to pack lunch, because I can treat you at that nice vegetarian café we once went to, Flora,' she said. 'What do you think?'

'How much time have we got?' asked Flora.

'Well,' said May slowly. 'Pat's coming about noon, and she said she could stay on until five, or possibly half past.'

Flora thought for a moment, and then said, 'The café would be really nice, Mum, but it will take more time than eating sandwiches, and I think I'd rather have the extra time at the shops. What do you think, Tracy?'

'I'd rather do that too.'

'All right,' said May. 'We'll pack up some food to take with us, and if you see a nice T-shirt or something while we're out, I'll get it for you instead of the lunch.'

'Flora's face lit up. Thanks, Mum,' she said. 'But it doesn't *have* to be a T-shirt, does it? It could be makeup or sandals or something else?'

'Yes, yes, that's what I meant to say. Come on now, my loves, we'd better quickly pack up some food.'

When noon came, the three were waiting in the hall for the arrival of Pat.

'Where's she got to?' asked Flora, hopping from one foot to the other.

'Here she comes now,' said May, as she saw her friend walk up the drive, and she opened the door to let her in. 'Hello, Pat,' she greeted her, giving her a hug. 'Thanks so much for bailing us out. I've left you some lunch in the kitchen, and just help yourself to anything else you want. Everything is the same as before.'

'I'll be fine,' said Pat. 'Have a good time, all of you. Don't worry if you're a bit late back, I can stay on till six if needs be. I've got my book, and I'll sit by the phone. Don't worry about anything.'

May, Tracy and Flora went out of the door and got into the van. Tracy and Flora squeezed together in the passenger seat, and Pat waved them off.

'I think I'll put the van in the park-and-ride,' said May thoughtfully, as she drove along. 'Then I don't have to worry about finding parking spaces, or about getting back when meter tickets run out.'

The parking area was extensive, and May had no trouble finding a space. A couple of minutes later they were boarding a bus for the last part of their journey.

'We'll have to decide whether we're going to stick together all the time or not,' said Flora through a mouthful of sandwich.

'I thought you two might like to explore the shops in the big precinct while I go off and see to the things I've got to do,' said May. 'We can arrange when and where to meet up, and then go on from there together. By that time you might have seen something that interests you, and we'll see what we're going to buy.'

'Okay,' Flora replied cheerfully. 'That suits us, doesn't it, Tracy?'

Once at the precinct they parted company after agreeing to meet under the large clock in the centre of the mall at around three fifteen. May hurried off to see to her business errands, and Flora and Tracy went into the Sock Shop.

'Hey! Look at these amazing striped tights,' said Flora, as she pointed out a dismembered mannequin's leg adorned with something that made it look rather like the bottom of a Belisha beacon.

'That's really cool,' said Tracy, as she admired Flora's find. 'And there are other colours of the same thing in these packs over here,' she added, pointing to a large cardboard box on the floor, partway under the display unit. 'And look at these!' She pulled Flora over to a stand that had a display of knee length socks in lurid colours, covered with silver stars.

'Whenever I come in here, I wish I could grab a pile of things and take them home to try! I hate having to choose between things, and wonder what will suit what I've got already. I just want to try things out, and then if they don't seem all right, toss them to one side and use something else. But I can't do that, because it's wasteful. I *wish* I didn't have to think about things like that!' Flora grumbled.

'I think I know what you mean,' said Tracy. 'It would be nice to be able to play with the things – like a sort of grownups' dressing-up box – and not have to think about money.'

'Hey, that's very good,' said Flora, with admiration in her voice. 'I think you've put your finger right on it. Unless I try a lot of things out, I can't get an idea of what really suits me. Then by the time I've worked it out, I've got taller, or wider, or both.' At this, she started hooting with laughter.

Tracy stared at her in amazement. 'It's nice to see you like this, but I'm not exactly sure what's so funny,' she said.

Between gusts of mirth, Flora managed to squeeze out 'It... just... suddenly... seemed... such ... a... hoot!'

'What did?'

By this time, Flora was managing to contain her laughter a little, and she said, 'I spend quite a lot of time feeling all peculiar about my body, but saying what I did suddenly helped me to see it as funny for once. It was such a relief that I couldn't stop laughing.'

Tracy started to realise more about one of the things she had wanted to talk over with her mum, and she knew now she didn't have to wait until she got back home to make a start. Here was her cousin talking about it, and all she had to do was to join in.

They went out of the shop, and back into the mall. Then Tracy began by saying, 'I'm a bit younger than you, but I'm feeling quite wobbly about my body sometimes too. I know I'm growing taller, and my breasts have been starting to come, but I haven't a clue what height or shape I'm going to end up. I'm a different shape from Paula, and Mum is different from both of us. But I don't know if I'm going to end up like Mum or not. And then there's *your* mum too. My mum and yours are different shapes. Actually, it's quite confusing, and the more I try to think about it, the more confused I get!'

'Hey, you might be younger than me, but you put some things really well,' said Flora. Then she went on. 'Although our mums are different heights, they both have quite big hips, but my mum has bigger breasts than yours.'

'*You* haven't got big hips,' Tracy said.

'And neither have you,' said Flora.

'But we both might end up like that,' they said together, and started laughing.

'The thing is, we just don't know,' Flora concluded; and then in a mock serious voice, she added, 'It's an anxious time,' before convulsing into giggles.

They walked on.

'I've just realised something really obvious,' said Flora suddenly. 'If the big hips thing starts happening, there's nothing either of us can do to stop it, even if we want to.'

'You're right,' agreed Tracy.

'But I know some people get into a big panic about it. I can panic a bit, but not as much as some people I hear talking about dieting – just about *all* the time. Hey, I've thought of something else...'

'What's that?' asked Tracy.

'I wonder if boys get into a panic about growing beard hair, and getting a deep voice.'

They stared at each other.

'I suppose I could ask Dad,' Tracy said.

'And if I was daring I could ask some boys at the Youth Club, but I don't know if I'll manage to. Come on though, we're supposed to be looking in the shops!'

The two girls linked arms and went through some revolving doors into what Tracy thought must be a department store.

'Let's look at T-shirts and underwear,' Flora suggested.

'Okay. And after that let's go to a shoe shop – I thought you said you might be interested in sandals.'

The time passed all too quickly, and soon they were making their way back to the clock, where they found May on a seat, scrutinising the passers-by for signs of them.

She had several heavy-looking bags with her. Tracy and Flora sneaked up behind her and made her jump by tapping her on the shoulders.

'Oh!' she shouted, startled. Then, when she realised who was there she said unnecessarily, 'You gave me a fright.'

'We've seen some things we want to show you,' said Flora. 'We'll help you with your bags so you can come and look.'

'That's the way to a mum's heart,' said May appreciatively, as the girls took her bags over, and headed back into the store.

'It's T-shirts for us,' Flora proclaimed, leading the way to the Teens section, where she pointed out a garment of an unusual design. The background colour was pale grey, but this was eclipsed by bold vertical strips of an Aztec-type pattern in bright colours.

'That's quite daring,' said May as she admired it. 'I'm not sure I would have chosen it myself, but I can see it suits you very well. You'll certainly be noticed in it! We'll definitely get this one.' She turned to Tracy and asked her what she wanted.

Tracy pointed to a pale pink T-shirt she liked that was hanging on the next rack. 'Are you sure?' she asked her aunt hesitantly, as May insisted on buying it for her.

'Yes, of course, love,' she replied. 'I'm grateful for all your help, and it's a treat for me being out with you both. Now, can we go for a cup of tea while I have a sit down?'

They found a table in the precinct in front of a small place that served tea and cakes, and chose some refreshments. May appeared to be much restored by this, and was enthusiastic about the idea of going to find the art shop. She asked the woman behind the counter if she knew of such a place. Luckily the woman thought she knew the exact shop, and gave May some detailed directions.

'Let's go in and have a look around,' suggested May when they had found it and were staring at the items in the window. 'It looks extremely interesting.'

Although the frontage of the shop was not very big, it actually had a large floor area, since it stretched back from the road quite a long way. The stock was plentiful and varied, and they were able to spend the next half hour happily absorbed.

On the way out, May noticed a few flyers pinned up just inside the door.

'Oh, look,' she said. 'There's a small exhibition of pottery, and as far as I can see from the address, it's not very far from here.' She looked at her watch. 'It closes at five,' she said, 'and it's half past four now. I'd really like to go and have a look – even if it's only for a few minutes. What do you two think?'

Flora scowled. 'I don't fancy that at all,' she grumbled loudly. 'Why do you have to go to *boring* things like that? It's not long before we've got to go home again, and I haven't had a chance to look at makeup yet.'

Tracy was puzzled. She knew that Flora liked makeup, and in

fact they had looked at some already today; but she wasn't sure that Flora was all that interested in looking at any more of it right now. She wondered what to say. Aunt May was obviously keen to see the exhibition, but Flora was in a mood, and it couldn't really be about makeup.

'Well, can we meet up at the bus stop around five?' asked May, reasonably.

'That's it! That just *proves* it!' shouted Flora. 'You just don't care about me at all!' And she started to storm off.

'Flora!' May called after her. 'It's all right, love. Let's all go and look at makeup together.'

Flora stopped, but didn't turn round. She stood with her back towards May and Tracy, and waited for them to catch up.

'I'm sorry, love. I didn't realise how important it was to you for us all to go and see some together,' said May, wisely. 'I know you go and look at things, but we don't often go together, do we?'

Flora made a grumpy sound, but Tracy caught sight of a flash of a smile on her face, and her shoulders didn't look all tight and hunched any more.

'Now. Where shall we head for? There's that nice chemist's near the bus station, or we could go back into the precinct. I saw a store with a number of displays on the ground floor.'

Flora skipped a little, and then stopped herself. 'I'd like to go back there,' she said.

'Good,' said May. 'I think that's the best choice.'

In the store May drew their attention to a basket of sale items. 'I don't know if any of these would interest you two, but they're good brands, and have been reduced to three pounds each. On the better names, that's a big reduction. Of course, they are probably last year's colours, but you might see something that catches your eye. I'll buy one each for you, and you never know, there might be something I fancy too,' she said with a twinkle in her eye.

Together they sifted through the contents of the basket. Tracy chose some sparkling pink nail varnish for Paula, and a small pot of special coloured lip balm for herself. Flora chose a twin-pack of eye shadow, and May chose a small pack of face powder. Tracy handed the money for the nail varnish to her aunt, who then paid for everything.

'Right, off to the bus now,' said Flora cheerfully. 'We can't hang about any more. We've got to get back to let Pat get away.'

Tracy was astonished about Flora's change in mood, and she glanced at her aunt.

May smiled back at her, and winked in a conspiratorial way. Then she said to Flora, 'You're quite right. Thanks.' And they all headed for the bus.

They arrived back at Welcome Home at a quarter to six, to find Pat looking very pleased with herself.

'Hello,' she greeted them. 'I hope you've all had a good time. I've been busy here. Everyone has booked in... *and*... I've got some surprise news for you!'

'What's that?' asked May with interest.

'Well, I had a phone call from the local college. Of course they wanted to speak to you, but I said I was your assistant, and asked them to tell me what it was about.' She was beaming from ear to ear, and could hardly contain her excitement. She went on. 'You don't have to agree, of course, but I've made a provisional booking for you.'

May put her bags down in the hall and said, 'Provisional booking for *what*? Come on, tell us!'

'Sorry, I'm so excited that I told you the last bit first. Well, they are looking for accommodation for some foreign students they're taking on. It's only for the autumn term to begin with. It's a sort of pilot scheme. They're starting up an English course specifically for foreign students, but it's a bit different from other courses like that. They're arranging some cultural outings as part of the course, and they're hoping that will attract students. It's certainly worked so far, because all the places were filled quite quickly, although they only started promoting it at Easter of this year. All they have to do now is help the students to find accommodation. That's where you come in.'

'Go on, Pat, tell me the rest,' May said excitedly.

'I've taken bookings for four students for the whole term,' she replied. 'When you get back to the college, you can offer to take more if you want, but after I checked your diary, I thought that two double rooms for the ten weeks seemed to be the best. It leaves you with enough rooms for the bookings you have already, with a bit to spare. Four students aren't too many to have around at once, and in any case, these ones could be fine. It would be a married couple from China, and two young women in their early twenties from Italy.'

May threw her arms round her friend and hugged her tightly. 'Pat, you're a genius!' she exclaimed. 'I'll phone in the morning to confirm. Who do I have to ask for?'

'I've written all the details down in your diary,' said Pat reassuringly. 'And I told them you'd phone about ten tomorrow. Of course, you'll have time to think this evening about whether or not you want to offer to take any more on as well. I wish I could stay to chat, but I must be off now. Let me know how it goes.'

She picked up her bag, and May went into her office and returned with some small cards, which she handed to Pat.

'Oh, thanks, May,' said Pat. 'I nearly forgot about those.' And she put them in her bag, and left.

'Auntie May... what were those cards?' asked Tracy a little hesitantly.

'I'm glad you felt you could ask, love,' May replied. 'Pat and I belong to a group of people who all help each other out. Each person puts on a list the sort of things they can do, and we pay each other in cards. Payment is normally one card an hour. In the summer I'm usually giving out lots of cards, but in the winter, I do quite a lot of things for others and earn a pile of them back again, ready for the summer.'

'Mum used to belong to a babysitting circle when Paula and I were younger that worked a bit like that,' Tracy reflected. 'What are the sort of things all the people can do?'

'Why don't we put these bags away, and get ourselves something ready to eat, and then we can sit down and I'll tell you more about it,' her aunt replied.

'Can we have beans on toast?' asked Flora. 'That would mean I could make it. And then...'

'Then what?' asked her mother.

'Then could you make some more of that brilliant salad stuff?'

'Yes, of course I could. I'm not sure if I've got exactly all the same ingredients, but I could make something similar. Would you like to give me a hand, Tracy, by chopping some herbs? If you take a sprig off each plant on the windowsill, and cut them up into small pieces with the kitchen scissors, that would be fine.'

They all set to work, and were soon sitting round the table.

'In answer to your question, Tracy,' said May, 'there's a growing list of people in our group, so there are always more things being added to what's on offer. Some people charge more cards for some things. For example, there's a solicitor with a young family. Solicitor's fees are usually quite high, so we've agreed he can charge two or even three cards an hour. Apart from that, he can only offer about four hours in any month because he already works long hours at his office. But there's a retired solicitor who offers a lot of very helpful legal advice for one card an hour. We've got people like Pat and myself who can do household things, and caring for people. We've got a plumber who offers a few hours a month. There are two people who do gardening. There are people who help to set up computers and repair them when there is a problem. I can show you the list sometime. It's in the office somewhere, but I suspect it's under a heap of things I'm trying to sort through at the moment.'

'That's *such* a good idea,' said Tracy. 'I hope that when I'm older I can join a group like that. How old do you have to be?'

'It certainly works very well around here,' agreed May. 'And you usually have to be eighteen to join our group.'

After they had finished their meal, May suggested that they watched some TV together. Flora had not been keen at first, but when she learned that what May had in mind was a documentary about the life of capybaras, creatures that looked very much like large guinea pigs, she was immediately convinced, and rushed through to the sitting room to find the right channel.

Chapter Eight

When all the breakfasts were finished the following morning, May phoned the number at the college that Pat had left for her, and spoke to the accommodation officer. Tracy and Flora waited quietly while she did this. They wanted to know all the news straight away.

When she came off the phone she said, 'That's it fixed then. They arrive on October 1st. The college is going to write to me with the details and send me a contract to sign. Apparently, I get payment directly from the college – they'll send me a cheque every month. I've said they can get back to me if they have trouble finding places for everyone. By then I'll have had time to have a good think about whether I could take any more or not. In any case, I suppose I could take a couple more for a week or two at the beginning of term, if they're still looking. What do you think, Flora?'

'It's really up to you, Mum,' Flora replied. 'The only thing is that you promised I could get my room back at the end of the summer, just before school starts up again.'

'Oh, yes,' said May emphatically, 'there's no doubt at all about that. There's no way I'd be thinking of using your room during term time.'

'And there's no way I could sleep in the attic when winter comes,' said Flora. 'I'd turn into an icicle!'

'Now, there's a thing,' said May. 'Miss Maitland once told me that she and her sisters used to wear woolly hats in bed in the winter, because there was no heating upstairs in the farm house.'

'No wonder she likes her hot water bottle even in the summer!' said Flora.

'Come on, we better get on with the cleaning,' urged Tracy.

'What's all the sudden eagerness?' asked Flora, with mock surprise. 'We have a little work-horse here I think, Mum.' She poked Tracy and then ran up the back stairs to collect the clean linen.

The morning's work completed, the girls were toasting sandwiches in the kitchen and discussing what to do with their afternoon and evening. Flora was beginning to get restless and irritable until her mother came up with an idea.

'How about getting the bikes out of the garden shed,' she suggested. 'They could do with a good clean, and the tyres and brakes checked. If they're working okay, you could go off for a ride somewhere.'

'Can't be bothered,' said Flora, rudely. 'And anyway, there isn't a helmet for Tracy, and I've probably grown out of mine. I seem to grow out of *everything*.' She slumped in her chair, pouting.

'You could use my helmet, and then Tracy could borrow yours,' said May patiently. 'I'll go and get mine from the cupboard and you can see if it fits.' She disappeared, and returned soon afterwards with a black helmet with a vulture on the front.

Flora cheered up immediately. 'I'd forgotten you had this really good one,' she said happily. 'I'll try it on straight away.' She put it on her head, adjusted the straps, and went off to look at herself in the mirror in the hall. 'It's *excellent*,' she called. 'Everyone will be really envious when they see this.' She reappeared in the kitchen. 'Come on Tracy, let's get the key to the shed, and go and have a look.'

'There are cloths you can use in that bucket at the back door,' May called after them as they went out of the room.

Flora opened the padlock that secured the door of the shed, and peered inside.

'I haven't ridden my bike since the Easter holidays,' she said. 'I got it last summer, but it was a bit big for me then, and I didn't ride it much. Mum had said it was no good buying one exactly the right size because I would grow out of it too soon, but actually it meant that I hardly rode it at all last year. We kept my old one, and I just kept using it that summer. It's still here. It'll be a bit small for you, but it'll be better than nothing.'

Together they moved May's bike out of the way, and lifted the other two bikes onto the concrete slabs.

'They don't look too dirty,' said Tracy. 'But I'll start dusting them down a bit.'

'I'll have a look at the tyres,' said Flora, and she started to press the front tyre of her new bike as hard as she could. 'This one's a bit low, but it's not too bad.' She took the pump from the mounting on her bike, attached it to the valve and started to pump vigorously. 'Hm... that doesn't sound right,' she said. 'I'll try the other pump.

Good job they've got the same fittings.'

This time the pump worked well, and she went round all four tyres, making sure they were hard enough, while Tracy finished off the cleaning.

'Right. Where shall we go?' asked Flora when they were ready.

'You'll have to say,' said Tracy, 'because I don't know where there is to go.'

'Well, we could cycle round and see if some of my other friends are in, or we could go along the back lane and loop round one or two country roads. That way we'd be going quite a few miles.'

'Can we go and see if we can find some of your friends,' said Tracy. 'I'm not sure yet how far I can ride on this until I've tried it out a bit.'

'Okay,' Flora answered. 'Melanie's been away on holiday with her family. I'm not sure if she's back yet, but we could cycle round and see. She was off for the last two weeks of term. Her dad's some sort of government officer I think, and they have their holiday weeks decided for them in the summer. That's why she was off school.'

'Where does she live?' asked Tracy.

'Remember the shops we went to for Miss Maitland?'

'Yes.'

'Well you follow the road that goes left after the library, and it's about another mile after that.'

'I'm up for trying that,' said Tracy, 'but let me ride down this road for a bit first, so I can be sure I've got the hang of this bike.'

Tracy set off down the drive and onto the road. There were a few worrying wobbles at first, but after that it all seemed fine; and soon they were heading towards their destination.

When they arrived at Melanie's house, they found it seemed empty and shut up. There was certainly no answer when they rang the bell. A neighbour who was working in his front garden leaned over the fence and asked, 'Are you looking for Melanie?' And without waiting for an answer he said, 'I'm keeping an eye on the house. They're away until the weekend.'

'Thanks,' called Flora. She turned to Tracy. 'You seem as if you're managing fine with the bike,' she said. 'Shall we go on a bit further?'

'Okay. This road is nice with all these big trees along either side.' Tracy could see that in places the trees were so huge that their branches had reached right across the narrow road, and had intermingled, so forming a kind of tunnel. The sun was by now quite hot, and Tracy welcomed the idea of cycling along in the shade of the trees.

'We'll have to keep cycling one behind the other though, as the road is a bit too narrow,' said Flora as she set off again. 'Just shout if I start leaving you behind, and you think I haven't noticed.'

'Okay,' Tracy agreed.

Flora continued, trying to speak over her shoulder as she pedalled. 'If we go along here for about another mile, there's a path leading to a track that used to be a railway line. The track is a walkway now, but cyclists are allowed along it too.'

Tracy pedalled along behind Flora, enjoying watching the shadows on the road from the leaves above – shadows that produced a dappling effect. It was certainly cooler along here.

As Flora had indicated, about a mile further on there was a break in the fence that ran along in front of the trees, together with a signpost. They stopped their bikes, and got off to walk across the road and along the narrow path until it soon opened out onto the walkway.

Tracy looked in both directions. 'Oh, this is so lovely!' she exclaimed, as she saw the mixture of broom bushes and tumbling wild roses that lined either side of the track. Below these she could see a variety of other plants, the flowers of which were familiar to her, but she could not name them. 'Which way shall we go?'

'If we go left, we could cycle as far as the bridge over the river, and then turn back,' said Flora. 'That bridge is downstream from the one we crossed when we were out for that walk with Mary.'

'How far is it?' asked Tracy.

Flora thought for a minute. 'I'm not too sure,' she said. 'But it could be about another three miles.'

'Okay then. I'll give it a try if you want,' said Tracy cheerfully.

Some time later they reached the bridge. Although it was a well-signed walkway, they had hardly encountered anyone on the way. There had only been a woman who was walking two dogs; and when she had seen them coming she had put the dogs on their leads, and held them to one side to let them past. Tracy and Flora had called 'thank you' to her as they pedalled past.

'That was really kind of her to do that, wasn't it?' said Flora. 'People do all sorts of different things when they see younger people like us coming on bikes. Sometimes they just walk on right in the middle of a path, so I have to get off.'

'I know what you mean,' replied Tracy. 'You never really know in advance what strangers are going to be like.' She paused for a moment and then said, 'This track is so nice that I wish we could pedal on for miles and miles.'

'Me too,' Flora agreed. 'But I suppose we should turn round now.'

'I've an idea,' said Tracy suddenly.

'What is it?'

'Do you think we'd have time to see Miss Maitland on the way back?'

'Hey. That's a good idea. She's bound to be pleased to see us, and we could get a drink while we're there. I'm thirsty.'

'Actually, I want to ask her about that book,' Tracy admitted.

'You're right!' exclaimed Flora. 'How could I forget! And I want to talk to her about when she first met Mum. Off we go then!' she finished; and she jumped on her bike and pedalled off at speed.

'Wait for me!' Tracy called after her. 'Remember I can't go as fast as you. This is just a small bike.'

'Sor...ry!' Flora shouted over her shoulder as she put on her brakes to slow down.

Having parked their bikes at the back of Miss Maitland's bungalow, Flora chained them together; and they rang the doorbell and waited for her to appear.

'We're back already,' Flora pronounced cheerfully as, after a while, Miss Maitland appeared at the door. 'We've got things to ask you about.'

'Come on in then,' said Miss Maitland as she pushed the door wide open to let them in. 'It's good to see you both, whatever the reason for your visit.'

Flora made her a cup of tea, but got two large glasses of water for herself and Flora. 'We're really thirsty,' she proclaimed as she handed one to Tracy. 'We've been out on bikes.'

'Well, what is it that you've come to ask me?' said Miss Maitland, invitingly.

'We want to know more about how you met Mum,' said Flora. 'She's told us how you were both at the meeting at the medium's house, and I know why she went there. But I don't know why *you* went there.'

'That's easy to answer,' Miss Maitland replied. 'Do you want a long answer, or a short one?'

Flora looked at Tracy, and then back at Miss Maitland. 'How about a medium one?' she asked, and spluttered as she started laughing at what she had just said.

'I wanted to try to understand more about some things I had noticed about myself – things I had noticed particularly after my parents died and I had moved to this house.'

'What were those?' asked Tracy, sitting upright in her seat, and leaning forward with an intent expression on her face.

'One of the things I had been noticing was that I knew things about people without having to be told. It only happened from time to time, but it was so obvious to me when it did.'

'What kind of things?' asked Flora eagerly.

'Well, for example, I knew straight away that your dad had left, even though your mum hadn't told me, and neither had anyone else – and I could see pictures in my mind of how it had happened too.'

Flora was impressed, and said so.

Miss Maitland went on: 'Actually, I also had some sense of how he had left.'

'Did you tell Mum?' asked Flora.

'Not straight away. It didn't seem right. And anyway I wasn't completely sure if what was in my head was definitely to do with her. But one day, after we had known each other for quite a while, your mum wanted to tell me how it had all happened, and I knew then that what had come into my mind was true, and really had been about her situation.'

Flora stared at her. She seemed lost for words. Tracy had other questions she wanted to ask, but she thought she had better not say anything at the moment. She reassured herself that if there was no time to ask them during this visit, she could easily come on another day. She sat quietly and waited for Flora to speak. She could see that Flora was struggling. She was sitting with her right leg crossed over her left, and she was bouncing her right leg up and down in small, agitated movements.

When she did speak, it sounded rather aggressive. 'Why didn't you tell me this before?' she snapped. 'You've known me all my life, and you never told me.' She sunk her teeth into her lower lip.

'I didn't think it was my place to,' said Miss Maitland quietly. 'Perhaps if I'd been your gran it would have been all right, but I'm not, and it was really up to your mum to decide what to say to you, and when to say it.'

'Well, Mum only told me this week about how she first met you,' said Flora, sounding edgy. 'And she only told me because I pushed her into it. She was doing her usual avoiding thing, and I just told her she *had* to tell me.' Her leg showed more agitation, and she bit her lip so hard it bled a little. 'And... I'm really angry that you know more about my dad than *I* do!' she burst out.

'Maybe I just know different things about your dad,' continued Miss Maitland in calm tones. 'I've never met him face-to-face, but you have seen him many times.'

'But you *know* things about him without even seeing him.' Here Flora's voice took on a kind of wail; and Tracy, who had already been feeling uncomfortable, began to feel worried.

Miss Maitland had obviously noticed her discomfort, and she said, 'It's quite right that Flora is telling me how upset she feels. All of this is very important to her.' Then she turned back to Flora and said, 'Would you like me to tell you exactly what I could see in my mind? After that, whatever else you want to know, you must ask your mum.'

Flora's leg stopped its agitated jumping movements, and she sank back into her chair and considered this. 'But I want you to tell me *everything*, and I want you to tell me it *now*!' she insisted.

'Of course that's how you feel,' said Miss Maitland, soothingly. 'But it wouldn't be right for me to tell you things that aren't mine to tell. If you and your mum both asked me to tell you everything I knew, that would be different. But your mum isn't here at the moment, and she doesn't know what we're talking about, and hasn't had time to think it through. It would be very wrong of me to say more than I am free to say at the moment.'

'I know,' agreed Flora, miserably. Then she became forceful again and said, 'Dad tells me nothing, and Mum says very little. I just want to know *everything*, and I want to know it straight away!'

Once again Miss Maitland was gentle and understanding in her response, and once again Flora seemed to relax a little. And this time she stayed relaxed. She turned to Tracy and said, 'I'm so glad you're here. We'll learn a bit more about him now, and then we'll go back and talk to Mum.'

Tracy thought again how surprising it was that Flora wanted to include her in these conversations about her dad. After all, Flora's dad was only her uncle. She had never known him, and he wasn't really a relative of hers as he had only been married to Auntie May, and had left her before Tracy herself was born, so he wasn't really exactly part of her family. She didn't need him, and she certainly didn't need him like someone needs a dad. Flora needed him because he was her dad, and he was certainly part of her. Tracy felt sad that Flora had so little of her dad, whereas she herself lived with her dad and saw him a lot. She had nothing in her own life that she could use to compare with Flora's experience, except that Dad had seemed so distant from her when he was in all that pain. But that was so different from hardly having a dad at all that Tracy pushed the memory on one side, and waited to see what Miss Maitland was about to tell them.

Miss Maitland leaned back in her chair and half-closed her eyes as she remembered back to the day when she met May. 'It was a Friday afternoon in October, I remember,' she began. 'I'd been looking forward to the meeting for about a month. It meant a lot to me to have found a group of people I might be able to talk to about my experiences. I arrived there early, and there were only two people there by then. I spoke to them a little, but they didn't seem keen to talk, so I sat quietly and waited. A few more people arrived, and then your mum came in, carrying you in her arms. I remember thinking what a beautiful child you were, and for a moment I felt envious of your mother, having a lovely child like you. But then I started to feel terrible pain, and I knew that the pain wasn't mine. Your mother looked quite calm, but as I looked at her I realised that not only could I feel her pain, but also I could see it. Of course, I couldn't see it with my eyes, but it was *as if* I could.

'She sat down next to me, and you gazed at me very intently. I looked inside my bag, and took out the embroidered handkerchief I always kept there. It was just for show really – I never ever used it. I handed it to you to play with, and you loved it. You pointed to the embroidered flowers on it and smiled and smiled.'

'Did I?' asked Flora. 'Did I really?'

'Yes, of course.'

'Go on, tell us the rest,' Flora urged her.

'Your mother was pleased at the contact I was having with you, and she smiled at me but didn't say anything. It was when she smiled that the pictures came into my mind.'

'What were they?' asked Flora, leaning forward in her seat as if she were afraid she might miss something.

'I could see your mother standing in a room with a man. I couldn't see you, but I could see both your mother and the man quite clearly. The man was shouting, and your mother was crying. She was begging the man to sit down and talk about something. After that I could see that he kept turning away from her, and she kept taking his arm, but he kept shaking her off. This went on for a while. Then he went out of the room, and I knew that he was leaving and wouldn't be coming back.'

Flora stared at her, saying nothing. Tracy sat and thought it was as if this person had actually been there when Flora's father left, although she obviously hadn't been.

'How old was I at that meeting?' asked Flora.

'I think you were nearly nine months, and your father had left about three months earlier.'

'That means that my dad left in the summer,' said Flora, half to herself. Then she looked at her pink watch and said briskly, 'We'd better get back. Mum will be wondering where we are.'

'Would you like to phone her before you go?' asked Miss Maitland. 'You can use my phone if you want.' And she gestured towards the handset on the low bookcase behind her chair.

'It's all right, thanks. We'll be home soon,' replied Flora. She stood up, and went across to Miss Maitland and surprised her by giving her a hug. 'Thanks,' she said. 'Sorry if I was rude.'

'Don't you worry,' Miss Maitland reassured her.

Back at Welcome Home, Tracy and Flora put their bikes in the shed, fastened the padlock, and went off in search of May. They found her in her office, slowly working through a pile of papers.

'It's my accounts,' she groaned. 'But it's best to keep them up to date.' She glanced up at the clock on the wall. 'Goodness, is it that time already? You two must be hungry. I'll come through to the kitchen and we can decide what to have.'

Tracy noticed that Flora looked as if she was about to say

73

something, but decided that she must have changed her mind, because she turned and headed for the kitchen. On the way through the hall she said, 'Please will you not say anything about Miss Maitland's for now.'

'Okay,' said Tracy with alacrity. The whole subject seemed very complicated to her, and she was glad that she didn't have to do anything about it.

When May joined them in the kitchen, Flora began straight away.

'Will you please sit down there, Mum,' she said in a grown up voice, 'and tell me now exactly how it was that Dad left, and exactly what happened.'

Tracy noticed that her aunt seemed to crumple a little in her chair; but her voice sounded no different from usual, and she drew herself up again as she began to speak.

'Your dad was always a bit of a boy at heart,' she said. 'I think he never really grew past the stage of wanting to go out, travel about and see his friends. It was all right before I got pregnant. We used to go out a lot together, and meet up with friends. We found the cheapest ways of going on holiday together, spending as much time travelling about as we could. We bought this house together. It was very dilapidated, and whenever we saved up some money, we went out and chose things for it, and were gradually doing it up.

'But once I was pregnant, I couldn't keep up with all he wanted to do, and of course I wanted to get ready for having a baby. He seemed to think that I could be pregnant, but just be the same as usual, and he got irritable. He would go out without me, but because he was nice to me when he got back, I thought everything was all right really.

'After you were born, things went from bad to worse. He loved you, but he couldn't bear me having to spend all the time I needed to take care of you in the way I thought was right. He went out even more often, and I saw less and less of him. There was nothing I could do.

'Then the day came when he said he was leaving. I tried to persuade him to stay – to talk things through – but his mind was made up. He had already packed his bags, and he left. He didn't want to see me again, so whenever he was going to see you, I had to arrange for someone to be in the house, and for me to be out. I would leave just as he was due to arrive, and I would come back just after he left. Each time he came, he would leave a note of when he would be back, together with any instructions. As you grew older, he would come to collect you and take you away for the day or the afternoon. Again I had to arrange to be out, and a friend to be here with you. Once you were seven he used to come and stand at the front of the house, and I would open the door so you could go to him, but I had to stand out of sight, because he insisted on that.

'Before you say anything, there's something else I'd like you to know. As the years went past, and I racked my brains for some explanation for his behaviour towards me, I gradually realised it might have something to do with what happened to him when his brother was born.'

'What do you mean?' asked Flora instantly.

'Your dad's brother was born when he was three. Apparently, after his brother was born, his mother spent all her time looking after the baby, and spent hardly any time with him any more. Before his brother was born he and his mother had been very close.'

'That must have been terrible for him,' Tracy said.

Flora and May looked at her, and May said, 'Yes, I came to realise that it must have been. But of course, he then went on to do to me what his mother had done to him. It was a mercy that he still wanted to see Flora. Maybe it was because she was a girl and not a boy. Maybe if she had been a boy, he would have disappeared completely.'

'Well, he's *almost* completely disappeared,' said Flora. 'He hardly ever comes. And when I'm out with him he just talks to me as if I was any old person. He doesn't talk to me as if he's my dad.' She got up and wandered off out of the room, deep in thought, but came back almost immediately to ask, 'Why on earth did you not tell me all of this before, Mum? You *must* have known I needed to know.'

May looked contrite. 'I am so sorry, love. For years I was wrapped up in my own pain about it all, and to be honest, whenever I thought of talking to you about it, I just backed away from it. I know that's no excuse, but that's the truth of it.'

'Is there anything else you haven't told me?' asked Flora.

'I'm not aware of anything, but there may well be things come out now that we're talking about it.'

'Does any of our house still belong to him?' asked Flora suddenly.

'No. I bought him out soon after he left. It was still more or less in a mess, and house prices round here at that time were quite low. I took out extra on the mortgage at the same time as I started the business. I had to work very hard to get the whole of the first floor ready as quickly as I could to start letting the rooms. But I managed.'

'I think I want to talk about something different now,' said Flora with a sigh. 'I'm hungry.'

Later, in the attic, the girls lay in bed talking through some of what they had discovered that day.

'I still can't work out why on earth Mum hasn't talked to me about all of this before,' said Flora crossly. 'How silly can you get? After all he *is* my dad, and he was her husband... Now there's a thing... I'll have to ask her when they got divorced, because I don't know that either. I know it was when I was quite small, but exactly when I don't know.'

'I've been wondering how much of this my mum knows,' said Tracy. 'The only thing she ever told me was that your dad went away when you were a baby, and that you hardly ever saw him. I wonder if your mum and my mum have talked to each other much about him. I expect they have, because they always get on so well together.'

'Oh no!' moaned Flora. '*Another* person who knew more about my dad than I did!'

'But remember one of the things Miss Maitland was trying to say. It's you who has met up with him since he left.'

'Oh yes, but he wasn't being a dad to me, so I can't really say I've known my dad or been meeting up with him. I've known a man called Tony who came from time to time and didn't see my mum, but that's all.'

Tracy couldn't think of anything else to say that sounded remotely useful, so she decided to change the subject.

'You told me the Youth Club is on every Friday evening,' she said. 'Does that mean we could go tomorrow?'

Flora brightened up. 'Yes. In the middle of all this, I'd forgotten about that. And there's someone coming to give a talk. I think it's going to be on bullying. After that, we'll have a discussion about it, and then we all sit round and have something to eat and drink while we chat.'

'We did a project on bullying when I was still at primary school,' said Tracy. 'One girl had a really good idea. Starting at the front of a jotter, she wrote about the life of a bully, and then, starting at the back of her jotter, she wrote about the life of a victim. The two stories met when they got to the middle of the book, and she wrote there how they learned about each other and how they then became friends.'

Flora was impressed. 'You should talk about that in the discussion,' she said. 'That was a really good idea. When I started school at first there was a girl who was horrible to me because I hadn't got a dad.'

'That's awful!' said Tracy.

'But it wasn't long before I discovered that she didn't have a dad either, and that her brothers had blamed her for their dad going away. So after that I just kept out of her way. Eventually her family moved away, and so she went to a different school.'

'I remember some boys making fun of me because of some red shoes I used to wear for school,' said Tracy. 'I told them to stop, but they just did it more, so I told Mum. She told me to say to them that they were making such a fuss because they wanted some themselves. It worked really well. They never bothered me after that.'

'We'd better go to sleep now,' said Flora. 'It's nearly eleven, and we've got our usual early start.'

Chapter Nine

Flora's alarm clock let out its familiarly harsh noise, and Tracy opened her eyes to see her cousin wriggling out of bed in an unusual way.

'My stupid period must have started while I was asleep,' she muttered darkly. 'It usually starts during the day.'

'I haven't had many yet,' Tracy commented. 'But none of them has started in the night. Do you want me to pass you anything?'

'No thanks. I always keep a pair of pants and a pad under my pillow – just in case.'

Tracy got up and made her way downstairs with her wash bag, leaving Flora to sort herself out. She was dressed and down in the kitchen well in advance of her that morning.

'Where's Flora got to this morning?' asked Aunt May, as if through the back of her head, as she stood working at the cooker.

'She'll be down soon, Auntie,' replied Tracy. 'I'll go and get the tables started in the dining room.' And she hurried into the next room, away from May's questions, as she didn't want to have to be the one to explain; and she set to work.

She noticed that Flora looked a bit pale when she arrived, but apart from that was no different from usual.

Over breakfast Flora told her mother, 'We're going to the Youth Club tonight.'

'That's nice, love,' said May. 'We'll eat a bit early then.'

Just before seven that evening, Tracy and Flora made their way up the road to St Peter's church.

'It's in the hall round the back of the church,' Flora explained as they walked along together.

They had put on their new T-shirts, and Flora had changed into some rather low-cut jeans with a kind of frill round the top. At first Tracy thought that the material of the waistband was fraying, but then she saw that it had been carefully designed to give this appearance. Having washed their hair, they had also spent quite a bit of time that afternoon putting makeup on each other. It had ended up as a rather long and complicated process, as they tried various schemes and combinations of colours.

'We haven't thought any more about asking any of the boys how they feel about changing into looking like men,' hissed Flora suddenly, as they went round the last corner and reached the door into the hall.

'No, we haven't,' agreed Tracy. She was feeling wobbly enough about the idea of entering a room full of complete strangers, and felt reluctant to take on anything else. She hoped Flora wouldn't say anything else to her about it on this occasion. Perhaps we could talk about it before next week, she thought. Maybe we could decide something then, if we are planning to come back again.

By this time they were in the hall, and Tracy could see a small number of people occupying the seats that were at the moment arranged in rows, all facing in the same direction.

One of the girls turned round when she heard them, and said, 'Hi, Flora. Glad you could come.' She came across and gave Flora a hug.

Flora turned to Tracy and said, 'This is my friend Helen.' Then she said to Helen, 'This is my cousin Tracy, she's here for the holidays.'

'Hi,' said Helen, smiling at Tracy.

'I'm supposed to be here for two weeks,' Tracy explained, 'but we're both hoping I'll be able to stay on longer.'

'Yes,' said Flora. 'It's great having Tracy sharing my room... and the work of course!' She nudged Tracy in a friendly way. Then she continued: 'It's a pity a lot of people are away on holiday at the moment, so she's only met Mary so far.' She turned back to Tracy, and said, 'Haven't you?'

'Yes, but we've found out that Melanie will be back at the weekend,' Tracy added.

'What do you think's on tonight?' asked Helen.

'I think there's a talk about bullying,' replied Flora.

'I was pretty sure it was that one tonight,' said Helen. She turned round and spoke to the two girls and the boy that were sitting behind her and said, 'Flora thinks it's the bullying talk tonight too.'

'Good,' said the boy in a fairly high-pitched voice. 'There's plenty in that.' He was quite small and slender, and Tracy wondered if he was speaking from his own experience.

'This is Graham,' said Helen, and she introduced Tracy and Flora to him. 'And here are Rebecca and Rebecca.'

The two Rebeccas giggled. 'You can call one of us Becky,' they said. 'That's easier.'

'And it's usually me who's the Becky,' said the girl with the ponytail.

The door burst open, and in came a crowd of about ten girls and boys who all appeared to be about Flora's age, or a bit older. After that, although everyone was introduced, Tracy found she couldn't remember all the names.

'We could use sticky labels if you want,' suggested Becky.

'No, I'll be fine,' replied Tracy, feeling slightly embarrassed, as she sat down next to her.

'Here comes the minister and the speaker,' said Helen. She jumped out of her chair and went to meet them, explaining over her shoulder, 'It's my turn to do all the welcoming and introductions bit.'

Tracy saw that the minister was a short round man wearing the usual kind of white collar. He seemed to be about the same age as her dad, she thought, whereas the man that was with him looked much younger. In fact he looked a bit like one of the new teachers at Castlehill High, who had come to start his first job.

Helen shook hands with each of the men, and then turned to the group and said, 'You all know our minister, Jim Mason, but I don't think any of you have met Mr Trevor Ewing from the Education Department. He's agreed to come along this evening to talk about bullying in schools, and what the plans are to try to tackle it. After that he'll stay on so we can ask him questions, and we can follow that with a discussion.'

She sat down, and everyone in the group clapped.

'Thank you,' said Mr Ewing. 'I thought I'd start off by giving you some facts and figures...'

Half an hour later, Mr Ewing finished his talk by saying, 'Thank you for your time.'

And everyone clapped loudly.

'That was a very interesting talk,' said Tracy to Flora, and then blushed because everyone else was quiet and what she had said was clearly audible.

'I'm glad you all liked my talk,' said Mr Ewing, looking at Tracy.

He took a deep breath. 'Actually, I was a bit nervous,' he admitted. 'I've never spoken to a church Youth Club before, and I didn't know quite what to expect.' He swallowed, and then said, 'Have you got any questions?'

Graham put up his hand, and said, 'You told us how there are plans to get people who are bullying to apologise, and to understand the effect they're having on other people, but I think it might be very hard to get that to happen. I want to know more about how it could.'

'That's a good question,' replied Mr Ewing. 'At the moment we're talking about plans to help older pupils to learn how to help when there's a dispute. And also we hope to teach them how to intervene in cases of bullying, so that agreement can be reached about what has happened, what harm has been done, and what can be done to put things right. It's all in the early stages at the moment, but that's some of what we have in mind.'

Helen put up her hand. 'Do you know of any schools where it's being tried out already?'

'Yes, there are various ones in the UK, and there has been some success,' Mr Ewing replied. 'It has led to a reduction in the number of pupils that are excluded, and it has helped in cases of bullying, and with pupils who find it hard to identify with school.'

Another girl put up her hand. 'Are there schools in other countries that have been doing this?' she asked.

'I believe that there are some in other European countries and in the USA,' replied Mr Ewing. 'Of course, there is a whole system of justice used by the Maoris in New Zealand that is based on this kind of thing. It's called restorative justice, and it works very well in quite a lot of cases of all kinds of social problems.'

Tracy turned to Flora. 'I'd like to learn about that,' she said, and then blushed bright red, as she realised that again no one else was speaking, and everyone could hear what she had said.

'I have some information sheets about restorative justice back at the office,' said Mr Ewing. 'I wish now that I had brought them along with me. Would you like me to send some to Jim here, and he can hand them out at your next meeting?'

Tracy nodded vigorously. 'Yes, please,' she said emphatically.

'I'll see to that,' said Mr Ewing. Then he glanced at the clock on the wall and said, 'I'm afraid I'll have to leave in a minute. I have another meeting I must go to. Is there just one more question?'

No one spoke, so Helen stood up once more and went to the front. 'I want to say "thank you" to Mr Ewing for giving his time to come to speak to us tonight,' she said.

Everyone clapped again, and the minister let Mr Ewing out of the door, then came back and said, 'Let's get our biscuits and drinks out now. Do you know who's on the rota for this week?'

One of the girls and one of the boys stood up and walked over to the kitchen area.

'Right,' said the minister. 'Now we'll rearrange the chairs so it's easier to chat.'

There was the scraping of chairs, and soon the boy reappeared with a tin of biscuits, closely followed by the girl who had a tray of mugs. One of the others jumped up and collected bottles of various soft drinks from the kitchen, and began to pass them round.

'I see we have a newcomer here,' said the minister, smiling at Tracy.

'I'm Flora's cousin, and I'm staying for a holiday,' she said.

'It's more like a help-a-day, actually,' Flora joined in cheerfully. 'And it's great.'

'I hope we'll see you again next Friday,' said the minister; and he went off to talk to some of the others.

Flora began talking to an older boy who was sitting on her left, and Tracy wondered for a moment if she was asking him about shaving. She decided the best thing was to speak to someone else, and she was relieved to find that Becky was sitting on her right, and she began to talk to her.

The rest of the evening was taken up with an interesting discussion about what each of them might do if they saw someone being bullied, or if they came to hear about some bullying.

At nine o'clock everyone had left, and the minister locked up the door of the hall behind them. 'Goodnight,' he called to Tracy and Flora, who had been the last to leave, as they had volunteered to give the floor a quick sweep.

'We just want to show off our team effort,' Flora had said to the astonished minister.

Back at Welcome Home, Tracy and Flora said goodnight to May, who was nearly asleep in her sitting room, and then went upstairs to lie on their beds and talk about the evening.

'It's a pity Melanie and Mary couldn't be there tonight,' mused Flora. 'It was really good. Perhaps Mum would let me have them both round for a sleepover one night next week, and then we could fill them in.'

Tracy felt excited. She couldn't have a sleepover at her house, because the room she shared with Paula was too small. But the attic here was huge, and there was plenty of room for four. 'I hope she'll say yes,' she said eagerly.

'I don't expect she'll mind so long as we don't make a noise, and we get up to start work for seven,' replied Flora.

'What about Mary and Melanie? What will they do while we're working?' asked Tracy anxiously.

'Oh, I expect they'll sleep for ages. They can have breakfast with us, and then they'll go home while we get on with the cleaning. I'll ask Mum tomorrow.' She was silent for a minute or two and then said, 'Did you see that boy I was talking to?'

'Yes.'

'His name's Gordon. He's quite good to chat to actually,' said Flora in light tones.

Tracy waited. She wondered if Flora had gleaned any information from him.

'He's a bit older than me,' Flora continued. 'He's fifteen already.'

Tracy thought how he had looked as if he might be shaving, but she couldn't be sure, and she had felt it would be rude to stare. He had had quite a nice deep voice though, she remembered. A bit like Dad's, she thought. 'Did you ask him anything?' she asked.

'Not about anything I was planning,' replied Flora. 'I like him. He said he would be coming next week. I hope he does,' she added in a rather dreamy voice. 'It's funny, you know, he's been coming for ages, but I hadn't noticed him much really. But now I think he's really nice...'

Chapter Ten

The familiar harshness of the noise of Flora's alarm clock woke Tracy at the usual time. With her eyes still shut, Flora leaned out of bed, slapped the top of the clock to stop the noise, and then fell back on her pillow again.

'Oh, *no!*' she moaned. 'I just can't *bear* it. I feel *ghastly*. My back hurts, my front hurts and I've got a terrible headache.'

'Shall I go and get your mum?' asked Tracy, concerned.

'No, don't bother. I expect it's just my period. It's often like this. I don't want her climbing up the stairs at this time of the morning for nothing.'

'Shall I start the work downstairs, and you can come later?' asked Tracy.

'That would be great. The only problem is that it's Saturday, and that means it starts being busy quite early on.'

'I could go and ask your mum, and then come back and tell you,' Tracy offered.

Flora looked at her gratefully. 'Would you really?' she asked. 'Thanks a lot.'

Tracy went downstairs to get washed, returned to put on her clothes, and then went down to the kitchen.

'Auntie May, could you tell me how many people are coming for early breakfasts this morning?' she asked.

'Just two tables,' May replied. 'Why do you want to know?'

'Flora's got a really bad period, and I wondered if it would be all right if she stayed in bed a bit. Can you manage with just me this morning?'

May looked surprised, and then said, 'That's really kind of you, love. I think we'll be able to manage the breakfasts without her. Can you run back up and tell her, and then we'll get to work.'

It had been hard work, but Tracy and her aunt managed the breakfasts together without there being too many delays. And they were sitting eating their own breakfast, when Flora appeared, white-faced, at the kitchen door.

'Oh, love,' said May, sympathetically. 'Come and lie down in the sitting room, and I'll get you a hot water bottle. You can't do anything while you're in that state.'

Flora tried to protest, but failed; and instead she made her way slowly across the kitchen and through the door into the sitting room, while May put the kettle on.

When she had tucked Flora up on the sofa, May returned to the kitchen and addressed Tracy. 'Do you think you could do the two rooms on the second floor on your own this morning, love?' she asked. 'There's a lot of work because everyone is moving on, and all the beds and towels have to be changed.'

'I'll help as much as I can, Auntie May,' Tracy replied seriously. 'I'll go and get started right away.' And she stood up and made for the bottom of the narrow stairs that led up to May's room, so that she could collect the linen on her way up to the second floor. I'll do the dark blue room first, in case there's something funny in the bin, she said to herself. Then I'll have got it over with. And I'll have to remember to use Flora's rubber gloves when I do the bathroom and the toilet. It's a good job she showed me yesterday what to do.

She put the clean linen and towels in a heap on a chair just inside the door of the dark blue room, and went to collect the black bag and the linen bag. As she approached the bin, she thought she could see something odd. Although she felt curious she was also anxious, and she advanced with her eyes screwed up, while she opened the top of the bin sack.

Just then she could hear movement on the landing. 'Hang on a minute,' said a man's voice. She turned and saw a young man coming into the room. 'I've left something behind by mistake,' he said, as he quickly grabbed something out of the bin and stuffed it under his jacket. 'Bye then, I'm off now.'

Tracy could hear him running down the stairs, and when she went towards the bin again, she could see the thing that had bothered her was no longer there. She relaxed, emptied the remaining rubbish into her bag, and then went round the other bins.

She worked hard, finishing that floor as quickly as she could, so that she could help her aunt on the first floor. May was surprised and pleased to see her as she descended the stairs carrying the upright vacuum cleaner.

'You're a blessing!' exclaimed Aunt May. 'Can you start the vacuuming in the yellow room, and then come into the green one when I go to finish in the pink?'

'Right, Auntie May,' said Tracy, as cheerfully as she could.

Midday saw May and Tracy carrying toasted sandwiches through to the sitting room, so they could sit with Flora to keep her company.

'Are you feeling any better, love?' May asked her.

'It's not quite so bad,' replied Flora, who still looked rather pale. 'This must be just about the worst I've had yet.'

'When did it start?' asked her mother.

'When I got up yesterday. But then it seemed to go away again until this morning, and then it was just *terrible*.'

'That seems to happen sometimes,' said May sympathetically. 'Especially when you're young. It can happen to older people too, but not quite so often I think. You'd be best to rest until you feel a bit better. Why don't we all stay in here for a while? You can stay lying down, Flora, and we'll all have a chat. You haven't said much yet about the Youth Club.'

Tracy began to open her mouth to say something, but Flora cut her short by saying quickly, 'I don't really want to say anything about that, but I wanted to ask if we could have a sleepover one night next week. I wanted to ask Mary and Melanie.'

'That sounds fine to me,' said May. 'Have you worked out what they'll do in the morning though?'

'Just leave it up to us,' Flora reassured her. 'You don't have to worry about a thing.' She brightened up. 'I can phone them this evening, and we can fix what night they're both free. I hope it'll be Monday.'

May turned to Tracy. 'I've an idea. I know we've phoned your mum a few nights this week, but we haven't had much of a chat with her. I could bring the phone in here and plug it in that socket over there.' She pointed to a socket in the wall by the sofa. 'And then we could all take it in turns to speak to her,' she finished.

'I'd like that,' said Tracy, happily. 'Maybe Paula will be there too. Next week she'll be packing to go off on holiday with Jenny.'

'That settles it,' said Flora, from the sofa.

'Settles what?' asked her mother.

'Tracy's definitely going to stay here longer, then.' She turned to

Tracy and asked, 'How long is Paula going to be away?'

'Two weeks.'

'Well you're going to stay here while she's away, isn't she Mum,' said Flora determinedly, as she addressed May.

'We can certainly ask her mum,' May agreed. 'I like having you here, Tracy, and it would be lovely if you could stay for an extra two weeks. Would you like to?'

Tracy's face shone. 'Oh yes, Auntie May. I'd *love* to. There are lots of things to do here. I like the work, and sharing a room with Flora, and seeing her friends, and Miss Maitland, and...'

'Shut up,' said Flora amiably. 'Let's just get on with the phoning, okay?'

May rang Tracy's house, and found her sister and Paula were in the process of going through Paula's wardrobe to see if she needed anything new for her time away with Jenny. Apparently they had discovered already that a shopping trip would have to be arranged sometime over the following week.

The following hour passed very pleasantly as they passed the phone between them in the sitting room, while Tracy's mum and Paula took turns at the other end.

Flora looked much better by the time the call was finished, and she was sitting up.

'Mum,' she said. 'I can't wait until I've saved up enough for us to get my computer. It'll be great when I can e-mail all my friends.'

'It'll be a while yet,' replied May.

'I know,' said Flora. 'But it doesn't stop me thinking about it. I keep trying to work it out. Do you think we'll have one by Christmas?'

'I hope so,' replied May. 'But we'll have to work out what to do about the telephone line.'

'What do you mean?' asked Flora, sharply.

'Well, when you're sending e-mails, people won't be able to phone me to make bookings.'

Flora's hand flew to her mouth. 'Oh no!' she exclaimed. 'I never thought about that. Oh, what on earth shall we do?'

'I can't promise anything at the moment,' said her mother, 'but I've been thinking.'

'Thinking what?' asked Flora urgently.

'We...ll,' said May slowly. 'Supposing those students who are staying this autumn have computers.'

'Yes?'

'And supposing they're hoping to send e-mails to their friends in Italy and China? Well I can't really let them use my phone line. I was wondering whether to bring in another phone line to use with computers.'

Flora brightened. 'That's brilliant, Mum,' she said.

'Now remember, I haven't promised anything. But if it works out, we could put a phone socket on the landing of the first floor for the students and you to share. You'd have to take it in turns, of course, and you wouldn't be able to stay on for hours and hours... We'll need to see how things go, and see what we can work out.'

By the end of this conversation, Flora was almost completely restored. She was still a little pale, but apart from that seemed fine. 'Can I try phoning Mary and Melanie now?' she asked. 'I want to see if I can get everything fixed for Monday.'

As it turned out, it took some persistence from Flora before she managed to contact her friends; but by the end of the evening, the Monday sleepover was fixed, and she and Tracy went to bed early to make the rest of their plans for that night.

Chapter Eleven

Sunday had passed quite quietly. Most of the guests were staying on for another night, so there had been only two beds to change. Flora still wasn't feeling entirely well, and she and Tracy had watched TV for much of the afternoon. In the evening, they had played Scrabble with May, and then they all had another early night.

Monday morning was the familiar rush to serve all the breakfasts; and it was while the two girls were eating breakfast with May that the post arrived. Flora didn't take any notice because, apart from an occasional postcard from a friend who was on holiday, it was rare that any of the post was for her. May had heard the letter box, and had gone to the hall to retrieve the post from the box that was attached to the back of the front door. She returned with a pile of mail and sorted through it.

'There's one for you, love,' she said, absent-mindedly; and she handed it across the table to Flora while she looked through the rest of the heap.

Flora looked at the writing on the front of the envelope, and Tracy saw that she went just about as pale as she had the day before.

'What's the matter?' she asked.

'I'm *not* opening it!' Flora shouted loudly.

'Sh!' said her mother, sharply. 'You know we can't have that kind of noise when we've got guests in. It gives a bad impression.'

'*I don't care!*' screamed Flora.

Tracy thought that even if Flora tried harder, she wouldn't be able to shout any louder. For the first time since she had arrived, May looked grim. She took Flora by the arm, almost pushed her into the sitting room, and shut the door. Tracy felt terrible, and wondered what to do. She didn't think it would be all right to phone her mum without asking; and anyway, Aunt May might come back any moment. She didn't want to do anything that might make things any worse, so she sat where she was. Flora was still shouting, but the door muffled the sound. Tracy could only hear bits of what she was saying, and she couldn't really make sense of it.

Just then, there was a tap at the kitchen door, and a pleasant woman came into the kitchen. She reminded Tracy of one of her mum's friends, but she didn't have time to think who that might be. The woman was wearing a summer-weight coat, and looked as if she was about to go out.

'Is May Brooks here?' she asked.

Tracy thought quickly, and then said, 'Yes. I'll just go and get her. Would you mind waiting in the hall for a moment.' She was so grateful that on more than one occasion she had heard her aunt say to a guest 'would you mind waiting in the hall for a moment', while she went to search for something in her office; this meant that she felt confident about saying it herself. She pushed the kitchen door to, and then knocked on the door of the sitting room. Flora was still shouting loudly, so she knocked harder and went in. May turned to her, but before she had time to say anything Tracy said, 'A guest wants to see you. I asked her to wait in the hall.'

Aunt May glared at Flora, and then hurried off.

'What was that letter?' asked Tracy.

'It's from *Tony*,' said Flora, with a sneer in her voice as she said the name.

Tracy pulled her shoulders back, braced herself, and said, 'Look, I know you're really angry about him, but it isn't your mum's fault, you know.'

Flora flopped down on the sofa. 'I know,' she said, miserably, 'but I was *so* angry when I saw his writing, all I could do was shout.' And she began to cry. Between her sobs, she managed to say, 'I've talked about him quite a bit recently. Usually, I don't mention him.'

Tracy sat quietly until her aunt came back; and when May saw Flora was crying, she sat down next to her and put her arm round her. 'I'm sorry I was cross with you,' she apologised. 'What's the matter?'

'That letter's from Dad,' sobbed Flora. 'I've just had enough of him!'

'I'm so sorry, love,' said her mother. 'I was taken up with the pile of bills, and I didn't realise when I handed the letter across to you that it was from him. What did it say?'

'That's just *it*,' said Flora, dramatically. 'I don't want to open it. I just want to throw it in the bin. I don't even want to *think* about him. Now that I know more about him, I don't have to hang around him any more, hoping that he might tell me why he left me. I don't need him any more!' she finished, emphatically.

'I can perfectly understand why you feel like that,' replied her mother. 'Would you mind if I have a look at what he's written in the letter though?'

'You can *have* the letter,' Flora said, her voice rising towards a shout again.

May went to the kitchen, and came back with the letter. Flora was silent as she opened the envelope, and read the note inside. 'Mm,' she said.

'Well, what does it say?' snapped Flora.

May read it out:

I'd like to buy you a computer for Christmas. I expect you'll soon need one for your school work. Please will you ask your mother if that will be all right. I will be in touch again towards the end of the school holidays, and hope to see you then.

Love, Dad

Flora threw herself flat on the sofa, screaming, 'I hate him, I hate him.'

Her mother went across to her, took her hand and said, 'I think there's a lot we need to talk about here. I'll have to see to the guests now, but I don't think I'll be all that long. We'll have a bit of a talk before we do the cleaning, and then we can talk some more later.' She turned to Tracy and said, 'I'm sorry, love. I can see there's a lot here where I've been at fault, and it's all come to head during your holidays.'

'That's all right, Auntie May,' said Tracy, desperately wanting to be as helpful as she could. Inside she felt in a turmoil, and wanted at least to send a text to Mum as soon as she could; but for now she thought she had better stay with Flora, who was so obviously upset.

After May had gone, Flora quietened down considerably. 'I'm really sorry, Tracy,' she said. 'It can't be very nice for you.'

Again Tracy was surprised that in the middle of something so important to Flora, she was able to think about how she might be feeling.

'I was worried,' Tracy said honestly. 'And I wanted to phone Mum.'

Flora looked at her with her eyes wide open. 'Hey,' she said. 'It's ages since I spoke to your mum, and we had that really good chat between us all on the phone yesterday, but I never said anything about my dad, did I?'

'No, you didn't,' Tracy agreed.

'Well, remember I was upset before about the idea of my mum and your mum knowing things about my dad that I didn't?'

'Yes.'

'Well, perhaps I really need to say something to her about that. But on a phone call and when I haven't seen her for ages... Well, that just wouldn't be the right time.'

'I can see how you might think like that,' agreed Tracy. 'I wouldn't. But then she's my mum and I just tell her what comes into my head.' She stopped for a moment as she remembered there were things she wanted to talk to Mum about that weren't exactly in her head, and how this had meant she hadn't been able to say anything yet. She thought it only fair to explain this to her cousin; and she spent the next few minutes talking to her about it.

'I'm glad you told me,' said Flora. 'I think we've both got the same kind of problem really. If we know what we want to talk about, then we can tell our mums or our friends, but if there's something to say, and we don't know exactly what it is, it can get stuck.' She sat in silence for a few minutes, and then pronounced, 'And I think when it's been stuck for a long time, it can just burst out – very loudly – like it did with me this morning. Dad's letter appearing when I didn't expect it took me by surprise, and I just started shouting.'

'Yes, you did,' agreed Tracy. 'You shouted very loudly, and I felt scared.'

Flora stared at her cousin. 'I am *so* sorry,' she said. 'I didn't mean to make you feel scared. I was so busy being upset myself that I couldn't think about anyone else.'

Tracy was relieved to be having this conversation with Flora. Although she didn't know quite why, it felt very important. Curiously, it reminded her a little of something Mr Ewing had been saying in his talk on Friday night, but she had no idea what it was.

Tracy and Flora sat together and began to talk more about their plans for the sleepover; but it wasn't long before May returned.

'That's seen them off now,' she declared. 'Let's just sit and chat for a while before we get on with the cleaning. There's quite a lot to do. But it won't hurt if we leave it for now.'

'Tracy and I have been talking,' said Flora, 'and I feel much better. Let's get the cleaning done now.'

'We...ll,' said her mother uncertainly. 'If that's what you really want to do. But we'll need to have a chat about that letter sometime.'

'Yes, I know,' said Flora crossly.

'I've got an idea,' said her mother. 'Shall I keep the letter for you? And when you're ready to talk it over, you can tell me.'

Flora brightened instantly, and agreed with alacrity. Then she turned to Tracy and said, 'Race you!' before dashing for the back stairs.

Tracy was surprised at the speed and the energy Flora applied to her work that morning. She had never seen her shirk, or work particularly slowly; but neither had she seen her working at this speed before. It was as if she had suddenly found a store of energy. After they had finished and had their lunch, Flora had asked her mother if they could get food for a midnight feast. May had agreed on condition they remembered about the mouse problem. Flora had been annoyed with May, pouting and saying '*How* could I forget?' before flouncing off; but Tracy noticed it wasn't done with much conviction. In fact it looked as if Flora thought she ought to flounce, but didn't really want to.

By half past two, the two girls were walking to the shops beyond Miss Maitland's. They had wondered about taking the bikes, but in the end had opted for a slow amble so they could chat on the way. They had tried to draw up a list before setting off, but had soon given up in favour of making decisions once they arrived at the supermarket.

'It's great that Mum's doing another of those salads, and she's defrosting a giant pizza,' said Flora, half to herself, as she looked round the shelves.

Tracy heard her, and agreed.

'So what shall we get for the feast, I wonder?' mused Flora.

After that, she seemed to disappear quite suddenly, and Tracy wondered where she could have gone. Searching round the shelves, she was surprised to find her at the section where the alcoholic drinks were displayed.

'What are you doing here?' she asked. 'We can't have any of that.'

'Why not?' Flora challenged her. 'I'm going to get a bottle of cider.'

'What will your mum say?'

'She won't know,' Flora replied determinedly.

Tracy felt uncomfortable; but decided there wasn't much else she could do. If Flora had made up her mind, that was it. She wandered down the shelves disconsolately, trying to think what she would like to eat. Midnight was a very odd time to eat, she thought. Whenever she woke up in the middle of the night, she didn't feel hungry. But then, perhaps if they stayed awake until then, she would feel hungry after all. She would have to wait and see. 'How about some mixed nuts?' she suggested.

'That's a very good idea,' said Flora. Nuts fitted her ideas about healthy eating, but they also made it feel like Christmas, which she always thought of as a time of eating anything that was around. She put a packet of them in her basket and said, 'Now, what else is there?'

'I liked it when we were eating fruit when Mary came round before,' Tracy said.

'Let's go and see what there is, then.'

There was a large display of fresh fruits next to the vegetables. Tracy and Flora chose four Kiwi fruits, some small oranges, cherries, bananas and a custard apple.

'I've never tried one of these before,' remarked Flora as she chose the custard apple. 'And Mum never buys bananas for some reason.'

To Tracy's surprise, there was no difficulty about the cider at the till. The assistant didn't look much older than Flora, and she made no comment as she checked it through with the other items. Tracy had never tried to buy any alcohol herself, and she was sure that Mum had said you had to be eighteen. She didn't ask Flora, because she was feeling very uncomfortable about it, and didn't want to think about it. In fact, she felt annoyed with Flora for putting her in this position. Perhaps I ought to tell her how I feel about it, she thought to herself; but she thought better of it and said nothing.

On the way back, Tracy suggested they call in to see Miss Maitland. 'I'd like to find out what she's marked in that book to read out to us,' she said.

But Flora was not keen, and they went straight back to Welcome Home.

Tracy had pressed her cousin about visiting Miss Maitland, and had got her to agree to go one afternoon that week. That had satisfied her, and she was happy to leave the subject for now. Once in the house, they took their bags straight upstairs.

'Put the food on top of the chest,' Flora said. 'That should mean the mice can't get at it.'

At seven o'clock, Melanie and Mary arrived at the door together. Each of them was carrying an overnight bag, and a plastic carrier bag.

'Hi,' Flora greeted them as she opened the door to let them in. 'Melanie, this is my cousin, Tracy.' She gave them time to say hello, then the four went upstairs to deposit their bags in the attic.

'We've both brought some food,' said Mary, indicating the plastic bags.

'Put it on the chest,' said Flora, pointing to where Tracy had put the food they had bought. 'We've got quite a lot now, but we don't have to eat it all!'

She and Tracy had brought spare pillows, duvets and bedlinen from May's cupboard for the others to use, and there were already two spare single mattresses in the attic. They were stored there, propped up at one end of the attic, and wrapped in polythene.

'We can get them ready later,' said Flora, taking charge. 'Let's go down and fix the pizza, and then we can come back up and have fun.

Down in the kitchen, Flora put the pizza in the oven, and went to the fridge to take out the salad. She read out the note that May had left on the top of the plate that was acting as a temporary lid on the large baking bowl she had used for the salad. 'Hope you all have a nice time. Come and get me if there's anything else you need.'

Tracy noticed that Flora looked quite guilty as she read this out, and she thought it must be that she was thinking about the bottle of cider she had bought, but she didn't say anything to her. The pizza was very big, and there was more than enough for each of them, especially with the large salad May had provided.

'I feel really bloated,' said Melanie, who was a tall slim girl.

'There's nothing here to get bloated on!' Mary told her, a little irritably.

Melanie corrected herself. 'Sorry, I should have said I'm really full up. I've brought a lot of fruit in my bag. I don't think I'll be able to eat any of it.'

95

'I've brought fruit too,' said Mary.

Tracy and Flora laughed. 'We got some this afternoon, but we got some nuts as well.'

'I've got an idea,' said Tracy suddenly. 'Why don't we bring all the fruit down here and make a fruit salad?'

The others stared at her.

'We could put the rest of Auntie May's salad out of this bowl into a smaller one, and then wash this up and use it for the fruit salad. And we could leave some in the fridge for Auntie May, so *she* gets a surprise as well,' Tracy finished in a rush.

'I like your idea,' said Flora immediately. 'What do you two think?' she asked the others.

Having agreed on this plan, Mary and Tracy went up to collect the fruit, while Melanie and Flora tidied up the kitchen and got the bowl ready. The others were soon back with the bags, and spread the contents across the table.

'How many different fruits have we got?' exclaimed Tracy in amazement.

'I brought apples, pears and grapes,' said Mary.

'And I brought strawberries, cherries, peaches and nectarines,' Melanie added.

'And we got Kiwi fruits, bananas, oranges, cherries and a custard apple,' said Flora.

'What on earth is a custard apple?' asked Melanie.

'I don't really know,' replied Flora, 'but I thought we could try one. We could leave it out of the fruit salad, and share it to see what it tastes like.'

'That means we've got ten different things to put in the salad,' said Mary enthusiastically. 'Let's wash the fruit and then we can share it out and cut it all up.'

The four girls worked on until the bowl was almost full to the brim.

'When we've mixed it up, I'll put some in a big jar for Mum and put it in the door of the fridge,' said Flora. 'Can you write a note, Tracy, and I'll put it in the door too.'

Tracy got a piece of clean paper out of May's writing pad and wrote:

Thank you very much for the lovely salad. We have made a fruit salad out of the things we got for the midnight feast, and there is some in this jar. Eat it at midnight!

Love, Tracy

Then she handed the pencil and paper to each of the others so they could add their names, before Flora put it and the jar into the door of the fridge.

Upstairs in the attic room with the bowl of fruit, together with dishes and spoons, the four girls made up the two extra mattresses and made themselves comfortable.

'Tell us a bit about your holiday, Melanie,' Flora said. 'You're the only one of us that's been abroad. It must have been exciting.'

'Yes,' said Melanie. 'It was... Well, actually... it wasn't all that good.'

'What do you mean?' asked Mary.

'I thought it was boring most of the time,' Melanie admitted.

'What!' exclaimed Flora incredulously. 'Three weeks in Amsterdam was boring? I don't believe it!'

'We were there for the last two weeks. Before that we spent a week in London. That was quite good, but Amsterdam wasn't.'

Flora gaped at her friend. 'But I've wanted to go to Amsterdam for years,' she said.

'I expect it would have been fine for me if one of you had been there as well,' said Melanie. 'But I was just stuck with Mum and Dad, and all they wanted to do was look at art galleries and museums, and things like that. It was all right for a bit, but after a day or two, I wanted to scream and run away.'

'Where was Robert?' asked Mary.

Tracy was puzzled. 'Who's he?' she said.

'Sorry, I should have said. I've got an older brother called Robert,' Melanie explained. 'He's eighteen now, and he didn't want to come with us. He went camping with some of his friends, and they're all going to Amsterdam together for a few days in September, before they start university.'

'How did you manage?' asked Mary.

Melanie instantly appeared furtive. 'Promise not to tell anyone?' she said.

The others nodded.

'I bought some cannabis from someone who was pushing it in the street, and I kept chewing bits of it.'

The others gaped at her; and then Mary asked, 'Didn't your parents notice, or realise something was wrong?'

'No. I had gone into a café to use the toilets, and I was to join them where they were waiting on a seat in a kind of square. The pusher must have followed me out, and I just decided it was an answer to my desperation. Fortunately I hadn't spent much of my holiday money, so I could afford some. When I started being affected by it, Mum thought I was sickening for something, and kept making me sit down to rest as we all went round the sights. After that I found it much easier. I didn't seem to care too much any more about how boring it all was. In fact, some of the things I'd thought were terribly boring before seemed to be quite interesting after all.'

'That's a bit different from my postcard story,' Mary commented.

'What was that?' asked Melanie.

To the great surprise of Flora and Tracy, Mary recounted her story to Melanie, and went on to tell her about the secret project. When she had finished, she turned to the others and said, 'It really helped telling you both last week. I've been doing some more drawings, and I felt fine about telling Melanie.'

'Have you brought any of your drawings with you?' Tracy asked.

'Well… yes… I have,' said Mary, a little uncertainly. 'I brought a couple in my bag, in case you asked.'

She unzipped a large pocket section of her overnight bag, and produced some cardboard. The others soon saw that sandwiched between two layers of thick cardboard were two drawings.

'They're *brilliant*!' gasped Flora, as she studied Mary's work before passing it carefully to the others.

There was a charcoal drawing of Tim asleep in his cot, and a pencil sketch of a plant in a pot, standing on a windowsill.

'How long did it take you to do them?' asked Melanie.

'I did most of the one of Tim after he fell asleep earlier than usual one evening. I had the whole evening to work on it then. Mum and Dad were busy as usual, and they didn't disturb me. The plant I worked on from time to time, because of course houseplants don't move about.' She paused. 'Well, they don't move about if you don't move them.'

'What do you mean?' asked Tracy, fascinated.

'I found out that if I moved a plant to a different place in the house, it would gradually move its leaves about. When you think about it, the answer is obvious, but because plants don't run about, you don't think they move.'

'It isn't obvious to me,' said Flora, with a puzzled expression.

Mary explained. 'Green plants are dependent on light. So if they are in a house where the light comes mainly from one direction, and you move them, they move their leaves so they still catch as much light as possible.'

Tracy was impressed, and said so.

'I didn't learn about it from a book,' said Mary. 'I just had to work it out for myself.'

Melanie laughed. 'I'm glad that your bad experience in an art gallery turned out to be something good. I'm afraid I wasn't able to turn *my* bad experience into something good!'

'*Promise* us you won't do anything like that again,' said Flora sincerely. 'That was terrible. Fancy going away on a holiday and ending up having to buy drugs so you can cope with it. Are you going to tell your parents?'

'I don't know. They'll go completely mad at me, I know, so I don't know if I can face it.'

Tracy burst out, 'We could help you.' Then she looked astonished at what she had said. 'I mean…'

'No. Don't say any more,' said Melanie. 'Thanks for the offer. You're probably right. But I just can't face it at the moment.'

'Maybe it's time for the fruit salad,' said Flora. 'Then, if you're all willing to listen, I've got something big to talk about.'

Despite her earlier predictions, Melanie had no difficulty in eating two large dishfuls of the fruit salad, which they all agreed was delicious.

'What are you wanting to talk about, Flora?' asked Mary.

'There's quite a lot, actually,' Flora replied. 'Tracy and I were going to tell you a bit about what happened at the Youth Club, and I…' Here she hesitated, but then made herself go on. 'I want to talk a bit about my dad, because quite a lot's been happening.'

'Shall I tell them about the talk on bullying?' Tracy suggested eagerly. 'It was so interesting.'

'Yes, go on,' said Flora.

'Oh, I didn't mean that I was going to do it first,' said Tracy with a note of worry in her voice; and she knew she felt anxious about the prospect of Flora starting to shout again if anything else went wrong about her dad.

'I'd rather we told them about the Youth Club first,' Flora insisted. She turned to the others. 'I hope you'll be able to come on Friday.' Then she turned back to Tracy and added, 'We'll be going again, won't we?'

'Definitely,' Tracy replied. 'I hope Mr Ewing will have sent those information sheets to the minister by then.'

'What's all this about information sheets?' asked Melanie.

Tracy began to explain, and the others listened quietly while she gave them an account of Mr Ewing's talk and the questions that were asked afterwards.

'Maybe you'll be a teacher when you grow up,' said Flora admiringly. 'That was really good. You remembered a lot more than I did.'

'Thanks,' said Tracy, looking a little uncomfortable. She hadn't meant to create a good impression; she had just been keen to tell the others as much as she could remember, because she had found it so interesting.

'Do you know what's on this Friday?' asked Mary.

'I think we're off doing some golf again, actually,' replied Flora.

'I'm not sure that I'll be able to come,' said Mary, sounding rather weary. 'As far as I know, I'll be in charge of Tim again. But I'll certainly come if I can.'

'How about you, Melanie?' asked Flora.

'Should be okay for me,' she replied. 'But let's get on with talking about your dad. It must be very important because you hardly ever mention him usually.'

Flora told her friends what she had found out from Miss Maitland and her mum about what had happened when her dad left; and then she went on to tell them about the letter that had just come.

'What are you going to do?' asked Melanie, obviously keen to know.

'I don't know yet,' replied Flora. 'I'd been saving up to buy a computer. Mum was going to put money towards it too, and I thought I would have enough by Christmas. And now here's this letter. I just don't know what to do.'

'What's the problem?' asked Melanie. 'Just get him to buy it, and use your own money for something else. That's what I'd do if it were *my* dad.'

'I feel so angry with him that I don't want him buying it for me,' said Flora through gritted teeth. Then she added, 'But I'm worried that if I say that to Mum she won't understand, and she'll try to persuade me to let him get one for me.'

'And I'm worried that you'll start shouting again if she does,' Tracy said. 'I wouldn't blame you,' she added hurriedly, 'but it is quite hard for me when you're shouting.'

'So now that means we've got two things,' Mary reflected. 'Flora's worried about telling her mum how she feels about the computer, and Melanie's worried about telling her mum and dad about the cannabis.'

'What about you as well,' Flora reminded her. 'I know you're feeling stressed out because of all that minding of Tim you have to do, and you really should be talking to your mum about it.'

'But I can't. She's too busy.'

'That's why I said something about it. It's another of these "I can'ts".'

'I suppose so,' Mary agreed. She turned to Tracy. 'What about you?' she asked.

Tracy took a deep breath. 'Mine isn't about Mum,' she said. 'It's about Flora!'

Flora looked astonished. 'But we're getting on fine,' she objected. 'Well, I suppose there's that shouting, but I promise I'll try hard not to shout like that again.'

'It's not that,' Tracy said, as determinedly as she could. 'It's that alcohol you bought. I wish you hadn't done it.'

Flora looked embarrassed. 'I was still feeling so angry,' she admitted, 'so I wanted to do something that Mum wouldn't like. I know I wasn't going to tell her, so she wouldn't know, but I wanted to do something behind her back that she wouldn't like.'

'What did you get?' asked Melanie eagerly. 'I've been trying out some different drinks when I was away with Mum and Dad – things they bought for me.'

'It's a bottle of cider,' Flora said sheepishly.

'Great,' said Melanie cheerfully. 'Where is it? Let's get it out.'

'I feel bad about it now,' said Flora.

'Oh. Don't turn into an old stick-in-the-mud all of a sudden,' Melanie challenged her. 'Come on, *I'll* have some.' She stood up and started searching round the attic room.

'I don't think I want to any more now,' Flora said firmly. 'I think I'll give it to Mum in the morning.'

'I think Flora's right,' Mary said. 'Don't put pressure on her, Melanie. It's really not fair.'

At this point, Melanie became extremely grumpy. 'You're all just *boring*. That's what you are – *boring.*'

The others stared at her. It was Flora who spoke first. 'I'm sorry if you're disappointed. Would you like to have a go with my makeup bag instead? I've got a few new things since you were round here last.'

Melanie seized on this alternative willingly, and soon they were all putting their best efforts into trying to make her look as attractive as possible.

And it was after one before they were all in bed and asleep.

Chapter Twelve

Flora had put her alarm clock on the other side of the bed, away from where the others were sleeping; but it still made its usual very loud noise. She slapped it hard, and it fell silent. She was surprised to see that none of the others stirred, and she got out of bed and poked Tracy till she woke.

'Sh!' she said, with her finger to her lips. 'It's time to get up.'

Tracy stumbled out of bed, and the two staggered down the stairs to get washed.

Down in the kitchen, Flora went straight to her mother and said, 'I've got something to tell you, Mum.' And without waiting for May to turn round or say anything in response, she said, 'Yesterday I bought a bottle of cider for the sleepover. I'm sorry I did that. We didn't drink it. I got it because I was feeling so angry. I'll bring it down when we go up to get the others for breakfast.'

Tracy was astounded, and she was very impressed with the way Flora had told her mother. She hoped fervently that her aunt would not be angry with Flora.

May turned round, looked straight into Flora's eyes and said, 'That was very good you told me, love. I've a great deal of respect for you. And, like I said before, we'll talk about your dad when you're ready.'

After that, Tracy and Flora went into the dining room and began to lay the tables.

The serving of breakfasts over for the day, the girls went upstairs to wake the others, but found them already awake and dressed, waiting for them.

'I told Mum about the cider,' said Flora casually. 'She was fine about it. I'm going to take it downstairs to her now. Are you coming to have some breakfast with us?'

Mary and Melanie were eager to learn how Flora had approached her mother, and were impressed by what had happened.

'That's made a start,' said Mary. 'I wonder if I'll be able to talk to *my* mum about how I've been feeling about looking after Tim?'

'I'm sure I won't be able to talk to *my* mum about the cannabis,' said Melanie, dramatically. 'It would be *hopeless*. It'd be *bound* to go wrong.'

Flora picked up the bottle of cider from where she had hidden it behind the chest of drawers, and led the way downstairs with the others following close behind.

At breakfast, Flora further surprised everyone by telling her mother what she felt about her father's offer to buy a computer.

May had looked thoughtful, and said nothing other than acknowledging how Flora felt, and telling her that she could understand why. It was only after the others had gone home again that she said more.

'Flora,' she said. 'Would you mind if I write to your father about all of this?' Flora gaped at her in astonishment. 'But you've *never* written to him,' she said. 'And what are you going to say?'

'I don't quite know yet,' her mother replied. 'I was going to try writing something out, and then we could talk about it, but only if you wanted of course. Then I could send it off.'

'I don't think I want to,' Flora said hastily. But having considered the idea for a few more minutes, she changed her mind and said, 'Okay then,' before dashing off to start the cleaning.

This morning, the contents of the bin in the dark blue room provoked a very loud yell from Flora, and Tracy ran to see what was the matter. She found Flora shaking all over, and seeming as if she was about to either cry or laugh, although Tracy couldn't work out which.

'I'm *sick* of these magazines!' she said, with a strangled sob.

'Let *me* do it,' said Tracy.

'No! Don't touch them,' ordered Flora. 'I'm going to get Mum.' And before Tracy could say anything else, Flora had disappeared out of the door, and she could hear her running down the stairs. Tracy sat on the upright chair near the door, uncertain about what to do, but she soon heard Flora and her mother coming.

May went straight to the bin, and when she saw what was there she said, 'You were absolutely right to come and get me, Flora. That's it! I'm not having anyone staying here again that I'm not completely sure about. I'm not having you exposed to anything like this again!' She seized the bin, emptied its contents into the black bag that Flora had been using, and started striding back towards the stairs. Tracy could hear her muttering loudly to herself. 'And I don't care if it means we're short of guests sometimes. I'll tell anyone that might do this that we're full up!' she pronounced angrily, just before she went out of earshot.

Flora looked at Tracy. 'Mum's really starting to get the right angle on things these days,' she said.

'It might be because you're telling her more about how you feel,' said Tracy. 'My mum always helps me if I tell her what's the matter. Perhaps you haven't been telling her things.'

'You might be right,' said Flora. 'But it could be something to do with you, too.'

'How can that be?' asked Tracy curiously.

'You and I talk about quite a lot of things, and I think that might have made it easier for me to talk to Mum. In this house it's usually just her and me and the guests, and I think I feel worried about her quite often. She works so hard, and I don't want to bother her. I try to sort things out for myself, or push them out of my mind.'

Tracy tried to digest this information. It was something she hadn't thought about before, and she felt she didn't really have anything to add. 'I'm just glad you're talking more to your mum,' she said. 'And if me being around has helped, then that's fine.'

'Let's get on with the cleaning,' said Flora. 'And then we'll decide what to do this afternoon.'

'I know what I'd like to do,' Tracy answered eagerly.

'What's that?' replied Flora, a little puzzled that her cousin seemed so certain. She had found Tracy to be someone who was easy to be around, and someone who usually fitted in with whatever was going on; and to have an immediate response from her about what she wanted to do this afternoon was quite different from usual.

'I want to go and see Miss Maitland, and see what she's found in her book. You know, the one she said she would read to us from if we wanted.'

'Okay, then,' said Flora. 'Let's do that.'

May had been glad to hear that they were intending to go and see Miss Maitland again, and she had given them a jar of marmalade to take round for her. It was marmalade that May herself had made.

'I buy Seville oranges in January,' she began to explain to Tracy.

105

Flora butted in. 'Yes, it's *horrible*,' she said. 'The whole house stinks of oranges. You can even smell it in the attic!' Then she added: 'But I suppose it's worth all that suffering, because the marmalade tastes really nice. I hope there's plenty left for us, Mum.'

'Yes, there is,' May reassured her. 'I don't give it to the guests.'

'I know,' said Tracy. 'We put out those little individual packs for them. Do you get those from the Cash and Carry?'

'Yes, that's right,' replied May. 'I do that because there's far less waste that way. I suppose it means there's all that packaging, but hardly any marmalade gets wasted.'

As they walked down the road, Flora spoke about Melanie. 'I wonder what she'll decide to do?' she said. 'I remember when she started smoking her mum and dad were really horrible to her. They shouted a lot, and made her stay at home in the evenings for ages. It didn't stop her smoking though. She just started again as soon as she could, and if they are suspicious, she tells them that some of her friends smoke and that's what makes her clothes smell. She even says how she thinks it's a bad thing that her friends smoke!'

Tracy was astonished. 'But that's terrible!' she burst out.

Flora agreed. 'I know there are things I don't tell Mum,' she said. 'But I don't think I would behave like that. And there's another thing.'

'What's that?' asked Tracy.

'Melanie's dad used to smoke until recently. In fact he used to smoke all the time. Melanie told me he found it really difficult to give it up, and while he was trying to, he used to go round in a bad mood all the time, shouting at everybody.'

Tracy felt profoundly grateful that neither her mum nor her dad had ever smoked. She felt curious about cigarettes, and wondered why there were so many brands in the shops when everyone knew how bad they were for people; but she never had any wish to try one out. 'Have you ever tried smoking?' she asked Flora.

Flora laughed. 'Don't sound so serious. Of course I have. *Everybody* tries it these days.'

Tracy stopped dead in her tracks, and stared at her cousin. 'When did you do it, and how did you get the cigarettes?' she asked.

'There are always people at school who bring them in,' Flora replied casually. 'All you have to do is ask one of them for one to try, and they just hand them round – so long as you give them some money of course. I first tried one when I started secondary school.' She laughed again. 'I choked on it, and threw it away. I vowed I wouldn't try to smoke one ever again. But after a while everybody seemed to be trying them, so I had another one, and I got on a bit better with it.'

'But they're really bad for you,' said Tracy earnestly. 'Really, really bad for you,' she added emphatically. She thought about all she had learned so far about how they damaged people's health, and began to panic at the thought of Flora suffering from some of these effects.

'Don't worry,' Flora reassured her, noticing that Tracy looked alarmed. 'I wanted to be part of the group that were smoking a lot at the time, so I felt I had to smoke a bit, but I never smoked much, and I don't now. Anyway, I expect you'll have a try one day soon.'

Tracy was horrified at the thought, and said so. 'I don't even want to think about trying,' she ended determinedly. She began to worry in case people at school tried to put pressure on her about it. What could she do if they did? But then she knew she would talk it over with Mum and Dad straight away. She was sure they would help her to deal with it. Her mind went back to the talk on bullying. She had been so glad that Mr Ewing and a whole lot of other people were taking this very seriously. Although she herself hadn't been bullied much, she certainly knew the kind of thing that could happen, and she certainly didn't want to get tormented at school because she wasn't willing to try smoking. She comforted herself with the knowledge that she belonged to quite a large group of people in her year, people who got on well together and had similar interests; and she hoped that this would help.

Flora hadn't said anything further, and Tracy noticed that she had a dreamy look on her face. 'What are you thinking about?' she asked.

'Nothing,' said Flora. 'Well, actually, I was thinking about the Youth Club.'

'So was I,' said Tracy.

'I'm looking forward to Friday,' said Flora. 'And I hope Gordon will be there again.'

'Which one was he?' asked Tracy. But then she remembered it was the boy who Flora had been talking to – the one she had said afterwards that she liked. 'Oh, yes,' she said. 'I remember him. Did you really think we might be doing some golf this time?'

'Yes. If it doesn't rain, I'm pretty sure we will.'

'I'd like that,' said Tracy, skipping a few steps. 'That would be really good.'

She knew nothing about the game so far, and looked forward to beginning to learn.

By this time they had reached Miss Maitland's gate, and they went up the drive and rang the bell.

After waiting, the door opened, and Miss Maitland's face lit up when she saw them. 'Come in, dears,' she said. 'Come and tell me all your news. And I've marked some places in that book, so if you've got time, I can read some out to you.'

'I've got a jar of marmalade for you from Mum,' said Flora. 'I'll put it in the kitchen.'

She went into the kitchen and put the marmalade into a cupboard; then she made some tea, and took it through to the sitting room. 'I've had a letter from my dad,' she said to Miss Maitland without any preamble.

'What did it say?' asked Miss Maitland.

'He said he would buy me a computer for Christmas,' replied Flora. But without waiting for any response she added, 'I don't want him to.'

Miss Maitland was silent for a while. It was clear that she was thinking; and Flora and Tracy sat waiting quietly.

'How did you feel when you got the letter?' she asked.

'I was angry,' Flora replied with honesty. 'I was so angry I couldn't stop shouting, and Mum was angry with me until she understood why. I was shouting just at the sight of the letter. Wasn't I, Tracy?'

'Yes,' Tracy agreed. 'It was quite scary, and I wanted to phone Mum. She hadn't even opened it when she started shouting, Miss Maitland.'

'That doesn't surprise me,' said Miss Maitland slowly. 'You don't usually talk about your dad, Flora, but we'd been talking about him recently, and you were quite angry and upset even then. I imagine it's not easy for you to cope with. You hardly see him, so you can't really discuss much with him.'

'If I try he just changes the subject,' said Flora agitatedly; and she started to squirm in her seat.

'That must be very difficult for you,' Miss Maitland sympathised.

'Mum said that she could write to him, and that I could see it before she sent it,' said Flora cautiously. 'What do you think?'

Again Miss Maitland became thoughtful. 'I think it's good that your mum is writing something, but whether or not it gets sent is entirely another matter.'

'What do you mean?' asked Tracy curiously. She was intrigued by this discussion, and wondered what would happen next.

'Well,' began Miss Maitland, 'it's a step forward that May is thinking of writing a letter. That in itself is something different, isn't it?'

'Yes, that's right,' Flora agreed, eagerly. 'And she wants me to see it too!' she added. But then she scowled as she remembered that she herself didn't want to see it. But was that right? Perhaps she did want to see it after all, she thought. Aloud she said, 'I'm not sure I want to see it, but maybe that's something to do with the angry feelings I get when I think of my dad. Do you think I should give it a try, and have a look at what Mum writes?'

'That's a decision you'll have to make for yourself,' said Miss Maitland wisely. 'But just remember that although you might have some angry feelings, the whole thing could lead to something a bit better all round.'

'Mm,' said Flora as she reflected about what Miss Maitland had just said. 'I think I'll talk to Mum some more about it all.' Then she said suddenly, 'Miss Maitland, have you ever had a boyfriend?'

Tracy was astonished at Flora's audacity. Her mum had taught her never to ask personal questions of older people, and here was Flora asking something that she really shouldn't. She felt quite worried about what would happen next. She kicked Flora as unobtrusively as she could to try to alert her to her mistake, but Flora could not be deterred.

'Have you?' Flora repeated insistently.

'Now there's a tale,' replied Miss Maitland, smiling at Flora.

Tracy was very relieved to observe this.

'Do you two really want to hear about it?'

'Yes,' said Flora. 'You do too, don't you Tracy?'

'Er...um,' Tracy mumbled, unsure about what to say. She hardly knew Miss Maitland, yet here she was being asked whether or not she wanted to know about things Mum had told her she mustn't ask about. She felt confused, and wriggled in her seat.

'Maybe Tracy doesn't really know,' said Miss Maitland. 'I could tell you a little bit about my first boyfriend, and then you can decide whether you want to know any more, love,' she said kindly.

Tracy nodded. 'I'd like that,' she said. Miss Maitland had helped her out of what seemed to her to be an insoluble dilemma, and she felt very grateful.

'I was a bit older than you two are now,' Miss Maitland began. 'About sixteen as far as I remember. It's a long time ago, of course, so I can't be exactly sure. With having a wife and three daughters, my father decided he wanted a young man to help on the farm as well. Just across the yard from the farmhouse, there was a derelict cottage. He decided to make it habitable again so he could have someone come to live in it who would help. He worked on it from time to time for well nigh over a year before it was ready.'

'What rooms did it have in it?' asked Tracy, who was already deeply involved in what she was being told.

'There was a door at the front, and when you went in there was a small bedroom to the left, and a larger room to the right that was the kitchen and a place to sit. The bathroom was in a lean-to at the back.'

'What happened next?' asked Flora, who was leaning forward in her chair, as if afraid to miss a single word.

'My father heard that the son of an old friend of his was looking for farm work. He was twenty-one years old, and more than ready to leave home.'

'Did he come?' asked Tracy.

Flora kicked her, and said, 'Of course he did. Didn't he, Miss Maitland?'

'Yes, he did,' she replied; and her voice took on a slightly dreamy quality that surprised Tracy. 'He came soon after the cottage was finished.'

There was a silence, which was broken by Flora urging Miss Maitland to continue. 'Go on,' she said. 'You've got to tell us the rest.' She turned to Tracy. 'Hasn't she?'

Tracy nodded. 'Please,' she said.

'I liked him as soon as I saw him,' Miss Maitland continued. 'He was a hard worker, and my father was pleased with his decision to take him on. He'd been with us about six months when it all started.' Here she fell silent once more.

'*What* started?' asked Flora.

Miss Maitland struggled a little. And then it was as if she had

110

fallen into a kind of reverie, Tracy noticed.

'He started leaving little notes for me. He always seemed to know exactly where I was working, and he would leave a note for me to find. He would put each note somewhere where I was bound to find it, but no one else would.'

'That's really cool,' said Flora, bouncing up and down in her chair as if she were much younger than she actually was.

Tracy wanted to ask what the notes said, but she wasn't sure if that was all right, and said nothing. But Flora had no such inhibitions and said, 'What did he write, Miss Maitland?'

'It wasn't so much what he wrote, but how he wrote it,' said Miss Maitland.

Tracy and Flora looked at each other with puzzled expressions. 'What do you mean?' they asked together.

Miss Maitland wavered for a moment and then said, 'He wrote on leaves and sometimes on old seed pods. And sometimes he would write a word using some twigs, or scratch a word in the earth near where I would be working.' After she said this Tracy noticed she seemed to change, and said in matter-of-fact tones, 'One day, my father found out about it all, and sent him packing.'

Although Flora pressed her to tell them more, Miss Maitland had obviously said enough for one day, and refused to be drawn.

'I'll read you a bit of that book if you want,' she offered. 'But I'm a bit tired now, and I'll need to have a rest in a little while.'

'Please read a bit, Miss Maitland,' begged Tracy.

'All right then,' said Miss Maitland, sounding more like her usual self. 'Pass it across to me.' And she proceeded to read out a section of the book that was all about the resident ghosts in the castle where the author of the book had lived as a child.

'I liked the bit where that woman ghost didn't know about how one of the rooms had been changed into a bathroom, and she would appear through the wall and surprise people who were having a bath,' Tracy laughed. 'That's really funny. I must remember to tell Mum when I phone home again.'

'We'll let you have your rest now,' said Flora, standing up from her chair. 'Is there anything you want me to get for you before we go?'

'No, I'll be fine. Just let yourselves out. And do come back again.'

'Thank you for telling us about your boyfriend,' said Tracy, and she turned and followed Flora to the front door.

Strolling back along the road, Flora and Tracy discussed what they had just learned.

'That was *amazing*,' said Flora. 'I wish I'd asked her before, and I wish there had been time to tell her about Gordon.'

'We can go back and see her again,' Tracy reassured her. 'She said so.'

'I know,' replied Flora dreamily. 'Perhaps we can go back and see her after we've been to the Youth Club again.'

'I want to ask her if she ever tried smoking,' Tracy pronounced.

Flora gave her a dig in the ribs; and starting to run, called over her shoulder, 'Race you!'

It was not long afterwards that the two arrived back at Welcome Home, gasping for breath and sweating.

'Mum!' yelled Flora as loudly as she could, as she reached the kitchen door and threw it open.

May looked up from the kitchen table, and smiled. 'I'm here. You don't need to shout that loudly. I can hear.'

'Mum, have you written that letter yet?' asked Flora.

Tracy marvelled at the speed with which Flora's moods and attitudes changed, but said nothing.

'As a matter of fact I'm in the middle of writing something just now,' May replied. 'Do you want to see how far I've got? It's far from perfect, but at least it's a start.'

Flora sat down, took the writing pad that May was using, and read out loud:

Dear Tony,

I expect it'll be a surprise to get a letter from me, but I thought I'd better try to write. Flora says you've offered to buy her a computer for Christmas. I think it's difficult for her to accept it while you and I have no communication, and I wondered if you'd be willing to meet up with me one evening soon to discuss her situation.

I've realised that it must have been very hard for you to have a baby in the house after what you went through as a child, and I'm sorry for anything I did that made it even more difficult for you.

112

I think that as years have gone on, we've been stuck in a pattern of behaving that doesn't help either of us, and I'm sorry for my part in carrying that on.

Flora jumped up and threw her arms round her mother. 'You're a star!' she said. 'Can we send it off straight away, and see what happens?'

May looked very surprised. 'You mean you want me to send it off just like this?' she asked.

'Yes. Let's do it now,' said Flora decisively. 'Just sign it while I get an envelope, and then Tracy and I will take it to the post box.'

May copied the address from the top of Tony's letter on to the envelope that Flora had brought from her office, sealed it, and put a first class stamp on it.

Outside once more, Flora said to Tracy, 'I don't know what Dad will do when he gets this letter, but at least Mum understands how I feel, and she's trying to do something about it, and that's the main thing.'

Chapter Thirteen

Tracy woke before Flora's alarm went off. She remembered straight away that it was Friday, the day of the Youth Club; but her heart sank when she heard rain thundering on the velux windows of their attic room. She had been looking forward to the prospect of learning something about golf; and unless the weather improved soon, she guessed it would be off. She reached over and switched Flora's alarm off. At least she would be spared its jarring sound this morning; and she could nudge Flora awake soon. She lay in her bed watching the sheets of water washing down the windows.

As she lay there, she realised that in addition to the sound of the rain on the windows, she could hear a less prominent sound of water, and it was a dripping sound. She jumped out of bed and began to search around the attic; and it was not long before she found a small pool of water gathering behind Flora's chest of drawers. She grabbed the towel that she had hung over the back of a chair, and put it on the water to soak it up and to catch the drips that were coming through the roof. She couldn't see exactly where the water was coming in, but she could see quite clearly the point at which it was dripping off the sloping part of the ceiling.

She shook Flora awake. 'Water is coming in,' she said urgently. 'We'd better go and tell your mum.'

Flora sat bolt upright. 'Where?' she asked.

'It's dripping down behind your chest of drawers,' Tracy replied. 'I've put a towel there to catch it.'

'We'll need to get a bucket,' said Flora. 'I'll get one from the store cupboard. I'll be back in a minute.' She jumped out of bed, and disappeared down the stairs. Tracy could hear her running back up almost straight away, and she reappeared carrying a yellow plastic bucket. 'Here we are,' she said triumphantly. She placed it behind the chest of drawers. 'I've put the wet towel in it for now,' she added. 'That should do until we tell Mum. Let's go and get washed now.'

When May heard the news, she groaned out loud. 'Oh no!' she said. 'I'll phone the roofer, but you never know when he'll be able to get here, he's always so busy. I don't deserve this, you know. I get him to check the roof every year, so he can look for any weak points and replace missing tiles. Let's get on with the breakfasts and I'll phone him at eight.'

When they were sitting eating their own breakfasts May said, 'I got the roofer, but he won't be able to come until next week. Can you two keep a bucket under the leak, and I'll give you some old towels to spread round it? That way we'll be sure it doesn't go through to the floor below.'

'Don't worry, Auntie May,' said Tracy eagerly. 'We'll keep an eye on it. Won't we, Flora?'

Flora had her mouth full of toast, but she nodded vigorously.

The rain had continued almost unabated all day. Flora and Tracy kept checking the leak, and made sure there were no others anywhere else. Before they left for the Youth Club they changed the bucket so they could empty the water that had collected so far.

'I hope Mary and Melanie will be there tonight,' said Tracy happily as she hurried along with Flora through the rain.

'I hope Gordon will be there,' said Flora, who seemed to have temporarily lost interest in her friends.

They hung their lightweight showerproof jackets on the pegs in the hallway of the church hall, and found a few of the others had arrived before them. Tracy immediately recognised Helen, the two Rebeccas and Graham. There was no sign of Gordon yet, or Mary or Melanie. Flora looked despondent, but made an effort to speak to Becky.

Helen came over to join them and said, 'Jim Mason should be here soon. He's got some ideas for this evening, and he's got the sheets from Mr Ewing, so he'll bring those along too.'

'Oh good,' said Tracy. 'I was looking forward to seeing the sheets. What do you think his ideas are for the evening?'

'I think he's made a list of possible subjects to discuss, and we can choose from it,' replied Helen.

'That's a good idea,' said Becky cheerfully.

Tracy could hear some more people arriving, and she was glad to see Mary and Melanie with Gordon arriving just behind them, together with a group of boys of a similar age. She noticed that Flora brightened instantly as soon as she saw Gordon, and she went across to speak to him.

Mr Mason came in at the back of the group, and addressed everyone.

'Hello,' he said. 'Sorry about the rain. I might be able to fix some things, but I couldn't fix that.' Everybody laughed, and he went on, 'Tonight I've got a list of suggestions of things we could discuss, and I've got the sheets from Mr Ewing to hand round. I'll pass those round straight away, and then that's done.' He handed the pile of sheets to Helen who was sitting next to where he was standing, and she got up and began to pass them round. 'I'll read out the list. Of course, you can add to it if you want, and then I can read it out again and we can take a vote on which topic to have for this evening.' He read from his list: 'alcohol, drugs, electronic equipment for entertainment, mobile phones, TV violence, smoking, diet, families and anything else you might like,' he finished with a smile.

Graham put up his hand. He looked shy but determined at the same time. 'I think we don't get enough on sex education at school,' he said. 'Can you add that to the list, please?'

Mr Mason added it to his list, and Tracy noticed that most of the group were nodding their heads in agreement.

'What about citizen's rights?' said a tall serious looking boy, who looked a bit older than everyone else.

'Yes, I'll add that the list,' said Mr Mason.

'I'd be interested in that,' said Mary, 'but I don't think I'd want to talk about it all evening.' Most of the others nodded.

Then Mr Mason made a suggestion. 'How about we choose two subjects and split our time between them?' he asked. 'Tell you what, I'll call out the items, and I'll count the hands for each. Then we'll take the two subjects that come out top.'

Although this was a sensible idea, it turned out that everyone wanted to talk about everything; so Mr Mason cut his list up into strips, which he folded up and put into a serving bowl in the kitchen. 'I'll shut my eyes and stir them round and pick two of them out,' he said. He chose them and handed them to Helen, who read them out.

'Families, and sex education,' she said. 'That's good,' she reflected, 'they sort of go together.'

They shuffled the chairs into a loose circle.

'Shall I say something to start?' asked Mr Mason.

Everyone agreed, and he began. 'I have three brothers and sisters.

One of them, my brother, is two years older than I am. The younger ones are both sisters. One is two years younger than I am, and the other is four years younger than that. My father was a minister, and we lived in a huge stone-built house. My mother looked after everyone, including a lot of people who came to the church and needed help of one kind or another. We didn't have much money, and we were usually cold in the winter because we couldn't afford to heat that house. We all had to get dressed in our best clothes every Sunday, and usually we went to church twice on that day. Monday was my father's day off, but he spent a lot of it in his study, preparing his sermon for the following Sunday. I remember my little sister being born in the house. We lived in a place where a midwife would come to the house.

'We didn't have any sex education at school, although those who did biology as a subject learned about mammalian reproduction. I learned most of what I knew as a child from my brother, and I think he learned things from his friends. My parents certainly never spoke directly to any of us about it. I never heard of any parents who did in those days. I have often thought how silly that was. After all, none of us would have existed had not our parents come together sexually.'

There was a ripple of laughter from the group.

'You may well laugh,' said Mr Mason. 'It's ridiculous, but it's very serious too, and it still has consequences in our daily life.'

Graham put up his hand. 'I think it's silly that in our sex education classes all they tell us about is contraception and pregnancy, without saying anything about all the strong feelings people get about each other.'

The others nodded emphatically.

'That's certainly something we can talk about here,' said Mr Mason. 'I remember the first time I noticed a girl in that way, I just about fell over because the feelings were so strong!'

Everyone laughed again; and then Mr Mason continued. 'I remember when I was a boy, and I was helping my mother in the kitchen, I sometimes had very strong feelings towards her. I could feel quite overwhelmed by them. But those feelings seemed tame by comparison with the ones I got when I started being interested in girls later on.

'I remember too that I wanted to feel as close to my father as I did to my mother, but I could never get much time with him, and when I did, he always seemed distant. I feel quite upset even now, when I think of how sad I felt about that.'

For a moment Mr Mason looked as if he was going to cry; and Tracy was surprised to hear him say, 'I nearly cried there. And I just wanted to say that because I want you to know that it's all right to cry when you feel sad about something.'

Mr Mason stood quietly for a few minutes, and everyone waited.

'I'm wondering what might be the best way to go about this discussion,' he said reflectively. 'I have a suggestion, but the important thing is that whatever we do, it is with the agreement of everyone.'

Helen stood up and addressed him. 'I'd like to hear your suggestion,' she said. She turned to the rest of the group. 'Let's have a show of hands about it. Who else wants to hear Mr Mason's idea?'

Instantly, everyone put up a hand.

'Thanks for that vote of confidence,' said Mr Mason. 'This is my idea. I think from what we've said so far, there's general agreement that sexual feelings can be extremely strong, and that we could have a discussion about this. But I'm wondering if it might be best to start off by talking about strong feelings in general, and then start thinking about strong sexual feelings as a part of that more general discussion. What do you all think?'

'I think that's an excellent idea,' Gordon said. 'Does everyone agree?'

A ripple of eager assent went round the group.

Gordon went on: 'I don't find this easy to say, but I can feel very embarrassed talking about sexual feelings. I know that when I am talking about them, I can sometimes feel the feelings coming up, and I find that really difficult. I think it would help the discussion a lot if we followed Mr Mason's suggestion.' He looked rather embarrassed.

Flora turned to him and said with obvious admiration, 'It was really brave of you to say all that, Gordon. I don't think I could have.'

Mr Mason addressed Gordon and said, 'I have a great deal of respect for you, Gordon. I don't find it easy to say things like that myself, and you put a very important point very clearly. Well done.'

There was a rumble of approval from the group, followed by a brief silence.

Then Flora spoke again: 'I'd like to talk about angry feelings for a bit,' she said. 'What does everyone else think?'

Again everyone agreed, and Flora volunteered to tell them about her angry feelings about her dad.

This went well, and when she had finished Becky put up her hand. Mr Mason nodded to her.

'Thanks for that, Flora,' she said. 'It's helped me with *my* angry feelings. My dad hasn't gone away to live somewhere else, but he is away on business a lot, and I hardly ever see him. I used to think I was lucky because I had a dad, but now I can see that the important thing is what sort of contact you have with your dad, and not just where he lives. I have a lot of angry feelings about my dad, and I'd always thought there was something wrong with me, and that I should just be grateful that I had one, and that he had a job.'

'Do you think you might be able to say anything to your dad about this?' asked Mr Mason.

'No, I don't think so,' said Becky, 'but I'll think about what we've been saying.'

Melanie was the next to speak. 'My dad's quite a bit like Becky's,' she said. 'Well, he's away on business a lot, and I hardly ever see him. But I'm different from Becky because I don't feel angry. I'm just glad when he goes away. I know there's something wrong though, because sometimes I do things that my mum and dad would be very angry and upset about, but I keep it all secret.'

Mary was looking agitated. 'Can I say something too?' she asked.

'Of course you can, Mary,' said Mr Mason. He turned to Melanie and said, 'We can come back to you if there's more you want to say, Melanie.'

'I've just realised something,' said Mary. Her face was flushed. 'It came into my mind straight after Melanie said about keeping things secret.'

'What is it, Mary?' Tracy asked, wondering if Mary was about to talk about her art project.

'Recently I told Flora and Tracy how I sometimes eat up my little brother's leftovers when I'm looking after him, and that I do that even when I'm not hungry.' She paused, and then continued. 'I think it might be because I'm angry about having to look after him so much!' She blurted out this last sentence in a rush.

Mr Mason looked at Mary and said, 'That's very interesting, Mary. I'll have to think about what you just said. I used to look after

119

my little sister a lot when I was young. I loved her a lot, and I still do, but I think there were things about looking after her that I didn't always like.'

'I still think you should try to talk to your mum about having to look after Tim so much,' said Flora. 'After all, she isn't having to study any more.'

'But she's got to take phone calls about orders,' replied Mary in defeated tones.

It was Helen who spoke next. 'Your mum is in the house, but she's a bit like someone who's away on business a lot. My mum works from home, but she puts the answering machine on the phone after five o'clock, then we can have time together. It works really well. Do you think you could get your mum to do the same?'

Mary brightened. 'I could try,' she said. 'Thanks Helen.'

'We've been talking about some really strong feelings for the last while,' said Mr Mason. 'Can we talk a bit now about how strong these kinds of feelings are when compared with sexual feelings? I certainly remember having some sexual feelings when I was younger that were stronger than any other feelings I was having.'

Graham put up his hand and began to speak. 'The thing that's really hard for me,' he said, 'is that I'm just not used to them. Sometimes other kinds of feelings take me by surprise, but at least I'm used to them. These sexual feelings have only been coming in the last while, and I'm just not used to them.'

Most of the others nodded in agreement. Tracy felt a bit out of it, because she wasn't quite sure what they were talking about now. She knew she had started feeling a bit different when she saw people kissing on films and things like that, and she assumed that must have something to do with it all; but apart from that, she felt a bit lost. She heard Mr Mason's voice say, 'Of course, everyone is different. We just have to discover more and more about ourselves, and we do this only gradually. The feelings can be very strong at times, and that is quite normal. You don't have to worry or try to do anything about them.'

'I think I'm going to try to do something about my angry feelings though,' said Mary. 'I'm definitely going to try and get Mum to use an answering machine, like Helen's mum does.'

'Are you going to tell your mum that you feel angry?' asked Flora.

'I don't know yet,' Mary replied. 'I'll have to see what happens when I talk to her about the machine.'

One of the boys who had been there last week, but whose name Tracy didn't know, started to speak. 'My mum keeps giving me cuddles as if I was still a child, and I don't like it. It feels all wrong.'

Mr Mason smiled. 'I think it would be a good idea if I tell you that I don't always get that sort of thing right with my own children,' he said. 'When you have been a dad for years to a cuddly son or daughter, sometimes you can forget that things change when your children get older. I hope you'll be able to say something to your mum.'

'That's just it,' said the boy. 'I tried, but she's just the same.'

Another boy spoke up. 'I had that problem too,' he said. 'In the end I talked to my dad about it, and he got Mum to see what I was getting at.'

'That's a really good idea,' said the first boy. 'I hadn't thought of that. Dad never talks to me much, but I could try to talk to him.'

Mr Mason joined in. 'These dads who don't speak much... quite often it's because their own dads didn't speak to them. There are a lot of them who underneath long to be talking, but don't know how to go about it.' He laughed. 'I was one of those,' he admitted. 'And now my family can hardly get me to shut up!'

Everyone laughed.

'This is good,' said Gordon. 'I'm really glad I said what I did at the beginning.'

'Yes, it's really good,' agreed one of the girls. 'I haven't said anything tonight, but I've been thinking a lot. Can we have a discussion like this again soon, Mr Mason?'

'Yes, of course,' replied Mr Mason. He glanced at his watch. 'And now I think it's time to get the biscuits out.'

There was a loud hum of eager conversation between everyone as the biscuits and drinks were passed round; and at the end of the evening, Mr Mason had to threaten jovially to lock them all in for the night in a final attempt to get them to leave.

Later that night, Tracy and Flora stayed awake talking.

'What a relief!' said Flora with a big sigh.

'Why?' asked Tracy.

'Being told that when we get sexual feelings we don't have to do

121

anything about them,' said Flora.

'Why is that a relief?' asked Tracy, puzzled.

'Last week I got a lot of them when I was talking to Gordon,' Flora explained. 'And I thought that meant I had to do something. But now I know I don't have to, it just feels such a relief. There's so much to do, I don't feel I want to be doing anything new like that at the moment. There's all the cleaning, school work, friends, Miss Maitland, Dad and all that. I don't want to have to think about doing things about sexual feelings with boys yet. It's a big enough thing having the feelings, without having to do anything else!'

Tracy said nothing.

'Why aren't you saying something?' demanded Flora.

'I'm thinking,' said Tracy.

'Thinking about what?' asked Flora.

'I'm thinking about how there are a lot of adverts with people kissing on them. I've just realised that that's really strange,' Tracy replied.

'You're right!' said Flora. 'I hadn't thought about that before, although I must have noticed it.'

'I liked this evening,' said Tracy. 'It was really good. And I've got the stuff now about restorative justice that Mr Ewing sent. I'm going to show it to Mum and Dad when I get home. I want to find out if they know anything about it.' She lay quietly for a few minutes and then surprised Flora by saying suddenly, 'I wonder when your mum will hear from your dad?' She didn't tell Flora, but inside she felt quite excited. Perhaps this holiday she might get a chance to meet her uncle for the first time.

'I'm trying not to think about that letter Mum wrote to Dad,' said Flora. 'But actually it's on my mind most of the time now. I'm glad we posted it.'

'Where does he live?' asked Tracy.

'I don't know,' replied Flora. 'All we have is a PO Box number in London.'

'We'd better go to sleep now,' Tracy advised her cousin. 'Tomorrow we'll have to change all the beds again.'

Chapter Fourteen

Saturday morning was particularly hard work for them all. In addition to the usual breakfasts and cleaning, the man came unexpectedly early to look at the roof, and in the pink room a guest had spilt something sticky on the carpet, and it took a lot of work to clean it up. None of them had been able to work out exactly what it was, and May had had to experiment with a number of cleaning fluids until she found something that worked.

By lunchtime, they were all feeling worn out, and were glad to be relaxing round the kitchen table.

'It was very good of the man to come so quickly to mend the roof,' said May gratefully. 'That's one worry off the list. But it was an extra thing to deal with when we were so busy.'

The phone rang. May got up and lifted up the kitchen extension.

'Hello. Welcome Home,' she said. 'A twin room? I'll just go and get my diary.' She walked noisily towards the kitchen door, but to Tracy's surprise, she turned there and came straight back to the phone. 'No, I'm afraid I don't have one free,' she said. 'Goodbye,' she added rather abruptly, and put the phone down.

Flora stared at her mother in amazement. 'Mum,' she said. 'Why did you do that?'

May looked cross. 'I could just tell,' she said, her voice full of annoyance. 'I felt convinced it was the sort of person who would fill the bin with the kind of rubbish we don't want. I'm not risking any more of that!'

Tracy noticed that Flora was looking at May admiringly. 'That was great the way you did that, Mum,' she said, and she jumped up and gave her mother a hug.

'I wish I'd done it long ago,' May said, her voice filled with regret. 'It was seeing you in the state you were in the other day that brought me to my senses. I'm only sorry I didn't do this before.'

'Don't worry, Mum,' said Flora generously.

'I can't help feeling bad about it, love,' her mother replied.

Tracy took a deep breath. 'What are the magazines and things about, Auntie May?' she asked.

May looked at her across the table and said, 'Some people like to look at magazines of women dressed up in hardly any clothes – clothes covered in frilly bits.'

'Is that so they can get sexual feelings?' asked Tracy.

'I expect so,' her aunt replied. 'But I wish they wouldn't use my house for it. After all, it's quite a private thing. There's nothing wrong in having the feelings, but there can be things wrong in what you do with them. And if anyone decides to have these magazines, I don't think it is all right to leave them in a bin where any of us has to see them when we're doing the cleaning. It just isn't right.'

There were more questions that Tracy wanted to ask; but she wasn't sure that this was quite the right time, so she decided against it.

It was Flora who spoke next. 'I think I'll phone Mary and see what she's doing this afternoon,' she said.

'Perhaps she'll have Tim,' said Tracy eagerly. 'I'd like to play with him again. He's great!'

'Give her a ring, love,' said May. 'I'll have to be here as usual for the guests, and to answer the phone. I've been wondering about using the answering machine a bit more, but there doesn't seem any point when I have to be here anyway to book people in and out.'

'We were talking about that sort of thing at the Youth Club last night. Weren't we Flora?' said Tracy.

Flora nodded.

Tracy went on. 'Several of the mums run businesses from home, and some of the people at the Club found it quite difficult.'

May looked interested. 'It's good you were talking about these things,' she said. 'I know you want to phone Mary now, Flora, but I'd like to hear about it sometime.'

Flora looked pleased. In fact, she looked very pleased. She didn't say anything, but went to the phone, and was soon arranging to meet Mary that afternoon.

When she put the phone down she said to Tracy, 'She's definitely got Tim, and we're going to meet in half an hour at the same place as we did last time.'

'Oh, good!' said Tracy, who had jumped up from her chair and was bouncing up and down. 'And we can ask her if she's said anything to her mum yet.'

'What's that about?' asked May with interest.

'We'll tell you all about it later,' said Flora cheerfully, as she dashed off to get ready.

The two girls were soon at the corner where they had met Mary before, and could see her hurrying along the footpath pushing the buggy. As she came nearer, Tracy could see that Tim was asleep.

'Hello, you two,' said Mary. 'I'm so glad you phoned. After our talk last night, I've been bursting to talk to Mum about how I feel, but she hasn't got time for it today, *and* I'm having to look after Tim again until he goes to bed.'

'That's bad,' said Flora sympathetically, and Tracy nodded in agreement.

'Well, it might not be quite so bad,' said Mary determinedly. 'I did manage to get through to her that even though she was so busy we *had* to have a talk, and she said we could later this evening. She didn't ask me what it was about. She was too busy. But at least I made a start,' she finished proudly.

'Hey, that was really good!' exclaimed Flora admiringly.

Mary smiled and then said, 'Actually, I think it's got something to do with having talked to you two, and then everyone talking at the Youth Club last night.' She fell silent, and the three walked along together in silence, apart from the familiar rattling sound of the wheels of the buggy.

After a while Mary said, 'All of that's made quite a difference. I remember thinking when I was trying to get through to Mum today that at least I knew other people who knew something about how I felt. I realise now that I'm talking to you that that made the difference between giving up and keeping on trying. I'm not like you, Flora, I don't seem to be able to shout at Mum. I either say something, or I keep quiet. If I'm saying something, and I don't seem to be getting through to her, I usually shut up quite quickly.'

Tracy was listening very carefully to everything Mary was saying. She had a feeling it was all very important, although she wasn't sure quite why. The main thing was that she liked Mary and Tim very much, and she was glad that Mary was going to be talking to her mum that evening.

Suddenly, Mary stopped the buggy. 'I've just realised something!' she exclaimed. Tim started to stir, so she hurriedly walked on.

'What is it?' asked Flora.

'I had to give Tim his lunch just before I came to meet you, and I've realised that I threw his leftovers away, *even though* I felt hungry. I remember I was so busy thinking about all the things I was going to talk to Mum about this evening, that the bits were in the bin before I realised what I'd done. Then I made myself a nice roll with salad in it, put it in my bag with Tim's drink, and set off to meet you two.'

'That sounds *so* good,' said Tracy, who was feeling very pleased for Mary.

'And you *must* tell us what happens when you talk to your mum this evening,' added Flora.

'I will,' said Mary determinedly. 'Now, where shall we go today?'

'I'd like to go back to the play park,' said Tracy enthusiastically. 'It's such good fun.'

'Would you?' asked Mary in slightly disbelieving tones. 'Would you really?'

Tracy nodded emphatically.

'Of course,' Flora agreed. 'It's the best place for us to hang out when we've got Tim. 'And we've got to help with him if we want to see you in the daytime.'

'I think he'll probably sleep for a bit longer, so we could go somewhere else first,' said Mary cheerfully.

'Okay,' said Tracy.

'What'll we do then?' said Flora.

'Actually…' began Mary. But she didn't continue.

'Actually what?' asked Flora curiously.

Mary tried again. 'Actually…'

'Come on, tell us!' Flora insisted.

Tracy looked at Mary in a puzzled way. She couldn't guess what she was trying to say.

'Actually…'

'*Just say!*' Flora gave her friend a nudge. 'What's the problem about saying?'

'There's a small art exhibition in part of that big house at the other side of the park. You know, the one the Council took over last year. I'd like to go and have a look,' said Mary.

'Why on earth didn't you say so before?' asked Flora, clearly amazed at Mary's reticence. But without waiting for her friend to answer, she said, 'Come on then you two,' and strode off in the direction of a large house that Tracy could see in the distance.

Tracy's mind was whirling. All she could think of was Flora's reaction to Auntie May's idea of seeing the pottery exhibition when they were all in town together that afternoon more than a week ago. Flora hardly seemed the same person now. Tracy couldn't work out why this was, but she decided that she didn't need to know. The main thing was that they had all agreed they were going across to the big house. She turned her mind to herself. It was hard for her to work out whether or not she wanted to see the art exhibition that Mary was interested in, but she decided it didn't really matter. After all, she was out with people she liked, and that was the main thing. Actually, she thought to herself, I'm quite interested to see the house closer up, even if it turns out that I'm not keen on the art.

After five minutes of brisk walking, they had reached the front door of the house. To the left of the door there was a glass case mounted on the wall, and it had a poster inside it that Tracy could see advertised the exhibition. She read the details out loud: 'An exhibition of floral art on canvas by Tricia Penway.' In the centre of the poster was a picture of one of the paintings. It certainly looked very good, thought Tracy.

'Come on then,' said Flora. 'Let's go in.'

She opened the door, went in, and then held it open to help Mary in with the buggy. Tracy noticed straight away that all the floorboards were bare. They must be sanded and varnished, she thought, as she remembered how she had once seen some men working on a floor like this, and Dad had explained to her what they were doing. She didn't like to say anything to the others because, although there were quite a few people here, it was very quiet.

Mary went across to the first painting and stood looking at it with a rapt expression on her face. Tracy thought the picture was nice, and she wondered if there were any postcards of the paintings in the exhibition that she could send home to Mum and Dad. Of course, she remembered, Paula would have left today to go on holiday with Jenny. Fleetingly, she wished she had phoned her this morning to say goodbye; but she reassured herself with the memory of having spoken to her on Thursday evening when she had phoned home for a chat. I can get news of her when I next phone Mum, she reminded herself. Paula is bound to be phoning home quite often, she always does when she is away.

Mary was still staring at the first painting; and although Flora had moved on, she certainly seemed to be absorbed in what she saw, Tracy noted with surprise. She felt in her pocket to check the small purse was still there that she had carried the day before, and she went back to speak to the attendant at the entrance.

'Excuse me,' she said politely.

'Yes?' replied the woman in a pleasant tone. She was wearing a kind of uniform.

'Are there any postcards of the paintings for sale?' asked Tracy.

The woman looked embarrassed, and for a moment Tracy wondered if she had said something wrong.

'Thank you so much for asking,' said the woman. 'I had completely forgotten to put them out on display. You see, this is the first day of the exhibition, and we just opened at two o'clock.' She went behind a large wooden desk that stood inside the door, opened a drawer, and took out several heaps of postcards. 'There aren't many to choose from,' she went on. 'I think there are about five different pictures.'

Tracy looked through them and found one that showed the picture that Mary had been looking at. She paid the attendant, who handed the postcard to her in a small polythene carrier bag. She then went off in search of Mary and Flora who had disappeared into one of the rooms off the large hallway. Just as she caught sight of Mary, she also saw Tim begin to struggle in his buggy, and after that he started to cry.

Tracy noticed that Mary looked agitated and upset. She had never seen her look like that before, and she went across to see if she could help.

'I'll have to take him outside,' said Mary. 'It's no good trying to stay here now.' And she started to wheel the buggy briskly across towards the entrance.

Tracy went with her and held the door open to help her. She could see that Mary was crying.

'I'm so disappointed about not seeing all the pictures,' Mary said in muffled tones.

'Have you got many more to see?' asked Tracy.

'There are a few more in the room I was in, and then I think there's one more room,' said Mary.

By now Tim was howling, and tugging at his straps.

'Why don't we get hm out of his buggy and walk him round in

front of the house until Flora comes out?' suggested Tracy. 'Then perhaps Flora and I could walk him round while you finish looking at the paintings.'

Mary brightened up. 'Would you really do that?' she asked. 'It would make such a difference to me.' She let Tim out of the buggy, and she and Tracy each took a hand and walked him round the low bushes at the side of the area of paving stones that led up to the front door. Tim's crying was instantly transformed into happy chuckles as they wove their way round and round the bushes.

About ten minutes later, Flora appeared at the door. Tracy and Mary called across to her, and it was soon fixed that Mary could spend some time looking at the remaining pictures. Flora and Tracy devised a game of 'boo' around the bushes, that kept Tim busy until she returned. He had not seemed at all bothered as she walked away.

When she returned about fifteen minutes later, she was glowing.

'I met the artist,' she burst out. 'Did you see her arrive?'

'No we didn't,' said Tracy and Flora. 'We were busy with Tim.'

'She was really nice,' Mary continued. 'She came over to speak to me. And I found out she doesn't live very far away. We talked for a bit, and she said I could see her studio sometime. She gave me her card with her phone number on.' She jumped up and down excitedly, which was something that Tracy had never seen her do before.

After that she bent down to give Tim a hug.

'Oh no,' she said, laughing, when she stood up again. 'I'll have to change him. He's got a dirty nappy. It's okay. I always carry everything I need. It's in the bag on the buggy.'

She fetched the bag, and Tim lay down obligingly on the grass behind the bushes. Tracy and Flora entertained him while Mary cleaned him up.

'Right, that's that,' she said, as she put the dirty nappy into a polythene bag. She picked Tim up saying, 'Play park,' and strapped him into his buggy once more. After that she ran off down the path, with Tracy and Flora jogging alongside her.

Once again, the play park was busy with many children and families. Tracy noticed that there was much less litter this time, and she wondered if it was due to the effect of her aunt's phone call to the Council. They decided to take it in turns to help Tim with his activities. This meant that each of them could enjoy playing, but they had opportunities to talk as well.

The time passed pleasantly, and it was quite late in the afternoon by the time they were making their way back towards the place where Tracy and Flora would part company with Mary and Tim.

'I hope it goes really well with your mum this evening,' said Tracy sincerely.

'Me too,' added Flora. 'Actually, I've been quite surprised recently about what's been happening with me and my mum. So good luck!'

Tracy and Flora arrived back at Welcome Home to find May looking harassed.

'I'm glad you're back,' she said with relief in her voice.

'What's wrong, Mum?' asked Flora.

'I booked Mr and Mrs Temple in soon after you left. They are an older couple. Mr Temple didn't look very well, so I felt a bit worried about him. Anyway, they went upstairs, saying that he would lie down and rest. It wasn't long after that that Mrs Temple knocked on the kitchen door, and she asked me to call an ambulance! I've never had anything like this happen, not in all the years since I started this business. It gave me quite a shock. Of course, I phoned right away, and the ambulance came very quickly. Mr Temple's in hospital now. They're giving him tests to try to find out what's wrong. Mrs Temple is going to wait at the hospital with him. I phoned Pat for a chat. I just had to talk to someone about it all. But ever since then I've been looking out for you coming back.'

'You could have phoned me on my mobile,' said Flora.

'I know, love,' said May. 'But there wasn't really anything to say. I just wanted to see you both, and I knew you'd be back soon enough. I didn't want to spoil your afternoon.'

To Tracy's surprise she heard Flora say in a very adult way, 'Well, if anything like that ever happens again, I want to be sure that you would phone me on my mobile, and we can decide together whether I come back or not.'

'All right, love,' said May. 'I promise I'll do that.'

'What are you going to do about their room?' asked Flora. 'They were just booked in for two nights, weren't they?'

'I've been thinking about that, and I've decided I won't take any more bookings for that room until I know how long Mrs Temple will need it for. I can't risk having her worrying any more than she has to already. It wouldn't be right. I've got people coming at the weekend who I was going to put in that room, but I'll make sure one of the others is kept free just in case.'

It was late evening by the time a taxi arrived with Mrs Temple in it. May had been looking out for her as the evening progressed, and she opened the door as soon as she saw the taxi. She took her into the kitchen, sat her down, and put the kettle on.

'How is Mr Temple?' asked Flora politely, as she put a tin of biscuits on the table that she had collected from the cupboard.

'It's good of you to ask,' replied Mrs Temple. 'They're still not sure what it is, but he was sitting up in bed when I left, and he looked a lot better than this afternoon.'

May put a cup of tea in front of her, and she sipped it gratefully. 'It's really kind of you,' she said. 'And I need to ask you about the room. I don't know how long Ernest will be in hospital...' Here her voice tailed off.

'You don't have to worry about the room,' May reassured her. 'You can have it for as long as you need it. Just keep in touch about how things are going, and I can work round that.'

'I'm so grateful...' Mrs Temple began.

'You don't need to say anything,' May interrupted. 'I'm sure if our situations were reversed, you would be the first to help out.'

'Why yes... yes, I would,' agreed Mrs Temple, her face clearing. She finished her cup of tea, and then said, 'I think I'll go upstairs now. It's been a long day.'

Later, in bed, Tracy and Flora talked over the events of the day. Before she put out the light, Flora said, 'I can't wait to hear how Mary got on with her mum this evening.'

Chapter Fifteen

When Flora had phoned Mary the following afternoon, it was her dad who had answered. He had told her that Mary and her mum had gone off together for the day. Flora could hear Tim in the background, so she knew that Mary and her mum must be on their own, and she hoped that was a good sign.

When she phoned again after lunch on Monday, Mary answered.

'I've got lots of news,' she said happily. 'But I'm not free for a couple of days. Can we see each other on Wednesday?'

'I think so,' Flora replied. 'Give us a ring tomorrow and we'll fix it.'

'It all sounds a bit mysterious to me,' Flora told Tracy. 'But whatever it is, it sounds good. Mary seems fine.'

'I really want to hear her news,' said Tracy impatiently.

'So do I, but we're just going to have to wait,' said Flora.

'Let's take the bikes again today,' suggested Tracy. 'We could go and see if Melanie's in, and then we could call on Miss Maitland on the way back.'

Flora's face registered surprise. Tracy didn't usually have a plan, and if she did, she didn't usually come out with it like this. 'I don't mind doing that,' she said. 'But is there any special reason why you want to?'

'I loved cycling along that walkway,' said Tracy, and I'd like to explore it a bit more. I'd like to find out if Melanie's spoken to her mum about anything, and I want to hear more about the farm that Miss Maitland used to live on.'

'I think it's really sad that her dad sent that young man away,' said Flora dreamily. 'You know... the one who liked her.'

'I feel like that too,' Tracy agreed. 'And I think Miss Maitland does as well.'

They told May what they were planning to do, and they were soon setting off down the road. Flora was proudly wearing the vulture helmet again, and Tracy was wearing Flora's old one, which was the same colour of pink as her watch.

'Did you choose this helmet to match your watch?' asked Tracy as they pedalled along side by side.

'No. I chose the watch to match the helmet. And then my head got too big for the helmet,' replied Flora. 'I'm so glad that Mum had this vulture one. It's really cool. I hope some of my friends see me wearing it. They'll be really envious.'

They called round at Melanie's house, but again there was no one in. The neighbour popped his head over the hedge and informed them that they had gone away for a long weekend break, and wouldn't be back until Wednesday.

'Never mind,' said Tracy. 'Perhaps we'll see her at the Youth Club on Friday.'

They made their way along the road to the break in the hedge, and were soon pedalling along the walkway. This time, when they reached the bridge, they continued on over it, and followed the walkway for a few more miles.

'I'm finding your bike's fine now,' said Tracy, as she pedalled along easily. 'I was a bit worried before in case we went too far for me to get back.'

'I think we shouldn't go much further now, if we want to leave time to call in on Miss Maitland,' Flora advised her cousin.

'Can we just go round this bend to see what it's like?' begged Tracy. 'We can turn back after that.'

'Okay,' Flora agreed. She was surprised that Tracy was being so confident about what she wanted, but it felt all right.

The walkway was now skirting round a housing scheme, and there was quite a lot of rubbish at the side of the track, some of which looked quite unpleasant. And as Tracy pedalled round the bend, she misjudged her steering, her front wheel caught the edge of a pile of rubble, and she fell to the ground with a crash.

Flora jammed on her brakes, and jumped off her bike to help her cousin. She didn't try to hurry her into standing up because she was obviously in a lot of pain, and her breathing sounded strange. She stood patiently waiting, and trying to talk reassuringly to Tracy.

'Just take your time,' she said. 'I'm sure we can sort something out. The important thing is not to rush.' She wasn't sure if she believed exactly what she was saying, but it sounded good, and she felt calmer from having said it. She noticed that Tracy's breathing was getting a bit more normal and she wasn't making funny noises any more, but she showed no signs of wanting to get up.

At last Tracy said, 'I must have winded myself. I think the handlebars swung round and stuck into me, and that's what did it. At least I can talk now.' She paused for a minute or two. 'Please will you look at my knees. They feel horrible, and I'm a bit scared to look.'

Flora walked round her, bent down, and examined Tracy's jeans. The material over one knee was a bit torn, and there were dark patches on both knees.

'I don't know if there's any blood,' she said. 'Maybe it's just dirt.' She pondered for a moment. 'Would you like to try to stand up now? I can give you a hand.'

'Okay,' Tracy replied. 'Could you pull the bike away, please? That would help.'

Carefully Flora pulled the bike away from where it was tangled in Tracy's legs.

'Ouch!' exclaimed Tracy as she put her hands on the ground, preparing to stand up. She sat and looked at her palms, and it was then that she discovered that they were torn and bleeding, with grit embedded in places. 'Oh no!' she said.

'Let's have a look,' said Flora. She scrutinised Tracy's hands, and said sympathetically, 'That looks really painful. We need some clean water, and something to wrap them up in.'

Just then a large golden Labrador dog rushed round the bend, and when it saw Tracy on the ground, it came over and started trying to wash her face. Flora grabbed its collar and pulled it off. 'He's being friendly, but it isn't exactly what we want at the moment,' she groaned as she struggled to hold him back.

'Bracken! Come here!' said a voice. Flora turned and saw a woman coming along the track with two small children on bikes. The dog raced back towards her, and she put him on a lead. 'Can I help?' asked the woman, when she realised that Tracy had hurt herself.

'I think you might be able to help us,' Flora replied, 'but can I just phone my mum first?'

'That's a very good idea,' the woman agreed.

Flora took out her mobile and was soon speaking to her mother.

'And there's someone here who is offering to help us,' she finished.

'Shall I speak to your mum?' the woman suggested.

Flora nodded and told her mother that she was handing her phone to the woman.

'Hello,' she said. 'I live not far from here. I've got my two with me, and we're just on our way home. One of the girls seems to have quite a bit of grit in her hand. I think it would be good if she came back with me, and we can give it a good wash. Then we can phone you and decide what to do after that. I'll give you my phone number. We should be there in about five minutes.' She waited while May got something to write on, and then told her the number, slowly and distinctly.

Flora and the woman helped Tracy to her feet.

'Can you walk?' the woman asked.

Tracy took a few experimental steps. 'It's my knees,' she said. 'They hurt a lot.'

'Does the pain seem on the inside as well as on the outside?' the woman asked.

Tracy thought for a moment. 'I think it's mainly on the outside,' she said.

'Well,' said the woman. 'If we take it slowly, you should be fine.' She picked up the bike Tracy had been riding. 'Can you make your way along slowly with this?' she asked. 'I know it will be painful, but we haven't far to go. Just follow us.' She set off slowly along the track with the dog and the two little children, neither of whom had said anything. They had just stared at Tracy and Flora with big round eyes, and had watched while their mother had been arranging what to do.

It took nearly ten minutes to get to the woman's house. She let everyone in, and then showed Tracy the bathroom. Tracy was profoundly grateful that it was on the ground floor, as she didn't think she would manage stairs very well at the moment.

The little children seemed to like Flora straight away, and brought her a pile of books to read to them while their mother helped Tracy.

'Here's a dressing gown,' she said to Tracy. 'First we'll soak your hands in some water with a mild disinfectant, and then you must take your jeans off and put on this dressing gown and we'll have a look at your knees.

Tracy found that the soaking of her hands was not as painful as she imagined it would be; and she was glad to see most of the grit coming off almost straight away.

The woman brought some strips of what looked like an old sheet, together with a box of dressings.

'I'm afraid this is a bit makeshift,' she said as she patted Tracy's hands dry with a clean towel, put the dressings on and wrapped the strips round them. 'But it's all clean, and it will protect your hands meantime. I'll come back in a minute or two, when you've taken off your jeans.'

Tracy fumbled with the fastenings of her jeans and then carefully worked to get her legs out of them. She was relieved to see that her knees, although grazed, were not too bad. She put on the dressing gown, and went in search of the woman.

She found her on the phone, speaking to Auntie May. The woman handed the phone to her.

'My knees aren't too bad,' she told her aunt. 'My hands are the worst.'

'Pam was telling me,' said May sympathetically. 'We were just working out how to get you back here.'

'I'll be all right,' said Tracy bravely. She did not want to be a worry to her aunt, especially after all the trouble about Mr Temple. 'I'm sure I'll be able to ride back.'

'It's all right, love. We've been making a plan,' said May. 'Pam's husband will be home at five, and he'll be able to bring you both and the two bikes back here in his people carrier.'

'Shall I hand the phone back for now?' asked Tracy.

'Yes. Bye for now,' said May.

After she had finished speaking to May, the woman came and spoke to Tracy. 'I'm sorry, I should have introduced myself. I'm Pam, and my children are called Ben and Kate.' She looked across to where Flora was sitting with a stack of books, which she was reading to Ben and Kate, and said, 'They look as if they have found paradise! Come and I'll help you with your knees. And I've found a pair of shorts that might fit you. They're some my little sister uses when she comes to stay.'

She produced a pair of pale pink denim shorts with large flowers printed on them; and then she helped Tracy to clean her knees.

Afterwards Pam brought some drinks and cut up some apples for everyone to share; and they sat and talked and read more books until they heard Pam's husband arriving home.

'What's all this?' asked Dave, as he came into the living room.

Ben and Kate jumped up and each grabbed one of his legs.

'Flora,' said Ben, pointing to her.

'Taysee,' said Kate, pulling at her father's leg, as if trying to get him to join in.

'I'm afraid the girls have to go home now,' Pam explained.

Kate burst into tears. 'No no no no no no no!' she wailed, tugging at her father's leg.

'Kate, would you like to help Daddy to take them home?' asked Pam.

Kate stopped crying and went to get her shoes from the hallway.

'You come as well, Mummy,' said Ben.

'All right,' Pam agreed.

Pam explained to Dave what had happened; and he was soon loading the bikes into the back of the people carrier and securing them so they wouldn't slide about while he was driving.

On the way back to Welcome Home, although Tracy had to be careful with her hands, she kept Ben and Kate entertained with singing songs that she remembered Paula had liked when she was small. When they arrived, May came out to meet them, and Dave insisted on carrying the bikes through to the shed and locking them up before he drove off with Ben and Kate and Pam, who waved as they disappeared down the road.

'Now tell me exactly what happened,' said May, as they sat at the kitchen table. 'And I'll have to have a look at your hands and decide whether or not I'll need to take you to see the nurse tomorrow. Pam thought they'd be all right, but she wanted me to check. By the way, it's good news about Mr Temple. He's got some new blood pressure pills, and he'll be fine. He should get out of hospital tomorrow, and his son's coming up on the train and will drive them both back home in their car. After what's been happening, they just want to be back home for now.'

Tracy and Flora told May everything that had happened.

'It was lucky that Pam came along when she did,' said May. 'Accidents happen. They're never nice, but they're not so bad if someone like that comes along to help.'

The girls spent the evening quietly. They phoned Tracy's mum to tell her what had happened; and then finding there was nothing worth watching on the TV, they looked at the games in the cupboard and decided to play Scrabble. May joined them later, and was impressed by how well they could play. And although Tracy's hands were sore, her fingers were all right, and she had no difficulty in handling the letters.

Chapter Sixteen

Tracy didn't sleep very well that night. The pain in her hands and knees had woken her each time she turned over, and in some ways she was glad when she heard Flora's alarm go off.

'I don't expect you'll be able to do much today,' said Flora.

'I think I'll be able to help a bit if I'm careful,' Tracy replied. 'Anyway, I want to try. I'll get ready after you, and I'll come down to the kitchen.'

When May saw her she said, 'You'd better just sit here until I've got time to look at your hands.'

Tracy sat patiently at the kitchen table until Flora and May had finished the breakfasts and were ready to have their own.

'Now, let's have look,' said May; and she gently uncovered Tracy's hands. 'That's not too bad,' she proclaimed. 'I've no doubt it hurts, but they're doing fine. They're pretty clean, and I don't think we'll need to go and see the nurse. I'll get some clean dressings.' She disappeared up the back stairs, but soon returned carrying a number of items. She covered Tracy's hands with dressings held in place by a short length of bandage, and then gave her a pair of white cotton gloves to put over the top. 'That should do,' she said. 'There's plenty of protection there now. You'll just have to experiment and see what you feel all right about doing. Don't get them wet, though.'

'Thank you, Auntie May,' said Tracy gratefully. 'I think I'll be able to do some of the vacuuming.'

'Well, just be careful for a day or two,' advised her aunt. 'Now, let me see your knees.'

May examined Tracy's knees and pronounced that the worst thing was the bruising, and that the grazes were quite superficial and had begun to heal over already.

'It's Wednesday tomorrow,' said Flora half to herself, as she chewed the crust of her toast.

'What's happening then?' asked May.

'I'm hoping to see Mary,' Flora explained. 'We think she'll have a lot of news. Don't we, Tracy?'

139

'Why not invite your friends round for the evening again?' May suggested.

'Oh, thanks Mum!' said Flora enthusiastically. 'I will. Melanie's away at the moment, but she should be back tomorrow. I'll give her a ring then.'

By Wednesday lunchtime, Flora had managed to contact both Mary and Melanie, and she and Tracy spent the afternoon making a green salad and a fruit salad; while May, who had washed Tracy's torn jeans, sat and patched them with a piece of floral needlecord that Tracy had chosen from the drawer where May kept spare pieces of material.

'Do you want to sprinkle some sliced nuts on the green salad for a change,' she asked as she worked. 'Hazels are good for that.'

Flora looked doubtful. 'I'm not sure,' she said.

'You could put some out in a separate dish,' May encouraged her.

At a quarter past seven, there was a ring at the door, and Flora opened it to find Mary and Melanie had arrived together.

'My dad gave me a lift,' said Melanie, 'and he picked Mary up on the way. He doesn't usually bother to take me about,' she went on. 'I'm wondering if he's worried because someone got attacked last night. I don't know who it was, and Dad didn't say anything to me about it, he just insisted on giving me a lift. And he's coming back for us at ten.'

'Come in,' said Flora. 'Tracy and I want to hear your news. Tracy fell off my old bike on Monday and hurt her hands, but we've been making things for us all to eat this afternoon.'

'Poor Tracy,' said Mary. 'What happened?'

'She'll tell you herself,' replied Flora, as she took them into the kitchen.

Having exhausted the subject of the accident, Flora shared out the quiche that May had left out for them, and passed the salad round. 'Now, Mary, tell us what's been going on with your mum.'

Mary smiled broadly. 'It's great,' she said. 'Remember I was going to talk to her on Saturday evening? Tim wouldn't settle at first, so I was late, and Mum was busy with her accounts. It was after nine by the time we got started. It was difficult at first because I found that all I wanted to do was shout at her! I never thought I would feel like that, but I did. But after a while she said something that really helped. She said I looked angry, and she asked me if I was feeling angry with her. After that, it all rushed out. I couldn't stop talking, and she just sat and listened. I told her how I didn't mind looking after Tim, but I didn't want to be doing it all the time, and I didn't think it was fair that she was always expecting me to. I told her it had been going on for far too long, that I had my own life to lead, and that I couldn't have it when I was being Tim's mother. Yes, I even said that... Tim's mother! It felt good saying it, because it's true – I've been a mother to him for ages now.

'I didn't tell her about the food, it just didn't seem the point, but I *did* tell her about my art project.'

'Did you show any of your drawings to her?' asked Flora.

'Yes, I did,' replied Mary. 'And I told her that I've been invited to Tricia Penway's studio. She was impressed with what I've done, and she asked me if we could show Dad. I didn't want her to straight away, so she promised to wait until I was ready. And she took me away for the day on Sunday, and we went round a really good art gallery, and we talked and talked.'

'What's going to happen about you looking after Tim?' asked Tracy.

'Mum said that she and Dad would have to work it out between them, but she said she would be grateful if she could ask me to help out from time to time. She even apologised for assuming that I would keep on doing everything, and she's keen that we get back to me just being Tim's sister. I really love Tim, but if I'm doing a lot for him all the time, like I said before, I can't concentrate on doing things for myself.'

'That's great news!' said Flora. 'You've done really well.'

'Actually I feel really proud of myself. Whenever I've thought of talking to Mum before, just as I'm getting round to it the phone rings, or she remembers something she has to do, and then I give up. This time I was *so* determined. I knew that if the phone rang I would tell her to let the answering machine cut in. After all, other people's mums do that, so why can't she? Anyway, I didn't need to do that. She listened to everything I had to say, and she even asked me if there was any more I needed to tell her!'

'Was there?' asked Tracy, fascinated to hear about everything Mary had achieved.

'I told her that there might be, and she said we should talk again. She said we should talk again soon,' Mary finished, drawing herself up in her seat and looking confident.

Tracy was pleased for Mary. She had never had any difficulty going to her own mum to talk about things that were bothering her, and she felt sad to hear about other people's troubles. It must be terrible not being able to talk to your mum, she thought. But it was so good that first Flora, and now Mary, were able to. She looked across at Melanie, and wondered if she had got any further with *her* mum, but she didn't like to ask.

However, Flora didn't have any such inhibitions, and she turned to Melanie and asked, 'When do you think you'll be able to tell your parents about the cannabis?'

Melanie pulled a face. 'Never, I should think. It's just hopeless. I'm glad for Mary. It sounds really great what's happening now, but it's just hopeless in my house.'

'It can't be completely hopeless,' said Mary encouragingly. 'I used to think that about my home, and now look what's happening.'

'I know,' Melanie replied. 'But yours is a bit more straightforward. Most of it is about making sure you don't have to look after Tim all the time, and being interested in what you want to do. In my house, Mum and Dad just seem glad that my brother has just about left home, and they seem wrapped up in their own things. And anyway, I don't know what I'm interested in, so I wouldn't know what to say to them.'

Tracy was astonished. How awful, she thought. It must be terrible not to know what you're interested in. It was never a question for her. There were so many things that interested her. She didn't know what to say. But then something came into her mind and she asked, 'What was the last thing you were really interested in?'

Melanie looked surprised. 'I hadn't thought about that,' she said. 'All I think about is how horrible it is not having anything I really want to do. Of course, I like coming here and talking, but I mean things like Mary's art. I don't have anything like that.'

'What was it like being away with your mum and dad at the weekend?' asked Mary.

'It was okay... No, it wasn't,' replied Melanie. She continued irritably, 'Why do I keep saying things are okay when they're not? When I was telling you about the holiday in Amsterdam, I started off as if it had been fine.'

'I've been thinking about that,' said Flora. 'I think it's a bit like how so many people talk about the weather when they meet. It's sort of expected. With holidays I think people just say they've had a wonderful time, even if it's been horrible. Then we just go on and copy them. It's silly, isn't it? Mum and I hardly ever go away on holiday, so I've had a chance to think about what people say, and work out what's going on.'

Melanie stared at Flora. 'I'm impressed,' she said. 'I think you're right. And another thing is that Mum and Dad groan at me if I say I'm not enjoying myself. Last weekend was terrible. I was so glad to get back. Not that things are fine at home, but at least I've got my computer, and I can see my friends.'

Tracy surprised herself by asking Melanie again what she used to be interested in.

Melanie looked troubled. 'I try to be interested in clothes and makeup,' she said. 'And I like e-mailing people on my computer. I watch a lot of TV and pretend I like it, but actually, half the programmes are so boring.'

'What's your favourite subject at school?' asked Tracy, thinking about all the topics she was looking forward to studying when she went back after the summer holiday.

'I used to like French,' said Melanie mournfully, 'but then the teacher left. The one we have now is terrible! She can't even say the words properly. And the same happened with music. We used to have a great teacher, but he left too, and now we've got someone who's so boring I nearly fall asleep. The one that left used to give me clarinet lessons too. He always had something interesting to get me to play. He ran groups at school too. We did all sorts of things – jazz, and themes from musicals, as well as all the more serious stuff.'

'I remember him,' said Flora. 'I didn't do music for long, so I never had him, but he was always friendly to everybody. I never saw him doing anything nasty.'

'Flora and I have got quite a good French teacher at the moment,' said Mary. 'It's a pity you aren't in our set. We all thought you were one of the clever ones, because you were in the best set!'

They all fell silent. Melanie's situation sounded grim, and no one could think of anything helpful to say.

It was Flora who broke the silence. 'I know,' she said. 'Let's ask

143

Mum.' And without waiting for Melanie's permission, she went into the sitting room where May was sitting with her feet up, knitting a cardigan for herself. 'Mum,' she said. 'Can we come through for a bit? We've got something to ask you.'

'Of course you can,' May replied. 'Come through whenever you're ready.'

The girls finished their meal, tidied away, and then settled themselves comfortably in the sitting room with May.

'Now, what is it, my loves?' asked May.

Flora looked as if she was going to make a start, but to Tracy's surprise, Melanie eagerly told May everything she had been telling them, including the fact that she had bought cannabis when she was in Amsterdam.

May listened without interrupting until Melanie had finished, and then she said, 'I'm glad you decided to tell me all this. I'm sure there are things we can do to try to help, but it might take a while to improve things.'

Here Mary burst in. 'But things feel as if they're getting better once you're talking about them, even if nothing else has changed!' she said excitedly. 'Well, it's definitely like that for me.'

May went on: 'I think the first thing is to work out how to talk to your mum and dad about school,' she said. 'A young woman like you needs something in her education that she feels excited about, and it seems to me that the two things you really liked aren't being handled properly. I'm not wanting to be nosey, but I get the impression that your mum and dad aren't short of money.'

'I don't think so,' said Melanie.

'Well, then, they might be able to fix up some tuition for you, or something like that. And have they ever thought of doing an exchange with a girl of your age from France? Have you ever had a French pen friend?'

By now Melanie had brightened up considerably. After she had told May about the cannabis, she had been worried that she would insist that she told her mum and dad about it straight away. She wanted to be able to; but she knew she couldn't face it yet, and she didn't want the huge row she imagined would come from doing that. They were already unhappy with the way she was behaving, and that would just give them more reason to get at her. What Flora's mum was suggesting was something she felt almost certain her mum and dad would at least consider.

'By the way,' May went on. 'I wanted to ask you all if there is cannabis for sale from people at school. I was reading in the papers that it's quite easy to get at nearly all the schools everywhere now.'

Flora looked uncomfortable. She hesitated, and then said, 'Yes, there is. It's easy to buy some if you want. Actually... I bought a bit last term and baked it into some buns I made. But after I'd eaten the buns I felt all peculiar and decided I didn't want to have any more.'

'Was that the time I thought you were sickening for the flu?' asked May.

'Yes,' said Flora sheepishly.

'I wish you'd told me, but I'm glad you've told me now at least,' said May. She went on, her voice showing concern. 'There's so much around nowadays. It's not just the cigarettes and the sneaked drink of alcohol we used to have when we were young. It's all these drugs as well now. And although you all have sex education at school, there are problems with teenage pregnancies and all the illnesses that can come from getting together like that.'

Flora blushed bright red. 'Mum!' she said. 'I *wish* you wouldn't just start talking about sex, *and* when my friends are round!'

It was Mary who calmed Flora by saying, 'I'm not surprised you feel funny about it, Flora, but it helps me.' She turned to the others. 'How about you two?'

'I think it's really cool,' said Melanie enthusiastically.

'I don't mind at all,' said Tracy. 'She's my auntie, and she talks a lot like my mum does, so I'm used to it.'

'Oh well then,' said Flora. 'If it's okay for all of you, it's okay by me too. And since we're talking about sex...' Here she turned to Mary. 'How did you feel when your mum got pregnant with Tim? Did your mum and dad explain anything to you about that?'

'Not much,' Mary admitted. 'I remember they seemed all silly and giggly when they told me.' She pulled a face, and then went on. 'They did say it was a surprise though, so I don't suppose they'd exactly planned to have a baby.' She looked across at Flora's pink watch. 'Melanie's dad will be here in about half an hour,' she said. 'So we haven't got much time left.'

May spoke to Melanie very directly. 'Look, love,' she said. 'I hope you get on all right when you talk to your mum and dad about school.'

'Thanks,' replied Melanie.

May went on: 'I think what I'll do is come to the door with you when your dad arrives. I haven't met him before, so I'll just introduce myself and pass the time of day with him. And remember, if you want any help talking to them, just come back and talk it over here, or...' she thought for a moment, '... we might be able to find a way that I could talk to them too. We can put our minds to that if necessary. Now, don't let it get you down. You've got your life in front of you, and there's plenty in it for you. Now off you all go, and finish your chatting in the kitchen. I'm sure there are things you want to talk about yet.'

They went back into the kitchen, and were deep in conversation when the doorbell rang. May came through straight away and said, 'Leave it to me, girls.'

They heard her open the door and invite Melanie's dad in for a cup of tea.

Melanie was surprised to hear him agree, and Tracy jumped up and put the kettle on.

'Mum must have a plan,' whispered Flora. 'I think we can trust her.'

The others nodded, and began a conversation about an article on the front page of the newspaper that lay at one end of the table.

'Hello,' said Melanie's dad as he came into the kitchen. 'Flora's mum invited me in for a cup of tea, and it was an offer I couldn't refuse. Do you mind waiting for a few minutes while your taxi driver refreshes himself?'

Mary and Melanie assured him that that would be fine, and Flora watched expectantly while May got out some of her special shortbread for everyone to share.

They were soon passing round plates and cups of tea.

'It's nice to see you all,' said Melanie's dad.

Flora introduced Tracy, and Tracy explained that she was Flora's cousin, and that she was staying for a holiday. 'It's a working holiday really,' she said proudly. 'I'm learning a lot about Auntie May's business while I'm here.'

'Yes,' said May. 'She's a willing helper.'

'I wish Melanie was a willing helper,' said her dad rather disparagingly.

'Well, she's certainly a very pleasant and interesting visitor,' said

May spiritedly.

'And she's a great friend,' the others added.

He looked a bit startled, and sipped at his tea. He looked as if he didn't know quite what to say.

'It's fascinating,' May went on. 'She's got all sorts of interesting plans.' She winked at Melanie conspiratorially while her father's attention was on his second piece of shortbread. 'Of course, I'm hoping she'll be round again soon. Listening to her has certainly brought something into my evening.'

Flora kicked Mary under the table, and suppressed a giggle. She could see that her mother was in her element, and she was admiring her obvious skill.

Melanie's dad was mumbling through his shortbread, and May went on confidently. 'How about we make a date, Melanie? Can you manage this time next week?' She turned to her dad and said, 'Will you be able to spare her? Of course, if you're giving her a lift again, you're welcome to pop in when you come to collect her.'

By this time Flora was almost spluttering, and she had to get up and make a dash for the hall. She called over her shoulder, 'Excuse me, I'll be back in a minute.'

She went to the bathroom, splashed water over her face, and returned just in time to hear May saying, 'That's it fixed then.'

After that they went to the front door, and waved goodbye as Melanie's dad drove off with Mary and Melanie.

'Mum, you were *amazing*!' exclaimed Flora, hugging her mother tightly.

'Hey, hang on a minute, I can hardly breathe,' said May, laughing. 'But I must say, I rather enjoyed all that myself.'

Tracy noticed that her aunt's eyes were twinkling, and she seemed a lot brighter than usual.

Chapter Seventeen

When Tracy woke the next morning, she was relieved to find that not only had she slept through the night, but also her hands were much less painful. She put on a clean pair of cotton gloves and was able to help with the breakfasts again. There wasn't so much work to be done this morning she knew, as most of the guests were staying again tonight.

When they were eating their own breakfast just before ten, May heard the post arrive, and went into the hall to collect it out of the box. 'I'm expecting something,' she explained as she left her breakfast half eaten.

But when she returned, Tracy noticed that she looked a bit odd.

'Well,' said May. 'It's all coming thick and fast.'

'What is it, Mum?' asked Flora.

'It's a letter from your dad, love,' said May.

Flora dropped her spoon, and shouted, 'Don't just stand there. Open it!'

'All right, love,' replied May. 'But please try not to shout.'

'Okay,' said Flora. 'I'll try. But it's a big thing.'

'I know, love,' replied May, as she took a kitchen knife out of the wooden block and slit open the top of the envelope. She glanced at the contents of the letter, and then read it out.

May,

I am surprised to receive a letter from you. I thought we had agreed a long time ago we wouldn't correspond.

'Stuffy creep!' shouted Flora angrily.

'Hang on a minute,' said her mother, and read on:

But, having read what you say, I'm glad you tried.

'So?' said Flora, a little less loudly.

148

I've thought about what you say. But the past is the past, and we can't change it.

'It's like I said,' muttered Flora darkly. 'He's a stuffy creep!'
'Let me finish reading it out,' pleaded May.

I'm going to be passing through next Monday. Perhaps we can meet and discuss Flora's computer.

'That's it!' Flora muffled her shout by gritting her teeth. 'I don't want anything to do with him, ever again!'
'Look, love,' said May. 'I think I should explain. That's just the way Tony used to talk. The very fact that he's suggesting a way to meet me is a big thing for him. I know it sounds silly when he's pretending it's all to do with your computer, but that's not what he really means.'
'I just wish he could talk about things for what they really are,' said Flora tearfully. 'I've had enough of it all.' And she started to sob.
'There's a bit more,' said May, and she read out the rest of the letter.

Please tell Flora that I'm sorry I won't be able to see her this time. Explain to her that we've got some things to sort out.

Tony

'Did he say that?' exclaimed Flora. 'Did he really, really say that?' She jumped out of her seat, grabbed the letter and read through it to reassure herself that May had not added a bit of her own. 'But he might just be talking about the computer,' she said suspiciously, once she had confirmed to herself what he had actually written.
'I don't think so,' said May. 'And now I've got to get myself geared up for seeing him. He doesn't suggest a time or place. First I'll have to work out what to do about that.'
'He's written something on the back,' said Flora. 'It says:'

P.S. I'll meet you at the Woodlands Hotel at around eight.

'He doesn't give you any chance to say if that's convenient or not, does he?' sneered Flora. 'And he's been like that with me all my life!' She dumped the letter down on the table and gave an impression of flouncing off. But Tracy could see straight away that the flounce wasn't really a flounce at all.

'I think I'll phone your mum tonight, love,' May said to Tracy. 'I could do with a long chat about this. I need to get it all sorted out in my mind for Monday. You can have a chat with her first, of course. There'll be plenty of time for that, don't you worry. And I'll give Pat a ring straight away to see if she can come over and sit with you two and keep on eye on the business for me while I'm out.'

That afternoon, Tracy and Flora decided to visit Miss Maitland.

'No bikes today, though,' Tracy said ruefully. 'I don't think I could even grip the handlebars properly yet. Even though my hands are a lot better, it would hurt too much.'

'Don't worry,' said Flora. 'I wouldn't want to risk you having another accident. Anyway, I'd rather walk today. It gives us more time to talk.'

They were soon walking down the road in the direction of Miss Maitland's.

'I want to know what you think about my mum and dad meeting at the hotel,' said Flora bluntly.

'I think it's a good thing,' replied Tracy, 'but there's no way of telling what'll come of it.'

'I know,' said Flora. 'But I hate having to wait.'

'It's only a few days,' Tracy reflected. 'I know it seems a long time, but it isn't very long when you think about all the time you've waited so far.'

'I hadn't thought about it like that,' said Flora, surprised at her cousin's realistic way of looking at it.

'It'll feel really strange thinking about Auntie May and your dad being at the hotel talking together, while we're sitting thinking about it, waiting for your mum to come back,' said Tracy thoughtfully.

'It'll be weird!' said Flora. 'It'll be really weird. But at least there's one thing…'

'What's that?' Tracy asked.

'After the talking I've done about Mum and Tony since you came, I do trust Mum to do her best. I won't be sitting worrying about whether or not she's going to say a whole lot of useless things to him,' said Flora with relief.

'I'm glad that your mum's going to be having a long talk with my mum this evening,' said Tracy. 'I think that'll help her a lot.'

'And they can keep on talking to each other about it,' Flora added. 'You never know what else might come of Mum meeting up with my dad.'

By this time they had reached Miss Maitland's gate. Flora marched up the path and pressed the bell. After a little while, the door opened, and Miss Maitland was standing there, obviously delighted to discover who her visitors were.

'Come in, come in,' she said. 'I've been hoping you two would call in soon. I've got one or two things I can talk to you about. But first you must tell me your news.' She caught sight of Tracy's bandaged hands and said, 'Goodness! What *have* you done to yourself?'

They settled themselves in the sitting room with cups of tea that Flora produced as usual from Miss Maitland's kitchen, and Tracy began by telling her about her accident, finishing up with the account of how Dave and Pam and their children had taken her and Flora back to Welcome Home.

'They sound really nice people,' said Miss Maitland. 'What a good thing Pam came along when she did. And how are your hands now?'

'They're a lot better,' Tracy replied. 'Auntie May changed the dressings again before I came out. The only problem we can see is that there's one bit of grit still stuck in my right hand.'

'You'll need to keep an eye on that,' said Miss Maitland knowledgeably. 'Sometimes these things come out of their own accord, but sometimes they don't, and then they can fester.'

'I'll remember that,' said Tracy politely. 'Thank you.'

'You just let May keep checking, and she'll tell you if anything needs to be done,' Miss Maitland persisted. Then she turned to Flora and said perceptively, 'I can see you're bursting with some other news. What is it?'

'Mum's seeing Dad on Monday evening,' Flora burst out.

Miss Maitland looked astonished. 'Have I heard that right?' she questioned. 'You mean Tony?'

'Yes,' insisted Flora. 'My dad... Tony. Remember that Mum

was thinking of writing to him? Well, she did. And this morning we got a letter from him saying he'd meet her at the Woodlands Hotel on Monday.'

'You could knock me down with a feather!' exclaimed Miss Maitland. 'I never would have thought it.'

'His letter was all stuffy, of course,' said Flora.

'But Auntie May thought it wasn't as stuffy as it sounded,' added Tracy. 'And she's going to phone my mum this evening for a long chat about it.'

'That sounds very sensible,' Miss Maitland agreed. 'Will you tell her that you've told me about it, and tell her to give me a ring before Monday, or, better still, come down for a chat.'

'I'd like her to talk to you about it,' said Flora eagerly. 'You know so much about it, and you say lots of sensible things.' She turned to Tracy. 'It isn't easy for Mum to get out for long, is it?' she said. 'But I've got a plan.'

'What's that?' asked Tracy.

'We could ask her to come down in the van to get Miss Maitland and take her up to the house. It would only take a few minutes each way.'

Miss Maitland looked worried.

'What is it, Miss Maitland?' asked Tracy.

'I'm not very good without my chair,' she explained.

'I could come down with Mum and load it into the back of the van,' Flora offered. 'Let's phone her now, and see if we can arrange something.'

Miss Maitland agreed, and soon Flora was speaking to her mother. May was enthusiastic about Flora's suggestion, and arranged that she would come and pick Miss Maitland up the following afternoon, straight after lunch.

After that, Flora and Tracy told Miss Maitland all the news about Mary and Melanie's visit, and May's plan to help Melanie.

Miss Maitland clapped her hands together when she heard this. 'May can be very good at that kind of thing,' she said gleefully. 'You must come and tell me how Melanie gets on. It's different from my day, when father's word was law, and I'd like to think that your friend was getting on a bit better with her family.' She became solemn at the memory of her father. 'Now don't get me wrong,' she said. 'I loved my father very much, but he sometimes did things that hurt me a lot. I know it was because he thought he knew best, and I expect he usually did, but I'm not so sure he knew best about my Edwin.'

'Tell us some more about him, Miss Maitland,' said Tracy, sitting forward in her seat. Tell us some more about how he used to leave messages for you.'

'After you left here last time,' said Miss Maitland, 'I came to a decision.'

'What was that?' asked Tracy eagerly.

'I decided I was going to show you a photograph of him,' she said; and then she added, 'That's if you want to see it, of course.'

'Of course we do!' said Tracy and Flora together.

'Where is it?' asked Flora. 'I'll get it for you.'

'It's all right,' replied Miss Maitland. 'I've put it handy, just in case you came by and wanted to see it.' She lifted up a wooden box that she had on the table beside her, and put it on her lap.

Tracy could see that the box was carved all over the lid, but she couldn't see the design, and she didn't like to ask to see it at the moment. Perhaps I could ask later, she thought to herself.

Miss Maitland opened the lid of the box, and produced a long envelope.

'I thought you might be interested to see these too,' she said.

'They're very fragile though, so you'll have to handle them very carefully. But I'll get the photograph out first.'

Out of the box she took a photograph, which she passed to Tracy and Flora.

'That's him!' she said proudly.

Tracy stared at the young man who was standing in his working clothes, looking at the camera. 'He looks really friendly,' she said.

'Yes, he looks really friendly,' Flora agreed. 'And he's really good looking too!'

'I know,' replied Miss Maitland, with a pleased smile on her face. 'I'm glad you can tell that from the photograph. That's exactly what he was – friendly, and good looking.'

Flora handed the photograph back to Miss Maitland, who put it carefully back in the box.

'Who took it?' asked Tracy suddenly.

'That's a good question,' replied Miss Maitland. 'I don't rightly know. He never told me, and I never asked. It certainly wasn't taken at our farm. Oh, I forgot to show you... he wrote on the back of it for me.' Once again she took the photograph from the box and passed it across to Tracy and Flora.

'It says, "To my Louise, love Edwin",' said Tracy.

'Yes, that was his name, Edwin Lane,' said Miss Maitland, half to herself.

'That's a really unusual name,' said Flora as she passed the photograph back again. She watched Miss Maitland as she slowly replaced it in the box.

'Yes it is,' replied Miss Maitland, 'and it was then, too.' She said no more about it, but picked up the envelope. 'And now you can look in the envelope,' she said. 'I'll just pass it across to you, and you can look through the things inside. Take this tray to spread them out on.' She passed across the envelope together with a small tray that she kept at the side of her chair. 'But do be very careful,' she cautioned them.

'Yes, we'll be very careful,' Tracy reassured her, realising instinctively that this was a very important moment not only for Miss Maitland, but also for all three of them.

Uncharacteristically, Flora allowed Tracy to be the one who eased the contents of the envelope onto the tray and spread them out.

Tracy gasped. 'Oh! How lovely!' she exclaimed as she studied the tiny writing on some broad blades of what looked to her like grass. As she studied the writing, she could see that the pen strokes were almost completely even, and were formed in a very precise and exact way.

'I think he used to go down to the marshes and gather these rushes,' Miss Maitland explained. 'That's why they've lasted. You wouldn't get grasses quite as broad and tough as these. And he once told me he took some goose feathers and sharpened them to write with. He made his own ink too,' she finished proudly.

'How did he do that?' asked Tracy excitedly.

'He always kept that a secret, and I could never get it out of him,' Miss Maitland admitted. She went on: 'Most of the things he wrote on eventually crumbled away. I kept them for as long as I could, but they just turned into dust.'

'What were they?' asked Flora, now as fascinated as Tracy was. 'Do you remember?'

'Oh, yes,' replied Miss Maitland. 'I remember them as if it were only yesterday he left them for me. There were the seed pods of the plant that's called honesty – those were some of my favourites – and there were beech leaves and oak leaves. Sometimes he wrote on the inside of pods left over after we'd taken the broad beans out of them. He wrote on the leaves of cocksfoot grass too. Of course, if he left me a message written in twigs or scratched in the earth, I couldn't save that, and I had to make all those messages disappear straight away.'

'What did he say in those messages?' asked Tracy. 'All the ones here are short ones, like "To Louise... my love". What were the other ones?'

Miss Maitland looked uncomfortable. 'I'm not sure I should say what they were. They're private really.'

'I'm sorry,' Tracy apologised. 'I didn't realise I shouldn't have asked.'

'That's all right,' Miss Maitland reassured her. 'I should have told you right at the beginning.'

'Thank you so much for showing us all these things,' said Flora sincerely, as she put the pieces carefully back into the envelope and handed it back to Miss Maitland, together with the tray.

'There's one more thing I should have said,' said Miss Maitland.

'What's that?' asked Tracy.

'I should have said that I haven't shown these to anyone else... not even May,' Miss Maitland explained. 'I'm not going to make you promise not to tell anyone about them. That wouldn't be right. But what I'm going ask is that you only speak about them to people you really trust – people who would understand and respect what they mean to me.'

'Of course we will,' replied Tracy and Flora.

'There's something else,' said Miss Maitland suddenly.

'What is it, Miss Maitland?' asked Tracy.

'If you were talking to someone you think might learn in a good way from knowing about these, it would be all right to tell them, but I wouldn't want you to tell them my name, or Edwin's.'

'We *promise*,' said Tracy and Flora together.

'Miss Maitland, do you mind if I ask you about something else?' Tracy said uncertainly.

'Of course not, dear.'

'Did you ever try smoking?'

'As a matter of fact, I once did. Do you want me to tell you about it?'

'Yes, please,' Tracy and Flora said together, and then giggled.

'As we grew older, my sisters and I were allowed a day in the town every month, and if it was a quiet time at the farm we were allowed to go together. Of course, if it was a busy time, our father couldn't spare us all at once. Well, one day we were all sitting on the bus going to town, and Doris, that was my middle sister, said, "I'm going to buy a packet of cigarettes today". Annie, my older sister, was horrified at first, but then she admitted she wanted to try some too. And that's what we did. When we got there, we went straight to a shop and bought a packet of twenty and shared them out. Then we spent the day practising.'

'Did you like it?' asked Tracy, fascinated.

'I'll let you guess. The only clue I'll give you is that I've never tried again!'

'I tried some too,' Flora told Miss Maitland. 'And I got a bit further on than you did. But I don't smoke now. I don't want to.'

'I'm glad to hear that,' said Miss Maitland. 'There's some that don't seem to suffer through smoking, but there are plenty who do. And I wouldn't like to see harm come to anyone.'

'*I've* never tried,' said Tracy emphatically. 'And I don't want to either. But there are plenty of other things I want to try.'

'What are those?' asked Miss Maitland interestedly.

'I'd like to know how to design and make clothes,' said Tracy. 'And I think I want to learn how to play golf. We were going to do some at the Youth Club, but then it rained, so we couldn't. And I'd like to make some furniture when I'm older.'

Flora turned to Tracy and gaped at her. She had never heard her cousin talk about making clothes and furniture, and she was astonished. 'Clothes and furniture!' she echoed, once she had found her voice again.

'Yes,' Tracy replied. 'And there's a drama group starting up at school on Wednesday evenings during term time. I want to join that. I'm a bit worried that there might not be enough places for everyone who wants to go, but Mum says if I can't get a place, we'll try and find one somewhere else.'

'Well now,' said Miss Maitland. 'You've got plenty to be getting on with. Have you got some ideas about the clothes yet?'

'Not exactly,' replied Tracy. 'But I'm looking round, and I'm working out what looks nice on different people. It's really good fun.'

'Why didn't you tell me?' asked Flora.

'I don't know,' Tracy replied. She thought for a moment, and then said, 'Maybe it's because I'm doing it all the time, I just don't think of saying anything about it.'

'There's Mary with her drawings, and now you with your clothes,' said Flora. 'I feel envious. I want something like that too.'

'You will have something of your own,' Miss Maitland comforted her. 'It's only that you're not sure what it is yet. It'll come to you in time. Just be patient.'

'I *can't* be patient!' Flora snapped. 'I want it *now!*'

Miss Maitland looked straight at her and said, 'You're doing a lot more things at the moment than you realise. Once you're a bit further on with them, I'm sure you'll soon know what else you want to do.'

To Tracy's surprise, Flora became calmer and said, 'Thanks for saying that, it really helps.'

'Now you two had better be getting along,' said Miss Maitland. 'I'd better have my rest.'

Tracy and Flora tidied away the cups and saucers, thanked her, and left.

Walking along the pavement, Flora and Tracy agreed that the afternoon's visit had been quite surprising in a lot of ways, and that there was plenty to think about. And back at Welcome Home they discovered that there was a hand-delivered letter waiting for them.

'What an interesting envelope!' exclaimed Flora. 'It looks like gift wrap!'

'Open it, and see who it's from,' Tracy urged her.

Flora slit it open with a kitchen knife, and opened the piece of paper she found inside. On one side was a simple picture that was obviously drawn by a small child; and on the other was a letter. It said:

Dear Flora and Tracy,

We hope Tracy's hands and knees are feeling better. This is a picture that Ben drew for you. We all hope we will see you again some time soon.

Love,

Pam, Dave, Ben and Kate

'I like that envelope,' said Tracy.

'Yes, it's really cool,' Flora agreed. 'I wonder where they bought it? Perhaps we could get some.'

Tracy pondered. 'Maybe Auntie May would know,' she said.

At teatime Flora told her mum about the letter and asked her what she thought about the envelope. May examined it closely and then said she was sure someone had made it. 'You two could make some one rainy afternoon if you want,' she said. 'I'm sure I've got paper and glue that you could use. And if you want to go round for a visit, I've kept a note of Pam's phone number, so you'll be able to phone and fix when to go.' After that she changed the subject rather abruptly by saying, 'I was going to phone your mum in a few minutes, Tracy. But how about you giving her a ring just now, and then when you've finished I'll take over.'

Tracy phoned home and had a long chat about all that had been happening. She didn't say anything about the letter from Flora's dad, as she thought it was best to leave that up to Auntie May. It was so good to talk to Mum and Dad, she thought to herself; but she was happy to be here with Flora and May, and helping at Welcome Home. She found that Mum and Dad were redecorating the living room while she and Paula were away, and Mum told her the colours they had chosen. Before she said goodbye to them, she asked how Paula was getting on, and learned that she was phoning every day, telling them about long days on the beach.

'I'm going to give the phone to Auntie May now,' said Tracy to her mum. 'She's got something very important to talk to you about.' She handed the phone across to May, and then she and Flora went up to the attic, deep in discussion about it.

It was nearly two hours later that they heard May calling up to them from the bottom of the attic stairs. 'Can you come down for a few minutes, and I'll tell you a bit about it?'

They ran downstairs, and settled themselves in May's sitting room.

'Your mum was very helpful, Tracy,' said her aunt. 'But that wasn't all. Your dad and I spoke for quite a while too, and he says he'll help in any way he can.'

Tracy smiled happily, and Flora said slowly, 'That's good. I've been wondering if Dad might manage better if there was another man, but I couldn't think of anyone we could ask to help.'

'You're a step ahead of me, Flora,' said May. 'I was just going to tell you both that they've offered to come up for a day or two. I left it that I'd think it through, and that I'd talk to you two about it, but already I've just about decided that I'll ask them to come. It would be such a help to me if they'd be here on Monday, and stay the night afterwards. I did phone Pat for a chat about it all, and she's free to come and sit with you on Monday evening, but it would be even better if your mum and dad were here, Tracy. I'll go and get the diary. I'm pretty sure I've got a spare room that night, but I'll check.' She stood up and went off to get it.

For once, Flora did not seem to have anything to say, and Tracy sat quietly, thinking. It would be great to see Mum and Dad, she thought; but it wouldn't be for an ordinary visit. It would be much more than that. She had a feeling that something terribly important could happen, but she couldn't begin to imagine exactly what it would be. She had never seen her uncle, and knew so little about him, so there was no way of guessing.

May reappeared. 'I've checked,' she said decisively. 'And the pink room is definitely free. How do you feel, Flora?' she asked. 'Shall we ask them to come?'

Tracy looked at Flora, and saw she appeared quite pale.

'I feel a bit peculiar,' she said. 'My head feels all funny.'

'When did it come on?' asked May, concerned.

'It came on slowly,' Flora replied. 'It started up just after you said that Tracy's mum and dad would come if we wanted.'

'Actually, I feel a bit funny too,' said her mother. 'But I think it's because I feel so glad I'm getting some proper help with all of this. We're going to be speaking to Miss Maitland tomorrow, and I had this long talk this evening. I think I should phone Tracy's mum and dad back straight away and definitely fix for them to come up.'

Flora leaned back in her chair. 'I want you to as well,' she said rather tiredly.

'If you suddenly needed to use the pink room, I'm sure Mum and Dad wouldn't mind sleeping in the attic with Flora and me,' said Tracy helpfully. 'And I could sleep on the floor so one of them could use my bed.'

'Thanks, love,' said May, gratefully. 'I don't think that'll be necessary, though. Now, I'll ring them and fix it all up.'

Back in their attic room, Flora said wearily to Tracy, 'I'm not sure if I'll manage the Youth Club tomorrow evening. There's so much going on.'

'Why don't we just wait and see?' said Tracy. 'With a bit of luck it'll be a nice evening, and we might get some golf after all!'

'You're right,' said Flora. 'Let's just wait and see.'

Chapter Eighteen

The following afternoon Tracy and Flora squeezed into the passenger seat of May's van again, and May drove to Miss Maitland's house, where they found her waiting for them at her front door. May helped her into the van, while Tracy and Flora collected her chair, pulled the front door shut behind them, loaded the chair into the back of the van, and climbed in beside it. They were soon back at Welcome Home, where the girls unloaded the chair and carried it into May's sitting room, while May helped Miss Maitland to make her way there too.

'I'll make some tea,' Flora offered; and she and Tracy disappeared into the kitchen, returning later with a tray of tea and biscuits to share.

'This is a real treat for me!' exclaimed Miss Maitland. 'A trip out, *and* waitress service.'

'The girls are such a help,' said May smiling proudly. 'And we usually find our way through any difficulty. Don't we?' she added, looking across at Tracy and Flora.

'I always like to see them come to my door,' said Miss Maitland. 'They're really good company. I'll miss them when the holidays are over.'

'We should have thought of having you up here like this before,' said May. 'Now we've managed once, we should fix it up again.'

'That would be very nice, dear,' Miss Maitland replied. 'But don't go putting any extra stress on yourself. I'll be looking forward to seeing you at my house again once your busy season is over.'

'So am I,' said May. 'Now, I should say that we've got a bit of news for you.'

'What's that, dear?' asked Miss Maitland.

'I had a long talk with Tracy's mum and dad last night, and as a result of that we've fixed that they're coming up to be here on Monday, and they'll stay overnight and go back home on Tuesday.'

'I *am* glad about that, dear,' said Miss Maitland sincerely. 'It's just what you need.'

'We're glad too,' Tracy and Flora added.

Tracy continued excitedly: 'I'm glad because I think Auntie May will manage better with Flora's dad if she knows my mum and dad are here with us, and that they'll be there to talk to when she gets back. And I want them to see the painting Flora and I did in the attic room too.'

'I'm so relieved that they're coming,' Flora added. 'I never imagined I would feel that way, but I do. I feel that there will be plenty of grownups around, so I don't have to be responsible.' Here she started to go pale again, and she struggled to keep speaking, but she managed. 'I've felt horrible about the whole thing for all my life as far as I can remember,' she said. 'And I've done my best to cope with it. But now I want someone else to sort out the mess for me. None of it was my fault, and I don't even really know how it all came about.'

'There now, dear,' said Miss Maitland, patting Flora's arm. 'It's going to be a big day for you on Monday. None of us can predict how things will work out, but we can do our best to try to help to make it better than it has been for you.'

'Do you and Tracy want to go off and do your own things for a while, or do you want to stay while I talk it over with Miss Maitland?' May asked Flora.

Flora sat and thought for a few minutes, and then said, 'I think I'd like to go. Tracy and I could come back later and you could tell us what you've been talking about.'

Tracy was relieved that Flora had chosen to do this. She had felt uncomfortable with the idea of being there while May and Miss Maitland were talking.

'We could go and write a letter to Ben and Kate,' Flora suggested. 'I'd like to talk to Mary about what's happening, but I don't feel ready to yet.'

'You could phone her later if you want,' said Tracy. 'I'll draw a picture to go with our letter to Ben and Kate. It's a good idea of yours to write to them.'

It was about an hour later when Tracy and Flora reappeared in May's sitting room. They had with them a picture that Tracy had drawn of the bikes, together with a letter they had written in coloured pens.

'I'll read it out,' said Flora.

Dear Ben and Kate,

Thank you for your letter, and the picture. The picture is very good. We hope to see you sometime later next week. We will phone to fix a time. Tracy's hands are nearly better, and Flora's mum has mended her jeans with nice material with flowers on.

Love from Tracy and Flora xx

'That's nice,' said May. 'I'm sure they'll be pleased. You can take one of the bigger envelopes from the office if you want. Then you won't have to fold the picture up too much. Louise and I have had a long talk, and it's been very helpful.'

'I'm not sure I want to hear anything about it after all,' said Flora uncertainly.

'That's fine, love,' May replied. 'It's really up to me to decide what to do, and I'm gradually getting some ideas sorted out.'

'I think I should be getting back now,' said Miss Maitland. 'It's been lovely to be here, but I really need to get back for my rest.'

May looked at her watch. 'I suppose you're right,' she said reluctantly. 'It's been so nice having you here, and I'd like to try to persuade you to stay longer, but it won't be long before the weekend guests start to arrive, and I have to be in for that.'

Tracy and Flora organised the carrying of Miss Maitland's chair once more, and they soon had her safely back in her house.

'Be sure to let me know what happens on Monday,' said Miss Maitland as she settled herself.

'Yes, and we'll see you again soon,' Tracy and Flora agreed as they prepared to leave.

Back at Welcome Home Flora said, 'I feel totally wiped out, but I'd definitely like to go to the Youth Club this evening. I think I'll be like Miss Maitland and have a rest.' She disappeared off up the back stairs, leaving May and Tracy in the kitchen.

'Is there anything I can do to help?' Tracy asked.

'I was going to do some work in the office while I was waiting for the guests to arrive,' her aunt replied. 'I'm sure I'll be able to find some things there that you can help with.'

The following couple of hours passed pleasantly as Tracy helped May to tidy her office and file away some papers, in between her booking guests in and Tracy helping with their bags.

Flora looked much better when she reappeared. The evening was fine, and the two girls later set off to the Youth Club hoping for a session at the Golf Club. In the event they were not disappointed. Mr Mason walked along with them to the club to meet the person who was going to help. Not many had turned up this evening, so they were kept busy most of the time.

'That was great!' exclaimed Flora as she and Tracy made their way back to Welcome Home later that evening. 'I'm really glad you persuaded me to think about going. I was concentrating so hard on the shots it meant I didn't think about my dad for a while, and I feel quite a bit better. It's a pity Mary and Melanie weren't here tonight. I'll phone them both sometime over the weekend. Perhaps they've got some news, and I can tell them to keep their fingers crossed for us on Monday evening.'

Although the weekend was quite busy dealing with all the guests and the cleaning, it was relatively uneventful. When Flora phoned Mary's house, she discovered that Mary and her mum had gone to London for the weekend to see an exhibition. Mary's dad sounded quite harassed. Tim was shouting, and he had had to get off the phone quickly because the business phone was ringing as well. When she tried Melanie's number there was no answer.

'I wonder if they're away again?' she said to Tracy.

'I expect we'll find out later,' Tracy replied. 'But we might have to wait until they come round again on Wednesday.'

'Oh yes,' said Flora. 'With all that's been going on I'd forgotten. It was *so good* the way Mum fixed that up, wasn't it?'

Chapter Nineteen

Flora had no difficulty in jumping out of bed when her alarm rang on Monday morning. 'Come on, sleepyhead!' she teased as she pulled Tracy's duvet off. Your mum and dad will be arriving this afternoon, and we want to have the work finished and our room tidied up.'

'You're right!' exclaimed Tracy, sitting bolt upright. Then her face took on a determined expression. 'I'll beat you down to the kitchen!' she said as she grabbed her wash bag and made a dash for the top of the stairs.

May was surprised when they arrived in the kitchen a full five minutes earlier than usual. 'Raring to go?' she asked in amusement as they jostled each other to begin the task of taking things to the dining room.

After all the work was finished and lunch was over, Tracy and Flora spent much time waiting just outside the front door for Tracy's mum and dad to arrive. They knew they were to come around three, but all the same, they wanted to be watching out. The sun was warm, and the doorstep was a pleasant place to sit. They chatted to each other inconsequentially while playing games of throwing small stones at a larger one some feet away.

It was half past three when they arrived. Tracy felt a lurch of excitement when she saw the familiar Ford Focus turn into their street and pull up outside Welcome Home. She opened the passenger door and hugged her mum even before she had a chance to get out. While she was doing that her dad got out, came round behind her and hugged her. Meanwhile Flora had gone to fetch her mother, and they appeared just as Tracy was dragging her parents to the front door.

'It's so good to see you, Babs,' said May, throwing her arms round her sister. 'And you too, Derek,' she said as she turned to Tracy's dad and gave him a hug. 'Come on in. The girls will take your bags up, and I expect they'll put the kettle on too. They're experts!'

Tracy and Flora grabbed the bags out of the car and set off up to the pink room at speed.

Tracy's dad locked the car, and then said, 'I think we might have quite a lot to go through before you set off, May. And Babs and I have been thinking. Haven't we?' he said, turning to her.

'Yes,' she said. 'Derek's been thinking of going up with you to the Woodlands Hotel this evening. You don't have to decide straight away. Just think about it, and see how you feel.'

'If you wanted I could drop you off there, and then come and collect you later, or I could sit and wait for you in the foyer,' said Derek.

'Come into the sitting room and sit down,' said May. 'And we can talk it through a bit. I don't know if Flora and Tracy want to sit with us. I'll ask them. They should be down in a minute.'

Again Flora opted not to be part of the discussion, so she and Tracy went back up to their attic room to make their plans.

'We'll find out later what they've decided to do,' said Flora. 'Your mum's bound to be staying with us. I'd like to sit and chat to her for a while, and then perhaps we could play Scrabble until my mum comes home. I don't know how late she'll be, but I definitely want to stay up. How about you?'

'Yes, definitely,' said Tracy emphatically. 'Definitely. Definitely. I want to be up when she comes back. And I hope that my dad takes her and brings her back.'

'So do I,' said Flora.

They lay on their beds for some time before running down the stairs to join May and Tracy's parents.

'That's it fixed,' May greeted them. 'Derek's going to give me a run up in the car, drop me off, and watch me go in. Then he's going to sit in the foyer and wait for me. That way I've got the option of asking him to come and join me and Tony if it seems the right thing at the time. I'll just tell Tony that Derek's going to be collecting me and he'll be waiting in the foyer, so then it won't seem strange if he sees him on his way out.'

'That's exactly what I wanted,' said Tracy happily. 'I wanted Dad to go with you, Auntie May, and stay there until you're ready to come back.'

Flora looked very relieved. 'It's great you're going with Mum, Uncle Derek,' she said.

'We'd better get to work to get something to eat now,' said May efficiently. 'Then I'll go and get changed, and we can get off. I'd like to set off a bit early, Derek, if you don't mind.'

'That's fine by me, May,' Derek replied.

Just over an hour later, Babs, Tracy and Flora were waving at the front door as May and Derek set off.

'Auntie Babs, will you come and tell us what you were talking about when Tracy and I were upstairs, please?' said Flora immediately. 'I didn't want to be in on the talking, but I wanted to know what you were all saying.'

Back in the sitting room, Tracy's mother explained a little of what had been discussed. 'We talked a lot about how your mum was feeling,' she said.

'How *was* she feeling?' asked Flora eagerly.

'One minute she seemed to be calm and determined, and the next minute she was feeling very wobbly. She wanted to be sure she had thought of the best kind of approach to make to Tony. It means a lot to her to get some sort of conversation going with him – one that will help your situation,' Babs explained. 'As she talked, it was clearer and clearer that she hoped she could make some sort of connection that would improve things for herself too.'

'That's a relief!' exclaimed Flora. 'I didn't want her to be doing this only for me.'

'That's exactly what I said to her,' Babs agreed. 'I felt sure that would be how you were feeling.'

'Mum,' said Tracy. 'Do you think I'll ever meet Uncle Tony?'

'I don't know,' her mother replied. 'I hope so, but there's no way of telling at the moment.'

'That would be really cool if you met my dad,' said Flora, digging Tracy in the ribs. 'Tell me everything you can remember about him, Auntie Babs,' she demanded.

Babs hesitated.

'Go on, Mum. Tell us!' Tracy insisted.

'You've got to remember it's fourteen years since I last saw him,' Babs began.

'Yes, I know,' said Flora impatiently. 'Just tell us! After all, he *is* my dad!'

'Please, Mum,' Tracy persisted. Then following Flora's approach she added, 'He *is* my uncle!'

Babs began to tell the girls everything she could remember about

Tony. At first Flora butted in after every few sentences, but as time went on, she said less and less.

When Babs had exhausted all her memories of Tony, Tracy got out the Scrabble and they tried to play a game. Although none of their minds were fully on it they produced a few good words.

At ten o'clock the phone rang. Flora grabbed it saying, 'Welcome Home.'

Although she was not the one who was holding the phone, Tracy could make out May's voice saying, 'I'm glad to hear I'm welcome to come home, love. I'm just phoning to let you know things went quite well, and Derek and I will be back soon.'

'That's it,' said Flora, as she put down the phone. 'I'm going to stand at the front door until they get back. They won't be long.' She dashed out of the room, leaving Tracy and her mum to tidy away the Scrabble.

When the Ford Focus drew up outside the house, Flora rushed to open the car door to let her mother out, firing questions at her without a break.

'Steady on,' said May. 'Let me get in, and I'll tell you all about it.' Then, back in the sitting room, May gave them an account of what had happened.

'I'll start at the end first,' she began. 'Tony and I are going to meet again. We've both got quite a bit to think over, and we agreed it would be best to arrange another time. So I'll be seeing him again in a couple of weeks.'

Flora bounced up and down happily, and Tracy was surprised that she waited to see what May would say next.

'I explained to him that you were saving up for a computer yourself. And I managed to get him to understand that you found it difficult to accept anything from him when he and I weren't in contact with one another. It was a bit of a struggle, but we got there in the end. I even managed to get him to start to think a bit about the time when he left us. That didn't go so well, but I certainly don't think it was a waste of time trying. He told me quite a bit about what he's been doing since he went away. I must admit, I found myself quite interested. I didn't feel irritated with him for talking on about it when I would have preferred that we could have talked more about other things. He told me to say to you, Flora, that he hopes he'll see you again in about a month. He said that he wants to try and get some of this straightened out with me first.'

'So he *does* realise how important it is!' said Flora triumphantly.

'That was certainly my impression,' May agreed.

'When are you seeing him again?' Flora demanded.

'In exactly two weeks,' replied May.

'Did you see him, Dad?' asked Tracy.

'I did, but only briefly,' Derek replied. 'We just exchanged a few words, shook hands, and then I went off with May. I would say he seemed quite pleased I was there.'

'Auntie Babs and Uncle Derek, can you come back again in two weeks?' asked Flora.

May looked as if she was about to say something, but Tracy's mum and dad responded almost immediately. 'We'll do our best to,' said Derek.

Babs nodded. 'We certainly want to do everything we can to help.'

'Paula will be back home by then. Won't she?' said Tracy.

'You must bring her with you if you're coming,' said May.

'I'll certainly ask her,' Babs replied. 'I expect she'll want to come. I'll bring it up with her when she phones us tomorrow evening. She knows we're up here, of course, and we've explained why.'

Tracy felt pleased. In fact, she felt *very* pleased. It looked as if Mum and Dad would be here again, just at the right time; and she looked forward to the prospect of seeing Paula again. They could show her the attic room with its mural, and maybe she could meet Miss Maitland, and some of the other friends she had made. 'Mum and Dad,' she said. 'You've got to come upstairs and see what Flora and I painted.'

'Yes,' May encouraged them. 'You must go up. Don't let's leave it until tomorrow, and then forget. It's really good, and you should see it.'

Tracy and Flora took Tracy's mum and dad up the back stairs, and then up to the attic. Babs gasped as she saw the mural. 'It's absolutely amazing!' she exclaimed. 'I didn't know that you two were so artistic!'

'Neither did we,' Flora explained. 'We just started painting, and this is what happened. Our friend Mary is *really* artistic. She's done some brilliant drawings in pencil and in charcoal.'

'Yes,' Tracy joined in. 'You should see them.' She turned to

Flora. 'Do you think she might come round when Mum and Dad are up again? I'd like them to see some of what she's done.'

'We can ask her when she's round on Wednesday evening,' said Flora thoughtfully. 'And we must remember to ask if she's been to Tricia Penway's studio yet.'

'Did you say "Tricia Penway"?' asked Tracy's mum.

'Yes,' replied Flora.

'She's quite a well-known artist,' Babs explained.

'Well, the paintings we saw of hers were really good,' said Flora; and she went on to tell her aunt and uncle about the visit they had made to the exhibition.

By this time May had joined them in the attic, and Tracy could see that she had to struggle to contain her astonishment that not only had Flora been to an art exhibition, but also she was enthusiastic about what she had seen.

'I've just remembered something!' Tracy exclaimed.

'What's that?' asked her mother.

Tracy rummaged amongst her possessions that were piled on a chair next to her bed, and triumphantly produced a small polythene bag. 'I was going to post this to you and Dad,' she said. 'It's a postcard from the exhibition.' She handed the bag to her mother.

Her mother opened it, took out the postcard and showed it to May and Derek, who studied it with interest.

'This is certainly a very good painting,' Derek pronounced. 'Did you say the exhibition had just opened the day you went there?'

'Yes,' Flora replied.

'Maybe Babs and I will have time to see it before we go home tomorrow,' he said enthusiastically.

'I'd like that,' Tracy's mum agreed.

'We could show you where to go,' said Tracy excitedly. 'We can take you when we've finished work. Can't we, Flora?'

May and Babs exchanged a knowing look, and May said, 'Perhaps your mum and dad will give us a hand with the cleaning in the morning, and then you'll be able to take them across a bit sooner.'

'That's a good idea,' said Derek, rubbing his hands together. 'You two can show me where the vacuum cleaners and the dusters are!'

'I think we'd better all get to bed now,' said May decisively. 'It's been a big day for all of us.'

It was not long before Tracy and Flora were in bed, turning over the news about Tony.

'It makes me feel excited,' said Tracy.

'That's how I feel as well,' Flora agreed. 'But I'm quite scared to admit it. After all we haven't a clue what will happen, and at worst it could all go wrong.'

'I think we should talk to your mum about it again tomorrow. I expect she'll tell us more about what happened.'

'Yes,' replied Flora. 'I expect she will. I didn't want to ask her any more, but by tomorrow I might be ready.'

'And we can talk to Mary and Melanie on Wednesday,' Tracy reminded Flora.

'Yes. That'll be good. And there's their news too,' said Flora, her voice beginning to sound sleepy.

'And we mustn't forget Miss Maitland,' Tracy said.

'I expect Mum will phone her,' Flora replied.

'But I'd like to go and see her,' Tracy insisted.

'I want to as well,' Flora agreed. 'And we'll definitely go before Mum sees Dad again.'

Tracy noticed that Flora had again called Tony 'Dad', but she didn't say anything about it. Things were certainly changing…

Chapter Twenty

The following morning, Tracy and Flora leapt out of bed at the first sound of the alarm, both saying, 'Race you!'

Tracy's mum and dad appeared about half way through the serving of the breakfasts, and tried to help; but Tracy and Flora insisted that they sat at the Pink Room table so that they could serve them.

Later on in the kitchen, Tracy could hear her mum and May talking to each other.

'I'm so impressed,' she heard her mother say. 'The girls work together so well as a team. I've been watching them, and the guests obviously feel very well cared for.'

'Yes,' replied May. 'Quite a number of them have commented to me when they were leaving, and some of them have left generous tips. By the way,' she added, 'I wanted to speak to you about money for Tracy.'

'Oh yes,' Tracy's mum replied. 'She'll need more because she's staying longer.'

'That's not what I mean,' May explained. 'I'd like to give her something, because she's helping so much. It won't be much, but I think she deserves something. She seemed uncertain about it when I raised it with her, so I said I'd speak to you about it, and she seemed satisfied with that.'

'Now don't go overstretching yourself, May,' said Babs. 'I'm sure Tracy's just happy to be here for the holiday, and if she's getting some tips, that's fine.'

'Well, I've decided I'll add my own tip,' said May determinedly. 'And I wanted to let you know.'

Tracy smiled to herself, and gave a little skip as she went off into the dining room to help Flora to finish the tidying.

After Tracy and Flora had finished their own breakfast, they took Tracy's mum and dad upstairs to start the cleaning. With two extra pairs of hands it was finished by eleven; and they all went downstairs to let May know they were setting off to see the exhibition.

'I wish I could come with you,' said May longingly.

'Well,' said Derek slowly. 'Why don't you and Babs take a run along, and I'll keep an eye on things here. I'm sure I'll manage. Flora could go along with you, and I know Tracy will stay here and keep me straight. Won't you Tracy?'

Tracy was very pleased at the idea, and agreed instantly. 'Yes, Dad,' she said. 'And then, after they come back will there be time for you and me to go to the gallery together?'

Her dad looked at his watch. 'Let me see,' he said. 'If your mum and May can be back here by one o'clock, we could go along there for half an hour. Will that do? I'd certainly like that.'

Tracy hopped from one foot to the other happily. It was a long time since she had done something with her dad on her own. First they would look after Welcome Home together; and then they would go to the gallery. 'See you at one,' she called out cheerfully to the others as they left through the front door. She turned to her dad and said, 'I'll show you where Auntie May keeps the books you'll have to use.'

Together they booked the remaining two couples out, and helped them with their luggage. After that there were a couple of phone calls that were enquiries about accommodation later in the season. Tracy's dad made provisional bookings, saying that May would phone back in a couple of hours to confirm.

As they sat at the kitchen table waiting for the others to come back Tracy said, 'I wish you had time to see Miss Maitland. Do you think you could see her when you come back again? She thinks she remembers meeting Mum once, a long time ago, but I don't think she has seen you before. She's quite old, and she doesn't get out on her own. Auntie May has known her ever since Uncle Tony left.'

'I'd like to,' her dad replied. 'I'll have to talk to your mum and see what time we can both arrange off work. This time, Monday and Tuesday happened to be her days off, and my boss let me take the time because I said it was urgent family business. Once we're back home, we'll see what we can sort out. If we can get just a little bit longer, then I'm sure we can call in on Miss Maitland. I'm on duty again this evening, that's why I've got to get back.'

Tracy nodded knowingly. She was used to her dad having to work in the evenings or at nights.

'I hope you can come,' said Tracy. 'And I hope you'll bring

Paula.'

'After that we'll have to think about when you're coming home again,' said Derek.

Tracy flushed a little, and then said determinedly, 'Dad, I definitely want to stay for the whole of the holidays. I miss you and Mum and Paula, but I really like it here, and I like helping Auntie May.'

'I'll have to check with your mum and May,' her dad replied. 'And you'll have to be back a few days before school starts at the very latest, because there will be things you need to get ready. But we'll see.'

Tracy relaxed. When Dad said 'We'll see' that usually meant that whatever it was about was going to happen. 'Oh good!' she said.

It wasn't long after that that the others arrived back. They were talking animatedly about the paintings they had seen. Tracy was glad to see Flora and her mother getting on so well about the exhibition, especially after that difficult time about the pottery. She had felt very uncomfortable about that, and had felt sad that Auntie May had not had a chance to do something she would have enjoyed. However, she had never heard her aunt complain about missing it, so maybe it hadn't upset her.

'Our turn now,' she said happily, as she took her father's hand and almost dragged him out of the door.

'Steady on,' he said, smiling. 'I'm as keen as you are, you know!'

At the gallery, not only did Tracy show her dad all the paintings, but also she showed him the bushes where they had played with Tim. He chuckled as she told the story of Tim dashing about. But the time passed quickly, and soon he was looking at his watch.

'I'm afraid we'll have to go back now,' he said. 'I'll tell you what. I'll give you a piggy-back to the car,' he added playfully.

'But you can't!' exclaimed Tracy. 'What about your back?'

'I know my back was bad for a long time, and that I felt I had to be careful for a while, even after I had it sorted out, but it's absolutely fine these days. Come on, climb aboard.'

Tracy didn't need any more encouragement. 'Come over to the steps,' she said eagerly. 'Then I don't have to jump up.'

When they arrived back at Welcome Home, the others were waiting at the front door with the bags to put in the car.

'You're late!' said Tracy's mum.

'I think we got engrossed in what we were doing. Didn't we?' said Derek, winking at Tracy.

'Yes, we did,' Tracy added happily.

'Never mind,' said Derek. 'Pass the bags, and I'll put them in the boot. Then we'll get off.'

Babs gave her sister a hug, and then she hugged Flora and Tracy. 'See you soon I hope,' she said as she got into the car.

Tracy could see her dad giving her a special wave as he turned the corner on to the main road.

'Mum,' said Flora. 'Will you tell us exactly what Dad said last night? Tracy and I want to know *everything*.'

'All right, my loves,' May replied. 'Let's get settled in the sitting room for an hour or so. There shouldn't be any more coming and going for a while now.'

Chapter Twenty-one

It was late on Wednesday afternoon, and Tracy and Flora were looking forward eagerly to the arrival of Mary and Melanie.

'I can't wait to tell them what's been happening here,' said Flora impatiently.

'Neither can I,' Tracy agreed. 'I wonder if Melanie has managed to say anything to her mum and dad yet.'

'I don't know,' replied Flora. 'But I know that Mum's definitely planning to get something started if she hasn't. I can tell by how determined she looked last week.'

'She might have forgotten with all that happening about Uncle Tony,' Tracy said uncertainly.

'No, she won't,' said Flora confidently. 'As soon as she sees Melanie, she'll remember. Trust me, I know.'

Seven o'clock came, the doorbell rang, and Flora let Mary and Melanie in.

'Dad's coming back again at ten, unless we phone him before that,' Melanie informed them.

'We've got a lot of news for you,' Flora began.

'So have I,' said Mary.

'And I've got a bit too,' Melanie added. 'It's all a bit odd, and I don't know what to make of it.'

'What do you mean?' asked Flora.

'I expect you'll understand when I tell you,' replied Melanie, not offering any further explanation.

'We've been a bit busy here, so we haven't made anything in advance,' Flora said apologetically. 'We can have beans on toast or toasted sandwiches, and we've got plenty of apples and dried fruit.'

'Hello girls,' called May through the door from her sitting room. 'Just make yourselves at home. If there's anything you want, come and ask.'

The day had been exceptionally hot, and none of them was particularly interested in food. After a toasted sandwich each, they set off up to the attic with a bag of apples. They arranged themselves comfortably on the beds, and then Flora said, 'I'm going to tell you some of our news first. My mum and dad met up on Monday evening, and they're going to meet again the week after next.'

'And my mum and dad came for the night so my dad could take Auntie May to the hotel where they met, and Mum could stay with me and Flora,' said Tracy.

Mary was gaping at Flora. 'Your dad!' she exclaimed. 'Your mum met your dad?'

'Yes,' said Flora, clearly pleased at Mary's astonishment.

Melanie was incredulous. 'But I thought you told me she hadn't spent time with him since he left when you were baby. How come they met on Monday?'

'We'll tell you more about that later,' said Flora. 'Now tell us what's happened to you.'

'There's something funny going on,' said Melanie. 'Mum came home from town the other day with some travel brochures, and she asked me if I wanted to go to Paris for a weekend with her! I was so amazed I didn't know what to say. So I just went off and watched a boring programme on the TV. I expected her to be annoyed with me, but she wasn't. She said she realised it must be a bit of a surprise, and that I could think about it and let her know by the end of the week. I can't believe it!'

'Do you want to go?' asked Mary.

'Of *course* I do, silly,' said Melanie. 'But I don't want to tell her yet.'

'Why not?' asked Tracy.

'I don't know,' replied Melanie. 'Well, I think I feel angry with her, so I want to make her wait. But it's really hard because I want to go, and I want to say straight away!'

'I think you should tell her tonight when you get home,' said Tracy. 'I think it's silly not telling her, even if you're feeling angry.'

'It's not *your* mum,' Melanie snapped. 'Oh, I'm sorry Tracy, that wasn't very nice of me to speak like that. It's just that I'm feeling excited and angry both at the same time, and I don't know what to do.'

'I think I know something about what you're feeling,' said Mary. 'I've been having a bit of it too. Mum keeps suggesting things we can do together, and I'm really happy about it, but I feel cross too. Sometimes I feel like snapping at her. I think it's something to do with not having had any proper time with her for ages.'

'That helps me a lot,' Melanie said reflectively. 'Now, Flora, tell us some more about what happened.'

The evening seemed to fly past. And when Flora heard the distant sound of the doorbell, she was sure at first it must have been something to do with the guests. But then she glanced at her pink watch and saw that it was ten o'clock.

'Oh no!' she exclaimed. 'Our time's up everybody.' Then an idea occurred to her and she said, 'I think we should stay up here for a few minutes.'

'Why's that?' asked Mary. 'We should be going.'

'I think it would be a good idea to leave my mum and Melanie's dad together for a little while before we go down,' said Flora with a broad smile on her face. 'After last time, I think Mum's got one or two things she wants to get across to him!' She thought for a moment, and then added, 'What I'd really like is to be a fly on the wall.'

'Perhaps we could sneak down into the hall and see what we can hear, if you're so sure that your mum's got some plan,' Melanie suggested.

'But they might hear us,' Tracy protested.

'Yes,' said Flora. 'I think it's best to trust Mum to tell me what happened, and I can tell you later, Melanie.'

Melanie agreed reluctantly, and the four only very slowly made their way down to the kitchen where her father and May were deep in conversation.

'Yes,' May was saying. 'I'm having some foreign students lodging here in the autumn term. Apart from the steady income, I think it will be a really good experience for Flora. I think if I weren't running a business, I'd have arranged an exchange with someone of Flora's age. Have you ever thought of that for Melanie? She's good at languages isn't she? I remember seeing some of her writing last year, and it was quite advanced for her age, and the others say she's very good at French. Oh...' Here she broke off. 'Here they are. How's your evening been girls?'

'It's been great, thanks,' said Melanie politely.

'Well do come again, any time. It's been a pleasure to have you here.'

Flora could tell that May was definitely saying this to affect Melanie's dad, although she wasn't saying anything that wasn't true.

'We'll phone you tomorrow, Melanie,' said Flora meaningfully.

'We must be off now,' said Melanie's dad. 'Thanks for everything.'

May stood with Flora and Tracy in the hallway as they said goodbye to their friends, and then they returned to the kitchen, where Flora insisted that her mother told them everything she had said to Melanie's dad.

'When we heard the doorbell ring, we stayed up in the attic to give you some time on your own with him,' she said. 'So now you've *got* to tell us about it.'

'That was good thinking,' said May admiringly.

'Well, I *am* your daughter,' replied Flora.

'It was quite easy, actually,' May began. 'Apparently he had taken to heart what I'd said about Melanie last week, and he was keen to talk to me. When he came in, he asked me straight away if I would mind if he had a word with me about her. Of course I agreed. He said they'd been having a lot of trouble with her, and just hadn't known what to do, and that after I'd shown that I enjoyed her company so much, it had got him thinking. He spoke to Melanie's mum the following evening, and they decided that they were going to try to show Melanie that they appreciated her, instead of being irritable with her. I must say I was quite surprised to hear him say that. When people get irritable with each other, it's the kind of pattern that can easily get very stuck, and a lot of blaming can go on.'

'Do you think it means that they like her really, if they're trying something like that so soon?' asked Flora with interest.

'I should certainly say so,' replied her mother. 'And I must admit that I do feel very guilty myself for not having done something about the situation with your father before now.'

'But it wasn't just up to you!' Flora said angrily. 'It was up to him as well. It's different with Melanie. She didn't know how to try any more, and she's not a grown-up.'

'You're right in a way,' May said in soothing tones. 'But I think that part of the problem between your dad and me was that he didn't realise he was being like a child. And it didn't help us that I was angry and upset with him for being like that. I'm trying to do something about it now, but I wish I'd seen before what I should have done.'

'I still don't think it's your fault, Mum,' Flora pressed. 'And in

179

any case, if you'd tried before and he'd not replied, *then* how would we have been feeling?'

'You're right, love,' May agreed. 'And I shouldn't dwell on what I might have done. It's best to concentrate on what we can do now. Maybe neither he nor I were able to do anything before. That's not very nice for you, but that's just the way it's been, and we're trying to find a way of changing it now.'

'Yes,' Tracy joined in. 'And if you'd tried before, maybe my mum and dad wouldn't have been able to help like they're helping now.'

'That's true,' May agreed, in slightly surprised tones. 'And I'll tell you something else.'

'What's that, Auntie May?' asked Tracy.

'There's something about having *you* here that's helped me too,' May explained. 'It isn't just the help you've been giving us with the business, or Flora having your company, it's something else as well, but I can't quite put in into words.'

'Having Tracy here makes it feel more like being in a family,' said Flora. 'We know that Tracy and Paula and her mum and dad are our relatives, and we see them from time to time, but it feels quite a bit different having Tracy actually living here.'

'I think that's it,' said May. 'I think you've put your finger on it. When it's just the two of us, it feels a bit like we're sisters running the business together. Oh, I know you're my daughter, and I never forget that, but living around each other often feels as if we're sisters. Having Tracy here, I feel much more like the mother all the time, and it makes me think a lot about how I wish a dad was here too. Maybe you don't know, but when Babs and I were young, our dad was hardly ever there. We didn't see him most of the time. As you know, he was a miner. In those days they worked very long shifts, and when he was off, he usually slept a lot. I didn't really get to know him until after he retired, and he didn't live for long after that. He was more like a grandad than a dad by the time he stopped working. He had to retire early because he had a bad chest. I'd left home by then, but Babs was still at school.'

'That's really interesting, Auntie May,' said Tracy. 'I must ask Mum about how *she* remembers him.'

'That's a good idea, love,' her aunt agreed. 'I really hope they can come up when I see Tony again. If they do, perhaps we can all have a bit of a chat about your grandad.'

Flora was sitting looking thoughtful.

'What are you thinking, love?' her mother asked her.

'I'm just thinking about something Mr Mason was saying at the Youth Club. Do you remember, Tracy? It was the week it was raining, and we were all talking about strong feelings.'

'Yes, I remember Mr Mason talked quite a lot,' said Tracy. After that she giggled. 'He said he used not to say much, but now his children can't get him to stop talking!'

'He said that his father hardly talked to him at all,' said Flora. 'His father was busy being a minister. And he was quite upset when he thought about it. Wasn't he, Tracy?'

'Yes, I remember that,' Tracy agreed.

Flora thought for a moment, and then said, 'Mum, were *you* upset that your dad didn't talk to *you*?'

'I don't think so, love,' May replied. 'After all, he was busy...' Here she broke off, and Tracy could see her face start to change. In fact, she looked quite upset.

'Yes,' said Flora. 'He was busy – just like Mr Mason's dad.'

May took her handkerchief out of her pocket, and dabbed at her eyes.

Flora went on: 'I hardly see my dad. And you hardly saw yours either, even though he hadn't gone away.'

'What you've both been saying is very important, and I'm going to have a good think about it,' said May determinedly.

'I'm really lucky,' said Tracy suddenly. 'I've got my dad back again.'

'What do you mean?' asked Flora with surprise. 'He never went away.'

'When his back was bad he went away inside himself,' Tracy explained. 'But now he's back again. I could tell when I was with him yesterday. It was great!'

'Melanie's dad goes away a lot. Doesn't he?' May asked Flora.

'Yes, he does,' Flora replied. 'But I think I know what you're going to say.'

'All right,' said May. 'Tell me what you think I was going to say.'

'I think you're going to say that you think Melanie's going to have her dad, whether he's away or not.'

May looked at Flora admiringly. 'You're a bright spark,' she said. 'Yes. If it's up to me, that's what she's going to have.' Then she added, 'I want that for you too, Flora, and I'm going to do everything I can.' She gave her eyes another dab, glanced at her watch, and exclaimed, 'Goodness! Look at the time. We'd better get off to bed, or else we'll never be able to get up in the morning.'

Chapter Twenty-two

'I'd like to see Miss Maitland this afternoon,' Flora told Tracy as they worked on the cleaning together. 'I know Mum's been on the phone to her and told her what happened about Dad, but I want us to go and talk to her ourselves now too.'

'That's exactly what I'd like to do,' Tracy replied. 'There's your dad, and a lot more we can talk about as well.'

'What do you mean?' asked Flora a bit brusquely.

'The most important thing to talk about is your dad,' said Tracy, hurrying to reassure her. 'But if there's time afterwards there are lots of things I'd like to ask Miss Maitland about.'

'All this about my dad is completely filling my head at the moment,' said Flora wearily. 'I wish it didn't.'

'It's *bound* to,' said Tracy sympathetically. 'I think about it most of the time at the moment, and he's only my uncle and I've never even met him yet. But he's very important to me because he's your dad, and he lived with my Auntie May.'

Flora relaxed. 'Thanks, Tracy,' she said. 'That really helps.'

The afternoon saw them pedalling down the road to Miss Maitland's, where once again they left their bikes round the back of her house.

Seated inside with drinks from the kitchen, they began to tell Miss Maitland everything that had happened.

'I expect Mum's told you most of it already,' said Flora defensively.

'I wouldn't worry about that,' Miss Maitland reassured her. 'Everyone experiences these things from a different angle, and it's important to talk about what it's been like for you two.'

Tracy said nothing, but was pleased that Miss Maitland had included her straight away like this.

'Yes, Tracy and I have got a lot to talk over with you,' said Flora.

The girls took it in turns to tell Miss Maitland how Tracy's parents had arrived, and how it had been decided that Tracy's dad would go up to the hotel with May.

'I knew Mum and Dad would come up with the right thing,' said Tracy proudly.

'I wasn't so sure,' said Flora. 'I'm so used to Mum and me mostly having to sort things out ourselves, I couldn't imagine what it would be like to have your mum and dad around. When I heard they'd offered to come, I knew straight away I wanted that, but I couldn't imagine what they might be doing to help except sitting with us. It was great knowing that your dad was at the hotel with Mum.'

'May told me that Tracy's parents are hoping to come up again a week on Monday, so they'll be here for the next meeting,' said Miss Maitland.

'Yes,' agreed Tracy. 'They've got to check about getting time off work, and they've got to speak to Paula about it all, because she'll be back home again by then.'

'Who is Paula?' asked Miss Maitland. 'Is she your sister, Tracy?'

Tracy nodded.

'I knew you had a sister, but I hadn't remembered her name. Where is she at the moment?'

'She's on holiday with her friend Jenny. She was invited to go with Jenny and her family on their holiday in Wales for two weeks.'

'There'll be a lot of news to swop when you see her again, won't there?'

Tracy nodded again, and then said, 'I hope she comes with Mum and Dad. Then she can sleep in the attic room with Flora and me, and we can show her the work we've been doing together.'

Miss Maitland turned to Flora. 'How are you feeling about all this about your dad, dear?' she asked.

To Tracy's consternation, Flora instantly began to sob. She looked at Miss Maitland, and was reassured that she did not seem to be worried at all. She looked as if she was just waiting patiently, so Tracy decided to do the same.

Flora's sobs went on for a good five minutes; but as time passed, the intensity of them started to decrease, and she was able to say a few words.

'I'm *so*... tired,' she managed to say.

And then, 'I want... things to be... different.'

And then, 'I don't... really know... what I... want.'

'That's only right,' Miss Maitland reassured her. 'I'm not surprised you feel weary and confused. You started things off by being able to see that you didn't feel all right about your dad buying a computer for you when he and your mum never saw each other, and you told your mum about that. The next bit is up to your mum and your dad, and Tracy's parents are helping with that. Just let them get on with that for now.'

Flora blew her nose loudly. 'That's what I want to do,' she said dismally, 'but it all keeps going on in my head – round and round and round in my head.'

'I told Flora that I think about it a lot too,' Tracy said to Miss Maitland.

'I think what I'm trying to tell you is that although you'll be thinking about it a lot, you don't need to be doing any worrying,' Miss Maitland said firmly. 'They'll all do the best they can, and we'll see what needs to be talked about after that. Flora, when are you seeing your dad again yourself?'

'Later in the holidays,' Flora replied in between sniffs.

'That's about right,' said Miss Maitland. 'We don't want it to be too soon.'

'I expect I'll just have to wait and see what happens,' said Flora reluctantly. 'Actually, even some of my friends who have their mums and dads living at home have problems.' She looked thoughtful. 'And there are a few girls at school who don't even have their mums.'

'That's terrible,' said Tracy aghast. 'How do they manage?'

'I know someone who lives with her dad, and there is someone else who lives with a foster family,' Flora explained.

'I could live with my dad,' said Tracy. 'He's really nice. But I'd *hate* it if my mum and Paula weren't there.'

'There are always problems to be dealt with, whatever the situation,' said Miss Maitland, 'and it's how we deal with them that makes the difference.'

'When my dad's back was bad, that was a very big problem for me,' said Tracy. 'And I couldn't think of anything to do.'

'And when my home help was ill, and I needed some shopping, at first I couldn't think what to do,' Miss Maitland added. 'To begin with I thought the best thing to do was to manage without. I knew that May would be too busy to help, and the people that can help out round here were away on holiday.'

'Then you thought of me!' Flora joined in. 'And it was a really sensible way of dealing with your problem. Wasn't it, Tracy?'

Tracy noticed Flora was being very grown up, and she wanted to be the same.

'Yes,' she agreed. 'Miss Maitland, you definitely made the right decision by phoning up to see if Flora could come. Just think, if you hadn't phoned for help, you wouldn't have got the things you needed, and we wouldn't have had all these interesting talks.'

'You're absolutely right, Tracy,' Miss Maitland replied. 'Now, if we look at Flora's problem... She asked for help by telling May how she felt about her dad's offer of buying a computer for her, and now she's waiting to see what's coming out of having done that.'

Here Flora broke in, 'And what's coming out of it is happening in stages. Isn't it? It's different from asking for help with shopping. When it's shopping, once someone has agreed to help, all they have to do is to get the shopping and bring it along. The help I'm getting started off by Mum thinking of writing to Dad. Then Dad wrote back. Then Mum talked to her friend Pat, and to Tracy's mum and dad, and to you. Then she talked to Dad. She's going to talk to him again, *and* Tracy's mum and dad are trying to see if they can come back to help next time. And the other thing is that we're talking to you about it all.' Here she paused for a minute, and then said, 'That's a lot of help. It isn't taking away my hurting feelings, but it's certainly a lot of help.'

'Flora,' said Miss Maitland. 'It's my belief that this help will all add up to some change in your feelings. It's just that we've got to be patient and let it take its time.'

'I don't want to be patient!' Flora's voice rose to a kind of screech.

'I can understand that, dear,' Miss Maitland soothed. 'After all, you've waited a long time already for help. The problem is that no one realised you were waiting.'

'I suppose so,' Flora acknowledged. '*I* didn't know I was waiting until I started talking to you and Mum and Tracy and my friends about Dad.'

Miss Maitland nodded. 'I think you're beginning to understand things a bit more now,' she said.

'Miss Maitland,' said Flora, with a sudden change of subject. 'I want to tell you about a boy who goes to the Youth Club. His name's Gordon.'

'Does he go to your school as well?' asked Miss Maitland.

'No. I don't know which one he goes to,' replied Flora. 'But I really like him.'

'Is he the same age as you?'

'No, he's fifteen.'

'Well, then,' said Miss Maitland. 'I hope you see him again at the Youth Club and have a chance to talk to him again. If he becomes a friend, he'll always be welcome here, remember.'

'Oh, thanks, Miss Maitland,' said Flora.

'There's one bit of advice I'd like to give you,' added Miss Maitland.

'What's that?' asked Flora.

'Never feel you have to rush into anything. You've got your whole life ahead of you, and you'll meet a lot of people along the way. Some of them you'll like, and some of them you won't. I'm glad you like Gordon, but the most important thing at the moment is to see what happens about your dad. And after that I've a hunch that you'll start to find quite a lot of things you're interested in.' Miss Maitland turned to Tracy and winked. 'I bet when you come and see her next summer – and I hope you will – that she'll have a new interest or two that will surprise you!'

'I expect they'll surprise me as well!' exclaimed Flora cheerfully.

As they pedalled back to Welcome Home, Flora and Tracy were quiet. Tracy thought about how full her life was. She had learned so much about the bed and breakfast business, there were a lot of new friends, and there was so much to think about. She wondered again if she might meet her Uncle Tony before the end of the holiday; but, of course, there was no way of telling.

As they pushed their bikes up the drive, May opened the front door and called out, 'That's good you're back. I've got Pam on the phone. The children got your letter okay, and she's asking if you'd like to go round for tea today. Dave would come and pick you up on his way back from work.'

Tracy and Flora looked at each other. 'That would be great!' they said, both at the same time.

May disappeared for a moment and then reappeared to say, 'That's it fixed. He'll be round for you at about five.'

Flora's pink watch revealed that it was already four thirty, so she and Tracy put their bikes away, and went to get a drink before Dave arrived.

'I wonder if I'll get to read the bedtime stories?' said Flora eagerly.

'I'd like to help with bath time,' said Tracy. 'Do you think we can?'

'We'll ask when we get there,' Flora decided.

It wasn't long before they heard Dave at the door, and they rushed to open it.

'I'll drop them back around eight,' Dave called through the door to May, who was coming into the hall from her office.

'How are your hands?' he asked Tracy.

'They're fine now,' said Tracy happily. She hadn't seen much of Dave so far, but she liked him because he reminded her of her dad; and the way Kate had pulled at his trouser leg had awakened distant memories of seeing Paula doing exactly the same thing when she was small.

'We're hoping to do baths and stories,' said Flora confidently.

'That would be great,' said Dave. 'That's exactly what Ben and Kate were saying, and we told them they'd have to ask you when you arrived.' He went on: 'I think they've been making a surprise for you this afternoon, but I can't tell you what it is. It's a secret,' he finished with an air of mystery.

Ben and Kate were standing at the door with Pam, waving excitedly when Dave drew up outside the house.

'We've been waiting here for ages!' exclaimed Pam. 'I don't know what I would have done if you hadn't been able to come. When Ben and Kate got your letter they insisted on doing some baking this afternoon and inviting you round. Come on in and see.'

Ben was tugging at Flora's hand, and Kate took hold of the leg of Tracy's jeans. They pulled the girls through the house to where the dining table was set. At the centre of it was a sponge cake with a candle in the middle. The table was laid with six places. Each place setting included a mug with an animal picture on it. Ben and Kate showed everyone their places. Tracy had a cow mug, Flora a pig, Dave's was a horse, and Pam's a giraffe.

'What's yours?' Flora asked Ben.

'A dog,' he replied, pointing to the picture on his mug.

'Let me see yours, Kate?' asked Tracy.

'Cat!' said Kate proudly pointing to her mug.

There was a large jug of orange juice on the table, and Dave poured some into each mug, while Pam helped Ben and Kate to carry plates of sandwiches from the kitchen and put them on the table.

'Ben and Kate have been helping with these,' she said. 'Haven't we, children!'

Ben and Kate agreed noisily.

She went on: 'There's cheese, and there's egg mayonnaise…'

'Oh, wow! My favourite!' Tracy could not contain her delight, and Dave chuckled.

'It's a good job they made plenty of them, otherwise you and I'd be fighting over them,' he said.

'There's a bowl of cress here that the children have been growing.' Pam pointed to a Bunnykins bowl piled high with cress. 'We grow it on the kitchen windowsill, and we take it in turns to water it. Ben wanted carrot sticks, so there's a pile of them here, and there's a dish of raisins. Kate wanted me to put some out.'

During tea, Tracy and Flora learned that Ben and Kate had planned a special bathtime, with extra toys to put in the water.

'There's a waterwheel,' Ben told them excitedly.

'And pump!' Kate squeaked.

'We do it together,' Ben explained. 'And I've got stories!' he pronounced, beaming at Flora.

Bathtime turned out to be uproarious. Pam and Dave couldn't stop laughing, and so much water escaped that Pam had to put down extra towels on the floor.

'It's a good job our bathroom is downstairs,' she said. 'We wouldn't be able to do this if it was upstairs, or water would be coming through the ceiling.'

'We had water through the ceiling at Auntie May's,' said Tracy. 'The roof was leaking, and Flora and I had to make sure we didn't let any of it go through to the room below us.'

'It's a good job you noticed it,' Dave remarked. 'A lot of damage can come from leaks.'

Storytime lasted for nearly an hour. Tracy and Flora took it in turns to read the books Ben had got ready in a heap for them. After that, Ben and Kate insisted on waving goodbye out of the window, as Tracy and Flora climbed into Dave's peoplecarrier, so that he could take them home again.

In bed that night, Tracy said to Flora in a sleepy voice, 'I feel really silly.'

'Why?' asked Flora.

'I've never asked you what you and your dad do together when you go out with him.'

'Well, if you're silly, I'm silly too,' Flora replied.

'What do you mean?' asked Tracy.

'I could have told you without you asking!'

'That's right. You could...'

After that, there was only the sound of gentle breathing as the girls fell asleep.

Chapter Twenty-three

The following day the weather was fine, and the girls were delighted to find that the Youth Club had once more been invited to the Golf Club. Although Mary and Melanie weren't there, Gordon was, and that pleased Flora no end. Tracy noticed that Flora chatted to Gordon in a less intense kind of way than she had before.

On the way back to Welcome Home, Flora said, 'Miss Maitland was right, you know. I'm glad I spoke to her about Gordon.'

'I like talking to Miss Maitland about *everything*,' replied Tracy. 'She says all sorts of interesting things.'

'I like talking to Gordon, and I sometimes get all these strong feelings when I'm talking to him, or when I think about him. But that's all it is – liking talking to him, and feeling strong feelings. It isn't anything else, because I don't really know him yet.' Flora laughed. 'I've only spoken to him twice so far.'

They walked along in silence for a few minutes; then Flora said, 'Come on! Let's jog back.'

'Okay,' Tracy agreed, and broke into a run.

They were soon back; and they found May sitting in the office surrounded by heaps of papers.

'I thought I'd try to get on with some of this,' she said wearily. 'This is the bit of the business that I find the hardest. Looking after the guests is usually fine, but I'm afraid I often let the paperwork get behind. Then I can get into quite a muddle – one that takes me a while to get out of.'

'If I don't keep up with my homework in term time I get like that,' Tracy sympathised. 'What I try to do is make a homework diary. I don't always stick to it,' she admitted, 'but it does help quite a lot.'

'That's a good idea,' May said thoughtfully. 'Would you two mind helping me to set a diary up some time soon? It would need to span the whole year.'

Flora and Tracy agreed, and Flora even admitted that she thought something like that might help her when she was back at school. 'I sometimes get into trouble for handing things in late,' she said. 'I usually rely on my friends to remind me about getting things in on time, and it doesn't always work.'

'Good! That's agreed then,' said May briskly. 'And now I've got some good news for you. Babs phoned while you were out. She and Derek and Paula are definitely coming a week on Monday, and they can stay two nights.'

Tracy bounced up and down with excitement. 'Hooray! Hooray!' she shouted, and then clapped her hand to her mouth. 'Sorry, Auntie May,' she apologised. 'I forgot about the guests.'

'I can't wait to tell Mary and Melanie,' said Flora.

'And Miss Maitland,' Tracy added.

'Yes, we must let Louise know,' said May. 'She'll be very pleased for us. And perhaps we could bring her up here again that Monday afternoon so she can meet the others when they arrive.'

'Perhaps we can make something, Flora,' Tracy suggested. 'Perhaps we could make a cake or something like that.'

Flora pulled a face. 'I don't want to,' she said; but almost immediately she relented and said, 'I've got a cookery book in my room. We could look at it in bed one night, and see if there's anything we could do.'

The weekend and the following week were busy. Welcome Home was full each night, and there was much changing of beds and cleaning to be done. As always, Flora and Tracy worked hard. Wednesday evening passed pleasurably with another visit from Mary and Melanie, who brought much news of how things were improving for them with their parents. Tracy and Flora told them of the impending visit from Tracy's mum and dad, together with Paula; and Flora spoke a lot about her feelings about her mother's next meeting with her dad. Melanie's dad seemed very relaxed when he came to collect her and Mary. Over a cup of tea, he chatted amiably to everyone for quite a while, asking interested questions and even cracking jokes.

After he left with Mary and Melanie, Flora burst out, 'That's *amazing*! Mum, you're a *genius*!' But she stopped half way along the hall, hung her head down onto her chest and mumbled miserably, 'I wish my dad would end up being like that.'

'I know, love,' said May as she put her arm round Flora; and

Tracy could see that she had tears in her eyes. 'I want you to know that I'm absolutely determined to do what I can. I think about it most of the time when I'm not working, and sometimes when I am. My head goes round and round it all. I think about how I first met Tony, how we got together, the day I found I was pregnant with you, the day you were born, the day Tony left, and all the years since then.'

'Do you, Mum?' said Flora, looking at her mother as she began to realise there was a side of her that she hadn't previously known. 'Do you really?'

'Yes, love,' May assured her.

'Mum, I think I'm going to write to Dad. I'll think about it in bed tonight, and I'll write it tomorrow. And tomorrow evening I want you to sit and tell me and Tracy about the day you first met Dad. You've never told me before.'

Upstairs in the attic room, Flora took a pencil and a notepad out of a box that stood on the floor next to the chest. 'I might make some notes while I'm in bed,' she said. 'But I'm not sure.'

'It's okay by me if you want to leave the light on,' said Tracy helpfully. 'I'm so tired I'm sure I'll fall asleep.'

At lunchtime the next day, Flora announced that she had written a letter and was on her way out to put it in the post box. She had given no indication that she wanted her mother or Tracy to read it before she sealed the envelope; and Tracy noticed that May had not suggested it.

When she returned she said to Tracy, 'What I'd like to do is to phone to see if we can go round and see Ben and Kate this afternoon.'

'I'd like that too,' Tracy agreed enthusiastically; and May added her own encouragement.

'Here's the number,' she said.

There was no reply when Flora rang, but she left a message on the call-minder; and not long afterwards Pam called back.

'We were out with Bracken,' Tracy heard Pam's voice say. 'You want to come over? That would be lovely. Can you come on your bikes?'

'That's it fixed,' Flora announced as she put the phone down. 'Let's get the bikes ready, and then we'll get off.' She went to collect the vulture helmet once more.

As the girls opened the door of the shed Flora said, 'I think we'll go round by the roads this time. I don't want you to go flying because of a pile of rubble again.'

'I liked the walkway a lot,' said Tracy, 'but I didn't like my crash. Roads it is!'

The afternoon passed very pleasantly with piles of story books, Pam's homemade lemonade, and various games of hide and seek, and 'throw the ball for Bracken'. When Dave came home after work, he offered Tracy and Flora a lift; but they declined, preferring to use their bikes instead.

That evening in May's sitting room, she told the girls the story of how she first met Tony.

'It was quite simple really,' May began. 'I met him at a friend's house. I was twenty-five, and the manager of a small boutique at the time. I had a circle of friends who were in the same kind of business, and we had a girls' night out every so often. We'd been to a film, and we'd gone back to the flat of the person whose turn it was to do coffee and nibbles that night.'

'What was her name? Is it someone I know?' asked Flora.

'It was Andrea... Andrea Greenleigh,' May replied. 'And no, you haven't met her.'

'Do you know where she lives?' asked Flora.

'No. She emigrated to Canada, and I lost touch with her,' May replied.

'Go on,' Flora demanded.

May continued: 'There was a ring at the door of the flat, and Andrea went to open it. She came back with two nice-looking young men. One was her brother, and the other was Tony, who was his friend. They sat down with us and stayed until the end of the evening. Tony was sitting next to me, and I felt very attracted to him.'

'Did you say anything?' asked Flora.

'I talked to him about the film we'd just been to see.'

'I don't mean *that*,' said Flora. 'Did you tell him you fancied him?'

'Of course not,' said May. 'I just felt attracted to him, and that wasn't a reason for saying anything about it.'

Tracy could see that Flora looked quite relieved; and she herself noted that May's behaviour certainly fitted with the kind of thing Miss Maitland had been saying.

May went on: 'I didn't think anything about it afterwards until I heard from Andrea that her brother had told her that Tony had felt attracted to me.'

'What did you do?' asked Tracy eagerly.

'I told Andrea that she could give her brother my phone number if it seemed right to do that, and I left it at that.'

'What happened next?' Flora asked urgently.

'Nothing. Well, not for a few weeks. It was about six weeks later that I had a phone message that someone called Tony had phoned and had left a number where I could contact him. Of course, I knew straight away who it was. I left it a few days to think about it, and then I phoned. And that was the beginning.' Tracy thought she had finished, but she went on. 'I wish now that I'd spent more time getting to know him – slowly, over a longer period of time. We should have spent more time with friends and with our families. I know that now, but at the time I didn't realise. I was too swept away with a lot of romantic ideas. All of that feels so nice at the time that you can easily forget there are other things that need to be thought about and seen to. I soon changed my job so we could go away more often together, and as I've said before, we did a lot of travelling about.'

'I must ask Mum and Dad how *they* first met,' said Tracy. 'I expect you know Auntie May, but don't tell me. I want them to tell me. I'll ask them when they come next week.'

'That's a great idea!' exclaimed Flora. '*I* want to know too.'

In bed that night, Tracy and Flora agreed that it had been good to get May to talk about how she had met Tony; and they made a pact to remind each other to get Tracy's parents to talk about how they first met.

Chapter Twenty-four

It was Monday, and the girls were lying awake in their beds long before Flora's alarm clock was due to go off.

'It's the big day!' sighed Flora. 'I wonder what'll happen.'

'I wish I knew,' said Tracy longingly. 'But I can't see into the future.'

'I think I'll just get up,' said Flora. 'I'd rather be getting on with something than lying here.'

'Okay,' Tracy agreed.

It was not long before they were both down in the kitchen. There was no sign of May, so Flora went off up the back stairs to see where she was. She found her fast asleep. The book she had been reading the night before had fallen on the alarm clock that she always put on the floor beside her bed, and had accidentally switched it off.

'Mum!' hissed Flora, shaking her mother gently. 'Mum, wake up!'

'What is it, Flora?' asked May sleepily. 'What are you doing here at this time? Is something the matter?'

'It's twenty past seven,' Flora informed her.

'Oh no!' May exclaimed. 'How can I have slept in?'

'Your book had fallen on the alarm clock, I think,' Flora explained. 'Tracy and I are ready. We could make a start.'

'Thanks, love,' said May as she got out of bed. 'I'll be down as soon as I can.'

Tracy and Flora set to work, and May appeared a little while later. 'And today of all days!' she exclaimed. 'I wanted to be calm today, and have no rushing, and now look what's happened.'

'It's all right, Mum,' Flora rubbed her mother's back in an attempt to comfort her. 'We'll help as much as we can. You'll be fine.'

'Thanks, love,' May replied gratefully.

When the breakfasts for the guests were over, the three were sitting once more around the kitchen table, when they heard the post arrive. Flora leapt up out of her seat and dashed into the hall. She came back carrying a pile of mail, and looking a little pink.

'I've got a reply from Dad,' she said breathlessly.

'Are you going to open it?' Tracy asked.

Flora took a knife, slit open the envelope and read the slip of paper she found inside.

'What does it say?' Tracy asked eagerly.

Flora looked secretive, but read it out:

I'll try. Dad

'But that's not a letter!' said Tracy disappointedly.

'I know. But it's the answer to the letter I sent,' said Flora determinedly. And although Tracy pressed her for more information, Flora would say no more. Tracy noted that her Auntie May said nothing at all.

When the cleaning and lunch were over, Flora and Tracy used a recipe they had found in Flora's cookbook to make a cake. It had taken Flora quite a long time to find the book, but she had eventually located it buried underneath a pile of old magazines in a corner of the attic room.

They left the cake in the oven, and at half past two they all set off in May's van to collect Miss Maitland together with her special chair. It was not long after Miss Maitland was comfortably installed in May's sitting room that the door bell rang. Flora and Tracy ran to the door to find Derek, Babs and Paula standing there. Derek was holding a large box of groceries.

'I thought I would bring a box of treats for us to share,' he announced cheerfully.

'Put it on the kitchen table,' said May from the back of the hall. 'And the girls will take your bags up. I've put you in the pink room again.' She greeted Paula. 'Hello, love. It's a good while since I last saw you. I think you've grown quite a bit.'

'My holiday in Wales made me grow up quite a bit,' said Paula. 'But I don't know if I'm any taller.'

Everyone laughed, and Derek said, 'Yes, Paula's got quite a tale to tell.'

'We've made you a bed up in the attic with us,' Tracy said eagerly. She was so pleased to see her sister again, and felt a rush of warmth towards her. 'We've got lots to tell you, too. Haven't we,

Flora?'

'Yes. It's a good job you're staying for two nights,' said Flora.

Tracy noticed that although Flora sounded pleased and confident, she looked a bit uncertain; and she realised that it might be hard for her to have Paula around at first, when something so important as this meeting tonight was about to take place. She wondered how she could make it easier for her, but couldn't think of anything to say. Instead she turned to Paula and asked, 'Have Mum and Dad told you all about Uncle Tony's meeting with Auntie May?'

'I know that Auntie May met him two weeks ago when I was in Wales, and she's going to see him again tonight,' said Paula.

'That's right,' confirmed Flora. 'And I think it's going to go okay.'

'You must come and meet Miss Maitland,' said Tracy. 'She's waiting in Auntie May's sitting room.'

'Yes,' said Flora. 'We'll take the bags up to the pink room, and then show Paula where she'll be sleeping. After that she can see Miss Maitland.'

The girls made their way upstairs, and soon Paula was admiring the sunflower painting in the attic room.

'That's good,' she said. 'But can I tell you about the police?'

'The police?' Tracy said in astonished tones, while Flora stood quietly, looking impressed.

'Yes. The police came when we were in Wales,' Paula explained.

'Why?' asked Tracy.

'Jenny's brother got into a lot of trouble. It was really scary,' Paula told them.

'Tell us what happened!' Flora demanded.

'Jenny's brother was supposed to be at the swimming pool with some of the boys he met there on holiday last year. He didn't want to come to the beach with us. He said it was too cold to swim in the sea. But he didn't go to the swimming pool. He did something really bad.' Here Paula's voice reduced to a whisper, as if she feared someone overhearing what she was about to say. 'The boys he was with went and bought glue, and they did something with it that made them feel very ill. The police found out, and they brought Jenny's brother back to the cottage in the evening, and had a long talk with Jenny's mum and dad about it. After he got better, Jenny's brother had to stay with us all the time. He was very quiet, and just read books, except when

Jenny's dad took him to things like archery. Jenny told me she thought her dad gave him a good talking to, but I don't know if he did or not.'

'That's terrible,' said Tracy in the same kind of whisper that Paula had used. 'What did Mum and Dad do?'

'Jenny's mum and dad phoned them the day after the police had been round. They explained what had happened, and asked if they wanted me to go home. They said it was all right for me to stay on if I wanted. So I did, because I wanted to. I had a long talk to Mum and Dad on the phone about it all, because I had felt scared when the police came round. Since I got back home, they've been explaining a bit about glue sniffing to me. It sounds horrible, and what it does to people sounds terrible.'

'It is,' Tracy and Flora said together.

'When I started at Castlehill High, the police came round and gave us a talk about it,' said Tracy.

'That's what happened when I started at secondary school too,' added Flora. 'Your holiday makes ours look tame!'

'Let me see your hands, Tracy,' Paula demanded. She examined Tracy's outstretched palms, and said, 'They don't look the same as when I last saw them. I was worried about you when I heard you'd fallen off a bike and hurt your hands. Mum and Dad tried to tell me that you were all right, but I wanted to see.'

'They feel fine now, and they're definitely nearly better,' Tracy reassured her. Then she said, 'Let's go down and get some cake,' as she suddenly remembered the cake in the oven.

They all rushed downstairs to find that May had rescued it long ago, and was slicing it up to share out.

Tracy heard her dad say to Miss Maitland, 'You've obviously been a great help to the girls. Thank you very much.'

'No, no,' she replied. 'They're as much help to me as I might be to them.' She turned and winked at Tracy and Flora. 'We've shared quite a lot. Haven't we?'

'Come and meet Miss Maitland,' Tracy said to Paula. 'She's really nice. We visit her at her house nearly every week and have some interesting chats.'

The cake was deemed to be excellent, and there was a hum of eager conversation between everyone.

At last, Miss Maitland said, 'Lovely though this is, I should be going soon. Can someone help me and my chair down the road?'

'Tracy and I will take you,' said Derek standing up. 'Can we take your van, May? I don't think I'll be able to fit the chair into my car.'

May passed him the keys, and she and Tracy helped Miss Maitland to the van while Derek carried the chair out. Together they took her home and got her safely reinstalled in her living room.

'Is there anything you need before we go?' asked Derek.

'I don't think so, thanks,' replied Miss Maitland.

'You can always give us a ring if you think of anything,' he said. 'It only takes a few minutes to drive down.'

Miss Maitland waved goodbye from her chair, and Tracy and her dad returned to Welcome Home to find the others working out a timetable.

'I'd like to be at the Woodlands by seven,' said May. 'Tony and I are meeting at seven thirty, and I really need time before that just to sit quietly for a while.'

'I can understand that, May,' said Babs. 'I think if you and Derek leave at about a quarter to seven, that should be plenty of time.'

'Yes,' Derek agreed, as he went through the door into the kitchen. 'Just name your time. I'm your companion and your chauffeur for the evening. Just tell me what to do.'

'It's such a help having you all here – including you, Paula,' said May, gratefully. 'I think I'd be quite agitated by now if you weren't.'

Tracy noticed that Flora was unusually quiet, and that she had a serene smile on her face. She wondered if it had something to do with the note she had got from her dad that morning. But she hadn't said anything more about it, or about the letter she had sent to him, and Tracy hadn't asked.

'Paula, what do you think about the sunflower mural?' May asked her.

'I'm jealous,' said Paula bluntly. 'I want to do a wall painting as well.'

The four adults stared at her, nonplussed, and there was a difficult silence.

It was May who spoke first. 'Well, since you've made the trip all this way to come and help me, I'd like to offer one of the walls of my bedroom. What do you think?'

Paula's face shone. '*Really?*' she exclaimed. 'Can I really paint on your bedroom wall, Auntie May?'

'Yes. Of course you can. I'll take you up in a minute and show you the wall. We'll have to put dustsheets down tomorrow to protect the floor from any splashes, and we'll have to find you some old clothes to wear. But yes, you can. You can do it straight after lunch tomorrow.'

'Wow!' said Paula, throwing herself into May's arms. Then she added generously 'Tracy and Flora can watch if they want.'

'I'd like to watch too,' said Derek with a twinkle in his eye. 'I'd like to see how it's done. I've never done a mural myself.'

'Tracy and Flora,' said Paula. 'Will you show me what to do?'

'Yes, of course,' said Flora nonchalantly.

'And I've brought my camera,' Babs joined in. 'So I'll be able to take a photo of the one in the attic and the new one that's going to appear in May's room.'

'It's nearly time for Derek and I to eat,' said May suddenly. 'But I don't feel like eating at the moment. In fact I feel a bit sick.'

'That's quite natural,' said Babs sympathetically. 'Derek can have a sandwich, and the girls and I can have something when you've gone.'

May looked relieved. 'That's one thing off my mind,' she said. 'I think I'll go up now and get washed and changed. You come up with me for a minute, Paula, and I'll show you which wall it'll be. Then you can be making your plans for tomorrow.'

Paula went off with May; and when she returned, Tracy saw that she was looking very content. 'Can we play Scrabble this evening, Mum?' Paula asked. 'Does Auntie May have a set?'

'Yes, she does,' her mother replied. 'I played with Tracy and Flora when I was here last time.'

Derek made himself a sandwich, and sat down to eat it. When May later reappeared, Flora gasped. 'Oh, Mum,' she said. 'You look lovely! And where did you get that beautiful necklace from?'

Tracy noticed that May's cheeks looked a little pink as she said, 'Your dad gave it to me after I told him I was pregnant with you.'

Tracy looked across at her mum and she could see that she looked a bit tearful.

'I hope it goes well, May,' said Babs, giving her sister a hug. 'Take good care of her, won't you, Derek?'

'Of course I will,' he said. 'Don't worry. We'll do what we can.'

And soon after that Babs and the three girls were waving goodbye to May and Derek at the front door.

'Now, what shall we do for our tea?' Babs asked as she closed the door. 'Shall we look in Derek's box of treats?'

The girls were keen to do exactly that, and she led the way to the kitchen to spread out the contents of the box across the table.

'Falafels. They look interesting,' said Flora.

'They're really good,' said Tracy. 'They're made out of onion and chickpeas and spices and things like that.'

'I've heard people talking about them, but I've never tried them,' said Flora. 'Can we have these, Auntie Babs?'

Paula was in agreement, and Babs put on the oven while she found a baking tray to put the falafels in.

'Shall we do some of this jasmine rice to go with them?' asked Babs, reaching for the kettle to heat up some water.

Paula bounced up and down several times. 'My favourite,' she said.

'We've got peas in the freezer,' said Flora. 'I'll get them.'

As they ate their meal, Babs and the girls talked about how they were looking forward to May and Derek's return later in the evening. Tracy noticed that Flora was unusually reserved, and she began to wonder if there was something wrong with her. But as she didn't look ill, she stopped feeling worried, and began to look forward to the game of Scrabble. Paula was a surprisingly good player, she remembered; so the game should be interesting.

The washing up took little time as there were four pairs of hands, and the first game of Scrabble was soon under way. Paula certainly managed some long words such as 'enviable' and 'quantum' that evening, and Flora was suitably impressed.

They were well into their third game when Flora thought she heard the door. She was about to get up when Derek came into the room.

'Where's May?' asked Babs anxiously.

'It's all right,' said Derek, smiling broadly. 'She's waiting at the front door. She's got a surprise for everyone.'

Puzzled, Tracy got up and followed the others to the front door where she stood between Flora and Paula, with Babs leaning over her shoulder. Standing in the street were May and Tony holding hands and waving. May turned to Tony and said, 'I'll make sure and give your message to Flora' before he hurried off in the direction of the main road.

'He did it. He did it!' exclaimed Flora triumphantly. 'That proves he really cares.'

'What on earth do you mean?' asked Tracy; but Flora said nothing, and would not be drawn.

'Well done, Mum,' said Flora, hugging May as she came through the door.

'Your dad gave me a message for you,' said May. 'He said that he would see you next week. He said he'll come round to collect you next Monday, and he'll come in and have cup of tea with us before you set off together.'

'Oh May! That's such good news,' exclaimed Babs, with tears pouring down her cheeks.

'Well, it's not all sorted out yet,' said May. 'We've a long way to go, and neither of us knows where it'll lead. But things are certainly on a better footing between us now, and that's the main thing. I could do with a sandwich now,' she added, surprised. 'In fact I feel quite hungry.'

'We kept something for you,' said Babs. 'I'll put it under the grill.'

'If you don't mind, I'd rather not talk about this evening yet,' said May, as she ate her food. 'I think I just want to go to bed.'

'That's entirely understandable,' said Babs. 'I'll go up with the girls and get them settled. Then I'll come and tuck you in!'

'I'd appreciate that,' said May gratefully.

Chapter Twenty-five

The following morning Tracy and Flora tried to tiptoe out of the attic room, but Paula was instantly awake.

'I want to help too,' she said determinedly, as she struggled out from under her duvet.

Down in the kitchen, the three girls found Babs and Derek preparing to make breakfasts for the guests.

'Where's Mum?' asked Flora.

Babs smiled. 'I stole her alarm clock last night after she fell asleep, so we're all in charge this morning. You two will have to keep us straight. Won't they Derek?'

'Yes,' he replied. 'We're relying on you.'

Tracy and Flora took Paula into the dining room and showed her how to lay the tables; then Flora went back into the kitchen to help with the cooking.

They were all sitting round the table eating their own breakfasts when May appeared, looked rather bleary-eyed.

'I feel all disorientated,' she said. 'I couldn't find the clock, and then when I saw my watch it was nine thirty. I got such a shock!'

'It's all right. Everything is under control,' said Derek. 'We've done the food, and we've even booked some of your guests out. They didn't seem to notice that it was Babs and not you!'

'I am *so* tired,' said May, and sat down suddenly.

'Why don't you go back to bed for a bit,' said Babs. 'The girls and I can bring your breakfast up to you.'

'I can do my mural later, Auntie May,' said Paula. 'So you can have a proper rest.'

May looked relieved. 'It's wonderful to have all this help,' she said. 'I'd like to take you up on your offer of breakfast in bed. And if you're willing to do your painting a bit later, Paula, then I'll have another lie down. Babs, there's one more thing I'd really like if we could fix it.'

'What's that, May?'

'I would love to have half an hour with Miss Maitland this

afternoon.'

Derek and Babs looked at each other, and Derek said, 'May, you can have a couple of hours or so if you want. We can hold the fort here. Can't we, girls?'

'Yes,' said Tracy. 'We can all do the work, and Paula will paint something nice for you.'

'Right,' said Babs briskly. 'Back up to bed with you. Breakfast will arrive soon, and after that the five of us will get on with the cleaning. Don't worry about a thing. We can phone Miss Maitland at lunchtime and tell her to expect you. And if there's anything that comes up that we're really stuck with this afternoon, we can always phone you there to ask what you want us to do.'

May went off upstairs, and everyone busied themselves. Tracy and Flora showed Paula and Derek what needed to be done to the rooms, while Babs made her sister's breakfast.

'Auntie May's having bed and breakfast this morning,' said Tracy cheerfully.

It was lunchtime when Flora and Tracy remembered something important.

'We were going to see if Mary could come round while your mum and dad and Paula were here,' she said.

'Yes. We were going to see if she wanted to bring some of her drawings round to show them,' Tracy added.

'Why not phone her now, and see if she can come round some time this afternoon?' asked May. 'She's welcome, even though I'll be out.'

Flora jumped up and went to the phone straight away; and Tracy could tell that it must have been Mary herself who answered.

'That's it fixed,' said Flora. 'She'll be here at about half past two.'

'Tell her that I'm sorry not be seeing her, and that if she's bringing pictures I hope I'll get a chance to see them another time,' said May as she got ready to go.

The evening was spent in the sitting room. May kept saying how grateful she was for all the help, and for the lovely picture of tulips that Paula had painted on her wall.

Paula was a bit upset at first when she realised that she was going home with her mum and dad the next day, until they told her that she could help with the decorating. After that she perked up, only to show more upset when she realised that when her Uncle Tony came to Welcome Home the following Monday, she wouldn't see him.

'It's really Flora's day, love,' her mother explained.

'But Tracy will see him!' Paula complained in a loud voice.

'I've got an idea,' said Derek. 'I know that Tony's planning to be seeing a bit more of May and Flora soon. We can keep in touch, and when there's a convenient time, I'll see if I can fix to bring you here to meet him properly. How about that?'

Paula's face glowed. Tracy could see she suddenly felt special. She was sad that Dad would be making that particular trip without her, but she could understand why; and she hoped it would not be very many months before they all saw more of Uncle Tony.

'You haven't told me yet if Mary brought some of her pictures round,' said May suddenly.

'Yes. She did,' Flora replied.

'They were extremely impressive,' said Babs. 'I think she has quite a gift. Tracy, Flora and Paula are good at painting murals, and Mary is good with pencils and charcoal. She told us she'd been to see Tricia Penway at her studio. The visit went very well I think, and there was some talk of her going back some time.'

'That's good to hear,' said May. 'Now, there are a couple of things we have to talk about before we go to bed.'

'I know,' said Tracy immediately. 'I know what they are.'

'Go on then, love,' May encouraged her. 'You just say what they are.'

'We have to decide about how long I can stay here. And we were going to talk about my grandad – the one who was the dad of you and Mum.'

'I think we should start with the first thing,' said Derek decisively. 'Tracy told me earlier that she wanted to stay for the whole holiday. I said that she'd need a few days at home before term starts so she can get ready.'

'What do you think, May?' asked Babs.

'I'd be delighted for her to stay on,' said May without hesitation.

'All we have to do is to decide on a date then,' said Derek. 'I'll try and organise to come up and collect you, Tracy. If I can't, perhaps May could put you on the train.'

Tracy felt happy… very happy. She said nothing, and waited.

'Let's have a look at the calendar,' said May, taking it down from where it hung on the wall. She studied it, and then said, 'I think we've got nearly two weeks left. If you go back sometime during the weekend after next, then you'd have a few days before school starts again.'

'Please can I stay until the Sunday afternoon?' asked Tracy eagerly. 'The weekends are busy, and I want to help.'

'Let's try for Sunday, then,' Derek agreed. 'I'll let you know as soon as I can about whether or not I can collect you. If I can't we'll book a seat for you on the train.'

'Now tell us about grandad, Mum and Auntie May,' said Tracy happily.

'Hey, this is good!' Flora said. 'He's the grandad of all three of us.'

The following hour proved to be very interesting. Although May and Babs had memories of their father that were more or less the same, some of their memories were quite different; and these differences became just as much a subject for conversation as the memories themselves.

The following morning, everyone took a share of the work; and when it was finished, Babs, Derek and Paula loaded their things into the car and set off for home.

'See you soon,' called Paula out of the car window. 'And you'll get a surprise when you come home and see the living room!'

'Oh no!' exclaimed Tracy as the car disappeared round the corner.

'What?' asked Flora.

'We forgot to ask my mum and dad how they first met!'

Chapter Twenty-six

'What sort of things do you do with your dad?' asked Tracy as she and Flora lay in bed late one evening. 'You were going to tell me before, but then we never got round to it.'

'I know,' Flora replied. 'I've been thinking about that. I've never said much to Mum about it, so I suppose it's just a habit now. I don't talk about it.'

'Did you mind me asking?' said Tracy anxiously.

'No. I didn't mind. It just feels funny, that's all,' Flora reflected. 'I'll tell you a bit about it if you want. But there's not much to say, actually.'

Tracy waited.

'We usually go to some kind of museum, exhibition, visitor centre or ancient monument – and things like that,' Flora explained. 'Once or twice we've been to an afternoon concert.'

Tracy felt puzzled. If she went to places like that on her own with her dad, the first thing she wanted to do when she got home was to tell her mum and Paula about it. There must be some reason why Flora didn't do that. Then she remembered that it was only since she had been here that Flora had been talking to her friends and her mum much about her dad at all.

'Has your dad met any of your friends?' she asked.

'Not as far as I can remember,' Flora replied.

Tracy was aghast. How awful, she thought. Her dad had met nearly all her friends, and she certainly talked to him a lot about them all. She tried again. 'Do you talk to him about your friends?' she asked.

'No, not really,' Flora replied, her voice conveying an apparent lack of interest.

Tracy didn't know what to say next. All she could do was hope that somehow what was happening between Auntie May and Uncle Tony would end up with Flora having something better than this with her dad. She was glad Flora saw him, but she wondered what they talked about if they weren't talking about Flora's mum, and her friends and things like that.

Trying again, Tracy asked, 'What do you talk about when you're with your dad?'

Flora's voice sounded bored as she answered. 'We just talk about whatever place we're visiting at the time, and he asks me about school sometimes.'

'Does he ever talk to you about himself?' asked Tracy.

'Hardly ever,' Flora replied. 'He once said he wasn't going to because he didn't want my mum to know anything.'

'That's *horrible*!' Tracy exclaimed. She clapped her hand to her mouth. 'Oh, I'm sorry…' Her voice trailed off.

'Well… actually… it was,' said Flora. 'And when Mum came back from seeing him that first time at the Woodlands, I felt really angry when she said he'd been telling her about his life, and she'd been interested to listen. I felt really, really angry.'

'But you didn't say anything,' said Tracy, impressed.

'I know. I wanted to, but I managed not to. I thought it wouldn't help.'

'I hope things are going to be different soon,' said Tracy sleepily.

'I keep thinking of the things Miss Maitland has said when we've been to see her,' said Flora. 'And that helps. But there's one thing I'd like to ask her, but I daren't.'

'What's that?' asked Tracy, almost asleep.

'I want to ask if she ever had any more boyfriends after her dad sent Edwin away. But I don't think I can. She might not want to say.'

There was no reply, and Flora looked across at Tracy, only to discover that she was fast asleep.

'You fell asleep last night,' said Flora accusingly, when Tracy woke to the alarm the following morning.

'I'm sorry,' Tracy apologised. 'Was there something you were trying to say?'

'I was saying I wanted to ask Miss Maitland if she'd had any more boyfriends, but I don't think I can, in case she didn't and doesn't want to say.'

'I don't want to ask her either,' said Tracy firmly as she jumped out of bed to grab her wash bag. She stopped, perched on the side of her bed and said, 'And I don't think we should. I'd like to go and see her again soon though, and I'd like to see Mary and Melanie again if we can. I'd like to see them before we see your dad.'

'I think that the Youth Club won't be meeting this week,' said Flora. 'Perhaps Mary and Melanie would come round here instead. That would be tomorrow evening. I'll phone them later today to see if I can fix it up.'

'And we could see Miss Maitland one afternoon,' Tracy added.

'We can't stay here chatting,' Flora suddenly said, alarmed. 'We're late!'

They arrived in the kitchen a few minutes late, and quite breathless.

May appeared relaxed, so Flora said, 'We're thinking of asking Mary and Melanie round tomorrow evening. Is that okay?'

'That would be fine,' May replied. 'But I've got an idea I'll tell you about at breakfast.'

Tracy wondered what her aunt's plan might be, and tried to guess while she served the guests.

When they were sitting round the kitchen table later, May said, 'How about thinking of going to see a film tomorrow evening with Mary and Melanie? I'd be more than happy to pay for it. Why not give them a ring and see. Perhaps Melanie's dad would be willing to give you a run along to the cinema?' She smiled at Flora and Tracy conspiratorially. 'Let's have a look in the local paper to see what's on.'

Having found that there was a choice between two good films, Flora was soon speaking to Mary.

'She can come,' she announced to her mother and Tracy. 'Now I'll try Melanie.'

When the phone was answered, Flora pulled a face and spoke in a polite way.

'This is Flora. I was hoping to speak to Melanie,' she said. 'But I think my mum would like a word with you if you've got a moment.' She put her hand over the mouthpiece and passed the phone to her mother. It's her dad!' she whispered.

'Hello,' said May. 'Yes, I was hoping to speak to you. The girls were thinking of meeting up tomorrow night, and I offered to pay for them to see a film. There seems to be a choice on at the Cameo. Would you be able to give them a lift?... Oh, good. You'll get back to us when you've checked with Melanie?... Bye for now, then.'

'Well done, Mum!' Flora congratulated her mother. She turned to

Tracy. 'Shall we go to see Miss Maitland this afternoon, or shall we wait until tomorrow?' she asked.

'Let's go today,' said Tracy instantly.

The afternoon saw them pedalling down once more to Miss Maitland's house. Just before they left, Melanie had phoned to confirm that her dad would collect everyone the following evening and then take them to the Cameo.

'I can't wait until Monday,' Flora said to Miss Maitland once they were settled in her living room.

Tracy found to her surprise that Miss Maitland was not her usual patient self.

'Neither can I,' she said. 'But we'll just have to. And I'll have to wait even longer, because I won't get your news until after that!'

'I've got some news, Miss Maitland,' said Tracy. 'I'm staying with Flora for almost a week after she sees her dad.'

'That's good news, dear,' said Miss Maitland. 'And it means that I'll see you again before you leave, I hope.'

'I'll definitely come again, Miss Maitland,' Tracy said seriously. 'I'll miss coming here once I'm back home again. And I'll miss Flora and Auntie May and everyone else.'

Flora looked glum. 'It'll be really weird without you,' she said. 'At least I'll be back in my old room soon after you've gone, so I won't be sleeping in the attic and wondering where you are when I wake up.'

'If Auntie May can let you have your room back just before I leave, I could help you to take your things back to it,' suggested Tracy.

Flora brightened. 'I'll ask her when we get back. I'd like that,' she said.

Chapter Twenty-seven

The trip to the cinema had been a great success. Melanie's dad had been very friendly. He had insisted on coming in with them to find out exactly when the film would finish, and had been waiting outside for them when they came out. He even prompted what proved to be a very interesting discussion about the film.

The weekend had been the usual extra flurry of cleaning and bed changing. Flora was eyeing up her room now, and was counting the days to the time when she and Tracy could start to put her things back into it. She was pleased that her mother had been so enthusiastic about their idea of moving the things just before Tracy went back home. And it would only be a week after Flora started school again that the Italian women and the Chinese couple would be moving in. Flora had begun to look forward to this, and she promised to let Tracy know all about them once they had settled in. Flora and Tracy had talked about how good it would be once Flora got her computer and they could perhaps exchange e-mails. Tracy felt sure that her dad would let her use his computer for sending messages to Flora.

And now it was Monday, and Flora and Tracy were waiting for Flora's dad to arrive. The breakfasts were over, and Tracy and Auntie May were talking about how they would share out the cleaning, when the doorbell rang.

'That's him,' said Flora, running towards the front door.

Tracy didn't know quite what to do. She had looked forward to seeing Uncle Tony again; but now he was here, she felt uncomfortable. She knew it was a very important day for Flora, but she didn't know where she fitted in. She decided to put the kettle on for something to do. Auntie May had gone out of the kitchen door, but was standing there to allow time for Flora to greet her dad. She could hear Flora say, 'You've got to come and talk to Tracy. She's been staying all summer,' and she began to relax.

'Hello, May,' said Uncle Tony. And Flora could see that he gave her a peck on the cheek. Surely that was a good sign, she thought. 'Hello, Tracy,' he said to her, holding out his hand. 'It's good to see you.'

Tracy took his hand. It seemed quite warm and friendly, and she relaxed a bit more. 'Hello,' she said. 'I've put the kettle on to make some tea.'

They all sat down at the table, and Tony said, 'We mustn't stay long. I've got something fixed, and in any case I have to admit it's a bit difficult for me being back here in the house.'

'It's a bit difficult for me too,' May said honestly, but she was smiling.

'Don't leave us out!' said Flora firmly. 'But let's get the tea and set off, Dad.' She became thoughtful. 'While we're out we could decide whether or not you might come in again for a bit when we come back.'

At first Tony looked defensive, but then he looked at Flora. 'Yes, let's do that,' he said.

The rest of the short visit was taken up with pleasantries about the weather, and a couple of topics currently in the news. Then Flora picked up her bag, and she and Tony left.

'That went a lot better than I could have imagined even last week!' exclaimed May. 'And there's no way of telling what will happen next.'

'We won't have to wait long to find out,' said Tracy. 'Auntie May, when we've done the cleaning and had lunch, can I help you with your office again, please?'

May looked very surprised. 'Of course, love,' she said. 'It isn't much fun, though.'

'I like learning what to do,' said Tracy firmly. 'And I want to learn as much as I can before I go back home.'

This conversation led to May and Tracy spending a quiet afternoon in the office, gradually working through many piles of papers that had built up there; and by late afternoon, the office looked quite different.

May leaned back in her chair and heaved a sigh. 'It's not perfect, but it's the best it's been for a long, long time,' she said. 'Thanks, love. You've been a great help. With all this being much more tidy, and my diary system about to get off the ground, I won't get in such a muddle again, I hope.'

Tracy felt very pleased that her aunt valued her efforts so much, and she was sure that Mum and Dad would be very proud of her when she told them. Added to that she felt she had learned a lot, and if she ever wanted to do an office job, her experience here might help her. She had heard at school that the older pupils had what they called a work experience week. Maybe when it was her turn to do that she could ask to come and do it with Auntie May.

At teatime the phone rang. May answered it, and Tracy could hear her mum's voice on the other end.

'We're fine thanks,' said May. 'They're not back yet, but it went well this morning, and Tony said he might come in again for a minute when he brought Flora back... Yes... I'll hand you over to Tracy now.'

'Hi, Mum,' said Tracy. She was eager to tell her about her afternoon in the office. Mum was clearly pleased and said she would tell Dad when he came in from his shift.

'He should be in any minute,' she finished.

Then Paula came on the phone. 'I'm not telling you what colours we're using,' she said, but not in a nasty way. 'You'll have to wait until you come back to find out!'

Just then, Dad came home and Paula handed the phone over to him. 'It's Tracy,' she explained.

'Oh, good,' said Dad. 'Tracy, I've managed to get the day off on Sunday, so I'll be able to come and pick you up.'

Tracy could hear Paula bouncing up and down next to him, singing, 'I'm coming too. I'm coming too.'

'That's it fixed,' she told her aunt when she put the phone down. 'Dad and Paula are coming to collect me on Sunday.'

'That's good,' May replied. Then she stopped and listened. 'I think that might be Flora's key in the lock,' she said; and she went into the hall. 'Yes, here she comes.'

Flora came into the hallway and Tracy could see that she was glowing. She looked happier than Tracy had ever seen her look before.

'Dad can't come in at the moment,' she said breathlessly. 'But that's okay, because he says he'll come back again very soon. When I told him that Tracy's going back home on Sunday, he gave me his mobile phone number and asked me to phone once I knew whether her mum and dad were coming to collect her or not. He said if they were he'd like to come round and see us all then!' she finished triumphantly. 'He said he wouldn't be able to stay for long, and that he wanted to know as soon as possible!' She stood and took a few deep breaths. Then she went on: 'We had a great day,' she said. 'We talked about *hundreds* of things.' She went into the kitchen and flopped onto one of the chairs. 'I'm hungry!' she announced.

'I'm not surprised,' said May, smiling. 'Let's cook something nice as a celebration.'

Over their food, Flora couldn't stop talking. In fact she was almost jabbering. Tracy didn't try to say anything, and she noticed that her aunt wasn't trying either. She could see that May was nodding from time to time and making encouraging sounds; but she made no attempt to say anything. After all, thought Tracy, there wasn't any room to say anything, even when Flora was eating.

'And I can't *wait* to tell Mary and Melanie and Miss Maitland,' Flora said, between gulps. 'And I want to tell Mr Mason at the Youth Club that my dad has started talking a lot, just like *he* did.'

There was a gap, so May said, 'You could give Mary and Melanie a ring after tea and let them know what's been happening.'

'And we could go and see Miss Maitland tomorrow afternoon if you want,' Tracy added. 'Remember how keen she was to see us again.'

'By the way,' said May, having found that Flora didn't have to speak all the time any more. 'Tracy's dad and Paula will be coming to collect her on Sunday.'

'I've got to tell Dad straight away,' said Flora, jumping up to the phone.

'Perhaps it'd be better to wait until we know exactly what time they're coming,' May advised her. 'Derek had only just found out he could get the time off, so I expect he and Babs will be working out this evening exactly what they're doing.'

'Okay,' said Flora reluctantly. 'I'll phone him tomorrow.'

That evening, Flora spent a long time on the phone to her friends. And in bed at night, she was still talking. Tracy tried to stay awake, but in the end her tiredness defeated her, and she fell asleep.

Flora was much calmer in the morning, and at breakfast remarked to her mother and Tracy that she realised that she had talked a lot the previous evening.

'I think that was a good thing,' said May. 'I've done a lot of talking with Babs and Derek and with my friends. I think it's very important. You'll be going to see Miss Maitland this afternoon, and if I haven't heard from Tracy's mum and dad again by this evening, we'll give them a ring. After that you can phone your dad.'

The trip along the road to see Miss Maitland was very pleasant. Tracy and Flora found her sitting on a folding chair just inside the front door, which was standing open.

'I hoped you would come along,' she said when she saw them. 'And the sun was so nice and warm, I thought I would wait here for you. I got my home help to bring this folding chair and put it here before she left. Why not sit on the step and tell me all the news?'

When Tracy had finished, she said, 'Well, that *is* good news.' She turned to Flora, 'I'm very pleased for you, dear. There's still a long way to go, but it all sounds as if it's going in the right direction. And I've got a hunch it won't be long before you're coming down to tell me about some new interests of yours,' she added.

Tracy and Flora tried to press her to say more of what was in her mind, but she wouldn't say any more.

'You know something, don't you?' Flora said. 'I can tell!'

'I can certainly see something,' Miss Maitland admitted, 'but it wouldn't be right for me to say what it is. I have to wait for you to come and tell me.'

'But you've *got* to say,' Flora urged.

'It's no good putting pressure on me,' said Miss Maitland.

Tracy noticed that she looked very determined – even more determined than Flora – so she said nothing.

Flora was pouting. Then she said suddenly, 'I've got an idea!'

'What is it, dear?' asked Miss Maitland cautiously.

'You could write down on a piece of paper what you can see, and you could keep it in your special box. And if what you say is right, and I come and tell you about something I'm interested in, then you can show me what you wrote.'

'That's a very good compromise, Flora,' said Miss Maitland. 'I'll do that this evening, I promise you.'

They stayed chatting on the front door step until it was time for Miss Maitland's rest; and then they helped her back to her living room, folded the chair she had been using in the hall, and put it away for her.

'And now I'll soon be speaking to my dad again,' said Flora with a contented sigh, as they made their way back up the road to Welcome Home.

Just as they arrived back, May called out to them. 'You've come at the right time. Babs is on the phone. She says she has to work on Sunday, so it'll be Derek and Paula that will be coming, and they'll arrive sometime in the early afternoon.'

Tracy rushed to the phone. 'Hello, Mum,' she said. 'Everything's going really well, and Miss Maitland has had an apparition... No, I mean a vision...' she burst out excitedly. 'Well... I think so. She's writing it down, and if it comes true she'll tell us what she wrote down.'

'That's exciting, love,' she heard her mother say. 'Do you know what it's about?'

'It's about Flora and something she's going to do,' Tracy replied. She handed the phone back to her aunt.

'That's certainly very interesting news,' she heard May saying to Babs. 'When Miss Maitland sees something like that, I've never yet known her to be wrong. But she's never very confident about it herself, so she doesn't say until after what she sees has really happened.'

'That helps me not to mind waiting,' said Flora to Tracy. 'I wish Mum would get off the phone now, and then I can phone Dad.'

When May put the phone down she said to Flora, 'I think Tracy and I have got a bit more work we want to do in the office. Haven't we, Tracy?' She looked meaningfully at Tracy, who understood straight away what she meant, and followed her into the hall.

Flora did not come through to the office for quite a while, and when she did, she was glowing in the same way as she had the day before, when she had just come back from her day out.

'That's it fixed,' she said contentedly. 'Dad's coming at two on Sunday. He's really pleased that Tracy's dad is coming. I think he wants to try to have a talk with him, but he didn't say exactly.'

The week seemed to rush past. It was no time before it was Friday and the Youth Club. True to her word, Flora told Mr Mason about the changes that were happening with her dad, and he had tears in his eyes when he told her how glad he was for her.

'Now remember,' he had said. 'If there's anything you think I can do to help, just let me know.'

'Thanks, Mr Mason. I'll remember that,' Flora had said confidently.

Most of Saturday afternoon and evening had been spent bringing Flora's things back down to her room. It was hard work – particularly with dismantling, carrying, and reassembling Flora's bed – but Flora and Tracy were determined. The chest stayed up in the loft, but everything in it had to be brought down. They brought one of the mattresses down as well, so that they could spend their last night together.

By bedtime both girls were exhausted, and they were glad to get ready for bed.

Tracy thought how strange Flora's alarm clock sounded the next morning. It sounded quite a bit different from when it had been in the attic room. Tired though they were, both girls were eager to jump out of bed and get on with their work. They wanted everything to be finished in plenty of time for the arrival of the two dads and Paula.

At lunchtime, Tracy noticed how relaxed Flora and May seemed to be. She felt sad that she would be leaving them soon, but she knew that their life was changing in a way that was going to help them, so she didn't feel worried about them. She and Flora had planned to phone each other every week, and she was sure that Mum and Dad would be happy for her to do that.

It was Tracy's dad and Paula who arrived first. Paula was having great difficulty in not telling exactly what the redecorating was like at home. She kept starting to talk about it, but each time she managed to stop herself.

Flora's dad arrived not long afterwards. After he had said hello to everyone, Flora invited him upstairs to see her room and then the attic room. When they came back down again, Flora asked Paula up to see her room, and Tracy went with them.

'I wanted you to see my room, Paula,' Flora said. 'But I wanted your dad and mine to have time to talk to each other. Do you mind if we sit up here for a while? Mum can come and get us if they need us for anything.'

It was about half an hour later that they could hear May's voice calling for them, and they ran downstairs to find a very relaxed atmosphere in the kitchen, and the two dads making arrangements to keep in touch with each other about something they had just discovered: they had a shared interest. Tracy couldn't quite pick up what it was, but she knew she could ask Dad later.

Tracy found it quite difficult to say goodbye to Flora, Auntie May and Uncle Tony, even though she had arranged to speak to Flora on the phone later in the week. Once she was home she would have to start preparing for school; and of course she would see how the decorating had turned out. It would be good to see Mum again, and to tell everyone more about her holiday.

Uncle Tony left at the same time – but he stayed on the pavement waving with Flora and Auntie May. Tracy wound the car window down so she could wave back while Dad drove away.

The journey home was pleasant, and the girls were quiet for much of the time. The sun was shining, but it was not too hot. Tracy loved watching the trees and fields and hedgerows rushing by, and Paula dozed.

As they neared Bankbridge, Tracy leaned forward and said, 'Dad, do you think I could go and help Auntie May and Flora again next summer?'

'I want to go as well,' said Paula, quickly emerging from what had appeared to be a sleeping state.

'I don't know,' Dad replied. 'We'll have to see nearer the time. But we can say something to May when we phone her.' He thought for a moment and then added, 'Maybe Flora would like to come and stay with us for a break before then.'

Tracy and Paula bounced up and down in their seats so much at the thought that Dad had to ask them to sit still.

'Hang on, you're rocking the car about too much,' he said cheerfully. 'But no wonder you're excited. I think it would be great if Flora can come and stay. I could go across and pick her up for half term, if May can manage on her own for a few days.'

A warm glow spread through Tracy as she looked forward to planning more good times with her cousin.

About the Author

Mirabelle Maslin was born in Birmingham in 1947, and moved to Bramhall, Cheshire, in 1952. She studied agriculture at Reading University, after which she worked in scientific research near Edinburgh until the birth of her three children – two sons and a daughter. Since then she has spent more than twenty years helping people with their problems, together with providing nutritional advice where appropriate. She began writing in 2001, and has completed five books, of which Tracy is the second to be published. The writing of Tracy was specifically requested by a young friend who had recognised the importance of Mirabelle's attitude towards young people and their difficulties – which she demonstrates throughout the story of Tracy.

Lightning Source UK Ltd.
Milton Keynes UK
13 October 2009

144903UK00001B/2/A